unnerving

twelve stories for a monthly dose of shivers

DESCENT

BLUE FORGE PRESS
Port Orchard, Washington

Unnerving Descent
Twelve Stories for a Monthly Dose of Shivers
Copyright October 2020
by Blue Forge Press

Cover art by Brianne DiMarco
Interior layout by Brianne DiMarco

First Print Edition, October 2020
Second Print Edition, April 2022
Third Print Edition, February 2023

ISBN 978-1-59092-910-0

For information about film, reprint or other subsidiary rights, contact blueforgegroup@gmail.com

Blue Forge Press is the print division of the volunteer-run, federal 501(c)3 nonprofit company, Blue Legacy, founded in 1989 and dedicated to bringing light to the shadows and voice to the silence. We strive to empower storytellers across all walks of life with our four divisions: Blue Forge Press, Blue Forge Films, Blue Forge Gaming, and Blue Forge Records. Find out more at www. MyBlueLegacy.org

Blue Forge Press
7419 Ebbert Drive Southeast
Port Orchard, Washington 98367
blueforgepress@gmail.com
360-550-2071 ph.txt

*to all the authors brave enough
to write about what haunts them*

CONTENT WARNING

This book is intended for mature audiences as these stories are purposefully meant to unsettle the reader. Some stories may include death, violence, gore, sexual assault, cannibalism, self-harm, or other dark themes. If one month's story is too intense, skip that month. While the editor and Blue Forge Press have selected and edited each of these stories, ultimately you are responsible for curating what you read.

For a full list of triggers by story, please write to:
blueforgepress@gmail.com

table of contents

unnerving

twelve stories for a monthly dose of shivers

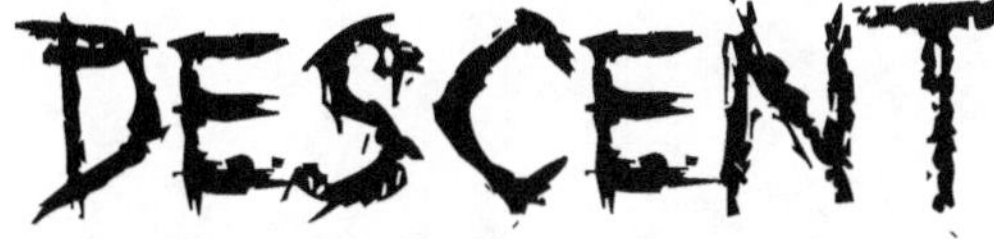

DESCENT

January

Forever and a Day
Jennifer DiMarco

I kept walking. I crossed at crosswalks and stopped with the signal; I didn't have a death wish and I wasn't acting like an idiot. I've never liked that stereotype about men: That we express every emotion as reckless anger. But if we did? That's the hot, steaming dish society served us. Which do you expect more: For a man to cry tears of sorrow or put his fist through the wall?

My father was a hole-in-the-wall guy. Which, in another context, might mean he liked discovering out of the way cafes or dive bars with great local ales. But here I mean: There were a great number of holes in the drywall throughout my childhood home from my father expressing a great number of emotions.

I'm not sharing that for pity. I'm just trying to illustrate what I'm not: I'm not my father. I handle my anger (and my other emotions, too) pretty darn well. And no. I don't use profanity. There's nothing manly about cussing.

I walked through Pioneer Square clutching my bulging manila envelope. Nine months. Nine long months I'd fought against everything inside that envelope. Stuck in a nightmare while the world moved on around me.

It was dusk in Seattle, Washington, the emerald green Pacific Northwet bathed in blue, purple, and black. The streets here in downtown near the waterfront were old cobblestone and red brick as slick as slug snot. (Do slugs have snot? Does "snot" count as profanity?) I grew up downwind of Capital Hill in a nondescript concrete block apartment with a disabled sister who died at nine and a mother who died by her own hand soon after. Grief and fury infested the thin coat of dust and skin cells and grime that came to cover everything after it was just my father and me. He loved my mother more than anything—living or dead—that had ever existed. His love for her was beyond my comprehension.

Until I met Maggie.

"Watch where you're going, faggot!"

I collided with the stranger at full clip, both of us moving at speed in opposing trajectories. It wasn't an awkward bump of arms or shoulders like when you brush past someone in a crowded space. This was a full body slam collision complete with recoil, rebound, and a deep breath of homelessness, resentment, and desperation. My fat manila envelope landed on the rain- and piss-soaked bricks, splattering oily water and muck onto my dress shoes and slacks. (What else was I supposed to wear to a divorce attorney?)

"Sorry, man..." My voice sounded hoarse and weak

despite my deep baritone that mimicked my father's far more than I'd ever cared for. Possibly why I wasn't much of a talker. I also knew enough not to argue with a stranger twice my size and a head taller than me wearing enough layers of clothing that he could be concealing an arsenal or a whole other person for all I knew.

"You're in the wrong place." He was glaring at me or maybe glaring at his hotdog with the works that, after our crash, was only a hot dog with half the works.

I started nodding, sidestepping to move on my way, ready to be gone, ready to be anywhere but here where, admittedly, I knew was not the best place for a thin, long-haired white man who wasn't packing, wasn't looking, and wasn't in a great head space. "I couldn't agree more."

He let me leave, his blood-shot eyes definitely on me as I passed, but he waited until I was across the street and the signal had changed before he called, "Don't litter, faggot!"

I looked back, though I didn't stop walking, and watched as the vagabond (Outcast? Drifter? Vagrant?) plucked my manila envelope out of the puddle and flung it into the nearest public garbage can. It landed on the overflowing refuse with a wet slap and I didn't go back to retrieve it.

"I'm straight," I muttered to myself as I turned my back again and picked up my pace. Night was falling and *I was in the wrong place.* My Social Security number, my phone number, address, description of my car, bank accounts and balances—all of that and more were in those documents. Maggie had left me everything, asked for nothing, taken nothing. Eight years of shared life and she was leaving with only what she had come with: Her clothes, her toiletries, and her teacup Borzoi named Feathers.

It all happened like that. The urine-soaked manila slapping home on the tsunami of other crap and I suddenly knew I'd never intended to return home, I'd never intended to return to my life in any way. I'd walked out of Gerald, Handel & Associates, leaving behind their dark mahogany and warm brass alcazar built from other people's pain, knowing my life was over. I should have turned left from their lobby, taken the wide, grand stairs that wove up the steep downtown hills and started the arduous but familiar climb home, but I'd turned right instead and (almost holding my breath) dove into the seedy cesspool that modern day *Sleazattle* had become after the fall of civility.

I was in the wrong place.

Because if I didn't have Maggie? Then everything was wrong. Everything. There was no way I could continue without her. Without Maggie I'd be putting holes in walls before I knew it. Maybe I already had.

It started to rain and I kept walking. I think I knew where I was going. But I was more aware of not having a jacket and how my long brown curls were turning into wet coils and sticking to the back of my cotton dress shirt with the vertical blue stripes that gave the impression that I was taller than five-foot-nine-and-nothing. I told myself I was just getting out of the deluge when I ducked into a covered stoop.

I looked down at my hands, bathed now in neon lights. The humming hiss of the cold cathode lights, their long glass tubes fitted with metal electrodes to ignite the hydrogen, helium, carbon dioxide, mercury, and noble neon that gave us the red, yellow, white, blue, and orange that painted our cities and drew our eyes. I was molten with waves of pulsing colors. I looked up. No signs for breweries or wine coolers or corporate logos, the storefront window was crowded with third eyes, pyramids of the Illuminati, cyclical snakes consuming themselves. And a single blood red sign (probably worth more than my condo up the hill) in a decidedly square OCD display font: Cacophonous Curiosities.

I went inside.

"Let me know if I can help you find anything." The twenty-something behind the glass counter filled with skull-shaped bongs didn't look up from his *Teatro di Freak* graphic novel. He wore a name tag upside down. It read Alistair, of course, in careful block letters.

I walked past the bins of polished tiger's eye and garnet, past the shelves of glass bottles filled with spider webs and dandelion puffs, and bellied up to the bar, so to speak. I shoved my wet hands in my wet pockets and was very aware of dripping rain on the floor. "I'd like to buy a plane slip. One determiner. One way." He looked up at me and I added, "Alistair."

"I'm sorry...?" He left it hanging as if waiting for something.

"John."

"Really?"

"No." I won't lie. I blushed. "Shawn."

Alistair grinned a little. "Yeah, Shawn, so here's the deal." He set his book aside and folded his hands into a single ball on the glass counter top. "We don't sell plane slips anymore. You'll have to go to PlaneMaster."

"They're not open until tomorrow morning." I held his gaze, unspoken things passing between us. I had never once in my life purchased anything illegal or even illicit. I never drank, had voted to legalize weed but had never used it, found cigarettes and cigars disgusting, and everything else just seemed dangerously ignorant. But I knew Cacophonous Curiosities had been busted and shut down for six months for undercutting the licensed planeslip dispensary a block away.

I took my wallet from my slacks pocket and fished out my debit card, sliding it across the glass to Alistair with a decisive and distinct sound that made me think of unsheathing a bayonet. "Pin is three, four, two, five." I saw his eye twitch and knew I had him. "There's four grand in the account." I broke eye contact and managed a weird half-shrug. "Right now."

"This is an emergency, right?" Alistair was a flurry of motion. Card taken. Card reader retrieved. His hands swiping, pinning, grabbing a notepad of forms, and clicking a blue ballpoint pen as if he were suddenly multi-armed Shiva; from my perspective, for my needs, he certainly had the power of a god. "Life or death?"

"Yeah, yeah." I was slow to catch up. This was happening! "Absolutely a life or death emergency."

Alistair was so efficient, even graceful, somehow mesmerizing in his fluid motions. Not everyone knew how to run a black market transaction but once you knew how, maybe it was a source of pride, maybe it was hard not to because Alistair moved through the process as if returning to a beloved art form; there was reverence in this downtown room. "You'll have to pay twice for the slip. My fee and the dispensary's fee. I passed the conductor test so I can legally sell if the dispensary is closed and it's an emergency but you have to buy round trip. There's no such thing has a one-way ticket."

"I don't want to come back."

He looked back at me suddenly, his hands frozen, poised in two separate tasks. "Dude." His face was a strange mix of pity and impatience. "I know."

I gave him a curt nod and he continued moving. Neither of us wanted to drag this transaction out longer than required.

"You sure you only have one determiner, Shawn?"

Alistair's expression was like words on a page. No one asked for just one determiner. If someone was slipping—especially someone slipping and not intending to come back—they'd ask for a dozen things to be just so, a dozen more to be guaranteed. If you were walking away from your *dimension*... you wanted to walk into paradise.

"I have to be married to Margaret Ayn Walker." I gave him her Social Security number because I'd heard that system often carried over.

Alistair's expression changed. Impatience was swallowed by pity as Mr. Not-Yet-Thirty decided he knew my whole life story, my entire sad existence. I was one of *those*.

Some whipped boy toy who'd been dumped and couldn't live without his soul mate, the love of his life, the angel that had stolen and shattered his heart. Whatever.

He could think whatever he wanted if I walked out of here with a green pill.

Alistair conjured up a HUD from the computing bar embedded in the counter. The semi-transparent display materialized between us like a shimmering purple fan of holographic information. From my angle it all looked like binary, alchemy, ancient alien hieroglyphics but that was probably just the privacy filter.

"Let's see... you've got some choices. You wanna be CEO at Araby Fair Online? Founder and majority stock holder of Top Dog Industries? Here's one with a private island and a mistress—"

"No!"

Alistair looked back at me through the purple HUD.

I took a breath and managed a tight-lipped grin. "Am I married to Maggie?"

Alistair kept looking at me for a silent moment that made the back of my neck prickle with cold sweat. Then he looked back at the summaries of dimensional gradients. "Listen, Shawn..."

I slapped my condo's keycard down on the counter.

Alistair stared at the card this time instead of me. The card was black on black, a matte finish with high gloss letters: Sky Tower.

"One determiner. Just one."

Ten minutes later, I walked out of Cacophonous Curiosities with one green pill, one red pill, and without my wallet entirely. I'd never need it again, anyway.

Alistair had given me clear directions: "Go straight to the pier next to the ferry dock. It's under construction. Duck under the tape, pop the green pill in your mouth, shove the red pill up your nose, and jump off the pier. The green is quick dissolve; you'll slip before you even hit the water."

"How will I know—"

"Listen! You'll enter gradient nine-fourteen-point-DX within ten feet of the target. Blow the red pill out of your nose and keep it safe until you want to—"

"I told you, I—"

"Dude." Alistair had reached across the counter and touched one of my cold hands. His were surprisingly warm. "I searched four-point-two million planes. In one of them—one!—you and your lady have the potential to be married. Just the *potential*! It's the rarest outcome and it's a hard ass life—"

"I want it."

Alistair had given in at last with a quiet, "It's your life, dude." But all I could think of was the saying, *It's your funeral.*

I was literally at the door of the shop, leaving with an almost intoxicated euphoria, when he tried a final, "Shawn, remember: The red pill is the only way back. They don't have planeslip technology in that parallel. If you lose the red pill, you're lost to that world."

Or found, I thought to myself but I was already booking it down the block, the chimes above Alistair's door like ethereal creatures singing.

I did not complete the slip prior to hitting the water. The cold, black waves came up to meet my falling body like a concrete wall and I swear I felt bones break even as I flailed and screamed and swallowed salt, brine and water.

But then I was dry, warm, reset… and standing in a cheap fiberglass tub with a ring of soup scum.

"What the fuck—" My voice but not me. The frosted plastic curtain was ripped back by Not-me to reveal actual me.

We looked at one another. Not-me blinked once, twice, rubbed a hand over his face. I smelled booze.

"Shawn? You okay, babe?"

It was Maggie. I could have cried. I could have shouted in joy. Instead I whispered to Not-me so she wouldn't hear, "Spider."

Not-me caught on quickly and despite his eyes still being as ugly wide as saucers, Not-me called back to her with humor in his voice, "Just a spider, Mag. One of those big ole brown ones."

"Eew! Hope you flushed it," she answered but I knew she definitely wouldn't come to the rescue now; Maggie hated spiders more than she loved anyone.

"Of course, yeah—" Not-me reached absently toward the toilet.

The moment he turned away from me, I struck. I didn't think about it. I hadn't thought about it. Not once in Cacophonous Curiosities, not once during the walk to the pier or floundering in the freezing cold January waters of the

Puget Sound. But obviously, on some level, I must have known exactly what to do.

I cracked my head that wasn't my head against the corner of the chipped pedestal sink with the mix-matched handles that both leaked. The sound was strangely duller than I expected and that gave me time to cough and run the water to further mask the sound of Not-me's body collapsing to the yellowed tile floor.

I shoved him to the side and thought about lifting him up and out the window (would I be strong enough?) but I wasn't sure how far up we were, where we were, or even if this were a house or—

I looked around me. *Oh my god....* It was my childhood apartment. I leaned forward heavily on the sink, staring open-mouthed at my own reflection in the cracked mirror.

I can't entirely say why this fact—that a dimension existed where Maggie and I were living in the low-income walk-up of my childhood—was what shook me. Killing *myself?* Not a problem. Having Maggie waiting for me in bed? Fantastic!

No wonder I'd known what to do and how to do it; I'd fantasized (Fetishized?) about killing my drunk, abusive father a hundred times exactly like that.

I pressed my thumb to my right nostril and blew the red pill out of my left. Then I dropped it into the toilet and flushed. I turned. If this were my childhood apartment....

I opened the little linen closet in the corner of the bathroom. The laundry chute was there, the lid rusting at the hinges. It went down two floors to the shared laundry room but each chute was locked at the far end and every tenant had their private key. I dragged Not-me's skinny self toward the chute, unable to look away from the impossibly large dent in the front of my face that stole the humanity from my features.

Not-me's body was swallowed to the waist when his eyes flickered open. He didn't look up at me but rather over at the sink of all places. "I knew..." he sputtered, so quietly I found myself leaning closer to hear him. "I knew it would come back to bite me."

I stomped on his neck then, once then again. Calling to Maggie about killing spiders and how I'd pick up a bug bomb tomorrow. She told me she wanted us to move and laughed. I laughed with her and shoved a now very, very dead Not-me down the chute. I think I heard him slide down the long channel and thump against the locked hatch at the bottom but I'm not sure because Maggie called to me.

"Sounds like a horror scene in there." There was still laughter in her voice but something more, too. She really was scared of spiders.

"Don't worry," I assured her, running the water in the sink again. "I'll clean up."

I felt around beneath the basin where Not-me had looked and found the ring almost instantly. Maggie would never have reached under there (note the extreme fear factor) so the hiding spot was flawless. It was definitely Maggie's size (five) and appeared to be antique white gold (her favorite) with a circle of small rubies around an impressive two-carat diamond. I'd seen the ring somewhere before but couldn't place it—perhaps at Pike Place when I was window shopping with Maggie a year ago?

I palmed the perfect moment, smiled and left the bathroom.

Maggie was sitting in bed with a paperback mystery, wearing her satin rose-colored pajamas that I'd always loved. As I crossed the room, she and I realized at the same time that I was naked. I faltered a step (quite the fact to leave out, Alistair!) but Maggie was tossing her book aside and grinning like the Cheshire Cat.

"My spider-killing hero emerges...." Her words trailed away into shock as I recovered my cool and went down on one knee. I'd already noticed she wasn't wearing a ring. Yet.

"Shawn, oh my god...."

The joy on Maggie's face as she realized what was happening almost burst my heart. I'd done it! I'd gotten her back and this time, I swore to myself on everything holy and unholy, I would keep her.

"Margaret Ayn Walker..." I turned my hand to reveal the ring, presenting it like a do-over, like a golden ticket, like a dream-come-true. "...will you marry—"

"Where did you get Jessica's ring?"

I'm not sure if it was Maggie saying her name—the god forsaken name I'd come to loathe with everything in me over the last nine months—or if it was the horror washing over Maggie's face, making her draw back, draw away as if in a slow motion of terror. But whatever it was, I remembered then where I'd seen the ring: On Maggie's hand at the attorney's office earlier today. On her ring finger. Symbolically if not legally.

I opened my mouth to speak, my head tilting in that way I had when I was thinking fast. But Maggie was backing up even faster now, pushing backward to put the bed between us. I had underestimated myself—or rather I had underestimated *not-myself*—and everything was unraveling.

"It was... it belonged to her grandmother. The police..." Maggie was moving toward the bedside charger where her phone sat. "They said it was gone when they found her body."

"Maggie." I couldn't think of what else to say.

The bedroom door eased open with a creak that made both of us jump. Feathers pushed into the room and took in the scene with black, black eyes and a long, eternally composed face. He looked at his mom then looked at me.

And growled.

february

When She Was Happy
Maxwell DiMarco

And what we're really excited about, John, is that the realization of this technology would not only save millions, but people of all ages and abilities could…"

Joanne's eyes slowly fluttered open to the sound of a television playing nearby, strands of her long, light-blonde hair in her face. With a drowsy groan, she lightly pushed the hair away from her eyes. This almost subconscious action allowed the young woman a view of the lamp upon the dark oak bedside table, the early morning sunlight streaming in through open blinds beyond… as well as an awareness of a skull-splitting ache in her head. Letting out a hiss of pain under her breath as she grasped at her temples, Joanne squeezed her eyes shut, and her world went dark once again.

The action didn't help the pain as much as Joanne had hoped. But it at least allowed her to turn off her unnecessary sense of sight, as she tried to focus on organizing her scattered thoughts.

"...so, Dr. Paxton, let's get on the same page here. You're telling me, that in just *ten years* time—potentially *nine,* if things go well—your team could unveil a fully-tested, finalized procedure..."

Despite her current discomfort, Joanne managed a small smile upon recognizing the voice of the interviewer. Relaxing on the couch and tuning into John Sager's early-morning talkshow was one of the rare moments of peace she still had in life...

Joanne's eyes reopened as a realization came over her.

Their television was downstairs. Joanne was in bed.

She wasn't at home right now.

Squinting against the sunlight as her mind raced, a series of hazy memories slowly started trickling back into Joanne's head: Yesterday was Valentine's Day. She'd gone out to Club Noble, her favorite night club—or, rather, it had been, when she and Marcus used to sneak in back in high school. Years had passed since Joanne last went out for a "night on the town," but that night, in the spirit of the most passionate day of the year, she'd decided to rekindle the spark that she'd left behind on Graduation Day.

Or, at least, that's the reason that she could remember. Going off of the throbbing in her head, Joanne could only dread what had ultimately transpired of this decision.

"Jesus Christ," Joanne blasphemed, slowly sitting upright and holding her face in her hands. "What the hell did I do last night?"

"Me."

"*Holy*—" Joanne's heart started upon hearing a voice speak up to her left; all drowsiness eradicated by adrenaline, she whirled to face the previously unseen speaker.

Sitting in the bed next to her was a brunette, average-sized woman around Joanne's age; maybe a year older at most. Her dark hair was trimmed into a neat bob cut, and though the blankets were pulled up around her as she eyed the television at the foot of the bed, Joanne could make out the straps of a blank tanktop. The fact that her bedmate was seemingly still clothed gave Joanne a brief reprieve from the increasing level of panic that had been gradually coming over her. But it came back in full force when the other woman turned her head from the television, eying Joanne with a casual smirk.

"Morning, blondie." The woman grinned, tilting her head slightly. Her voice was collected, yet tinted with spunk; a subtle southern twang helped accentuate the latter. "You sleep well?"

"I... m-morning..." Joanne briefly found herself at a loss for words. As she tried to find her voice—and fight back the persistent pain of her apparent hangover—she managed to lift a shaky finger to point at the other woman's tank top. "So... you... we didn't—"

Without missing a beat, the woman raised a hand to cut her off. "No, no, let me just set the record straight now: We very much did." She punctuated that statement by cocking dual fingerguns. "It's just, all the vodka had basically rendered you comatose when I got up myself. Thought I'd get the old morning routine out of the way while you got some beauty sleep... not that you need it, frankly."

Joanne's heart sank. "Oh, god," she bemoaned, falling back down onto the bed, the impact causing her to bounce slightly on the soft mattress. "Oh, god, what have I *done?* How could I do this to Marc? He's going to be so angry with me...."

"Marc... that's the name of the drunken asshole you're living with, right?" the other woman asked, her eyes drifting back to the television.

Joanne scowled; she quickly was becoming fed up with this woman's constant snark. Sitting back up with a frown, she once more turned to her unwanted bed partner. "That's the name of my *boyfriend,* yes. And for the *record,* he's not—"

"Who says he has to know?" her paramour once more interrupted, lifting a remote control to pause the program before turning back towards the blonde. "Blondie, this was just a harmless fling between two party chicks— can't speak for you, but I don't have any inclination to make a dramatic story out of this. And your boy toy already knew you were heading to the club; if he respects your freedom to a social life, he shouldn't bat an eye at you coming home with the sunrise. You're totally clear, hun."

Whatever Joanne wanted to say died on her lips, a hollow feeling beginning to fill her heart. "Marc... isn't like that." Pulling the blankets up to her chest, Joanne leaned away over to the bedside table, where she spotted her purse through her hazy vision. Reaching in, she fished out her smartphone as she continued her explanation. "If I'm not home on time, he'll text me relentlessly... asking where I am, when I'll be back, what I was doing... and then he'll start leaving voice messages."

There was a shifting behind her, a few moments before the television shut off with a barely audible click. "Of course he does... wish I could say I'm surprised." As Joanne took the phone in her hand and hesitantly turned it on, she only slightly acknowledged the other woman had shifted closer to her from across the bed.

"So, he's not just a psychopath... he's one of *those guys*, too, huh," the woman mused. The sentence could have been interpreted as a question, but it was clear from her inflection that she was more stating facts to herself. And to Joanne's surprise, for the first time she noticed an emotion besides snark in the woman's voice... was it distaste? Bitterness?

Anger?

Nevertheless, Joanne quickly came to her significant other's defense. "No, it's not like that... I mean, yes, I suppose he can be overbearing. But Marc's always had trust issues, ever since high school. Keeping in touch helps him overcome that... and to be honest, it really helps us *both* be more secure in our relationship."

"Mm." A barely audible murmur escaped the woman's pursed lips as she peered at Joanne's phone screen. Already, Joanne's finger instinctively readied to swipe into an unread text, her mind simultaneously trying to find an explanation for her absence... but that message never came.

"There's... nothing here?" Joanne couldn't believe her eyes.

If she ever wasn't at home and waking up in their bed by 6:30, Marc had *always,* on the dot, texted her to ask where she was. Now, starring at the barren notification feed, she wasn't sure whether to be relieved... or very, very afraid.

The other woman chose the former. Making a "tch" sound with her mouth, her tone lightened slightly. "Well, well... maybe the prick's got some respect for your privacy after all." The sound of shifting blankets told Joanne that the woman had gotten out of the bed, even as her own eyes remained staring down at her empty phone notifications. Then came the distinct sound of a creaky bedroom door opening. "I'm gonna head downstairs, blondie—make myself some eggs and toast. That sound good to you? Oh, and the name's Megan, just in case you didn't—"

"No, something's wrong here!" Joanne began shaking her head as she threw back the covers and briskly walked to the window, not even acknowledging that she was still completely nude. "He always texts me by now if I'm not home... there must be a bad signal, or something... if he thinks I'm ignoring him, then—"

"Hey, hey, calm down!" the other woman—Megan—briskly walked back across the room to stand a few feet behind Joanne. "It's all good, hun—our houses are both just outside of the city, remember?"

Having been fruitlessly holding her phone up to the window with the hopes of getting any unseen texts to come through, Joanne turned to her one night stand with a completely helpless expression.

"Oh... fuck, no of course you don't remember," Megan realized, awkwardly gazing down at the carpeted floor. "Okay, let's take it from the top, I guess...." After taking a moment to collect her thoughts, Megan looked back up at Joanne. "Last night, you told me you had a place over on Royal; I'm a fifteen minute drive from there, right off of Emilia Way. If nothing's showing up, then he hasn't sent anything. Plain and simple."

"Emilia Way," Joanne repeated, almost as if to reaffirm that Megan wasn't just saying what she wanted to hear. Megan nodded in response, placing a reassuring hand on Joanne's trembling shoulder.

"The way I see it, blondie, the fact that he hasn't messaged you is a good sign," Megan stated frankly, before laughing spitefully under her breath. "And actually, to be blunt: After what you told me happened between you two, I probably wouldn't be comfortable letting you leave if he had."

"Between—" Joanne reeled back as though she'd been punched in the gut. All at once, the memories of the previous night broke through her alcohol-induced haze like water bursting through a dam. Her prior black-out forgotten, she now felt almost completely sober, as the full events of the night flooded her mind.

All the plans she'd made for the day, that she thought he'd enjoy. A romantic, homemade dinner, followed by presenting him with two VIP passes to Club Noble's Valentine's Slowdance;

a trip down memory lane, to commemorate how far they'd come in their relationship.

That same dinner she'd painstakingly crafted becoming cold after two full hours of waiting for Marc to come home. And then Marc finally stumbling in the door drunk off his ass and lobbing a broken liquor bottle right into the center of the table.

The screams that been exchanged between them for nearly thirty minutes straight, culminating in a Joanne storming out the door, yelling over her shoulder that she was heading to the club herself, refusing to let Marc ruin her favorite holiday. That same man roaring obscenities after her like a demon from hell, throwing serving bowls of untouched food against the wall.

The long drive into the city, bitter tears running down Joanne's face as she drove in cold silence through the night, the VIP passes forgotten and pitifully torn up in the cup holder.

Finally getting through the line and walking up to that neon, LED-lit bar, bass pumping in her ears, and opening a tab with the intent to dance and drink the night away.

And then, Megan flashing a gorgeous smile as she sat down next to her.

"Oh—god—" Joanne could just barely choke out those two words. The hand holding her phone dropping to her side, she began rapidly blinking to clear her eyes of the tears that threatened to pour down her face. Joanne couldn't even look at the woman in front of her as Megan spoke up once more.

"You just remembered, huh." Again, it was technically a question, but Megan phrased it as a statement. And the answer was obvious to both parties involved.

Yet, as Joanne slowly looked back at the woman's solemn face, something compelled her to reply anyway. "Yes," she replied plainly. "Marc came home drunk... we had a huge argument. I went to the club alone. And that's... where I met you." Megan simply set her jaw in acknowledgement. "God, he... h-he must be so angry with me! How can I go home now, after..."

And then, before Joanne realized what was happening, Megan had pulled her into a deep, loving kiss. The brunette's eyes closed as her hands ran through Joanne's blonde hair, stroking her head and neck reassuringly.

As the two women broke their lip contact and met each other's gaze, Megan's eyes showed nothing but love as she promised with a fiery determination, "He can't hurt you anymore, Joanne. I won't let him."

The burning conviction behind Megan's words almost seemed to dry Joanne's wet eyes. For all of the five years she'd dated Marc—and even the full twelve she'd actually known him for—she had never had someone stand up for her like Megan was doing now.

"You... didn't have to say that," Joanne muttered, looking away.

But immediately, Joanne's face was gently turned back by Megan, who was looking at her with a small, confident smirk. "Maybe I did, maybe I didn't... but see, blondie, I wanted to. And ten years in MMA says that motherfucker had better not test my credibility."

Even though the subject was grim, Joanne couldn't help a smile from tickling her lips at Megan's words. "I...

appreciate that, Megan," she managed.

"No problem, hun," Megan replied. "One way or another, I'll help you get through to him. Everything's going to be just fine."

There was a silence for a time as they stood before each other... it was then Joanne noticed something about Megan. Despite her assertive personality, and seemingly being the older of the two... Megan was actually slightly shorter than Joanne was. In contrast, Marcus had always stood at an imposing six foot seven... Joanne found it strangely fun to be the tallest in the room for once. She wondered if she could get used to this feeling.

No. I can't do this.

Abruptly, Joanne pushed Megan aside and began to search the bedroom. "Where's my clothes?" she asked, tossing the sheets to the bottom of the bed. "I'm calling Marcus and going home."

"H-hang on, wait a sec here!" Megan stammered; though she tried to stay collected, her voice betrayed a surprising amount of panic. "Look, I get if you don't want to see me again. Fine by me, most women I bed don't. But you can *not* go back to that man!"

"That's my own choice to make. I can't just abandon Marcus based on a one night stand," Joanne rebutted firmly, finding her underwear and bra haphazardly discarded under the bed. Grabbing the undergarments in one hand as she tossed her phone aside with the other, she turned back to Megan as she began to cloth herself. "Yes, Marc might have bad days, but we're still dating! If I can just learn to communicate better with him, we can work out these problems over time. And he's held down a full-time office job so I can focus on maintaining our house; after we graduated he promised my *family* that I wouldn't have to work again! Even if it might not always seem like it, I *know* he must still care somewhere!"

Megan stared at Joanne, almost at a loss for words. "But, Joanne, you said—"

"Oh, so you *do* know my name!" Joanne snapped—this situation was pushing her to her breaking point. Courtesy be damned, she wanted to get home and forget this ever happened. "I met you *yesterday*, when I was drunk out of my mind—who are you to say what's best for me? I had a bad night with Marc, but maybe it was *my* fault, and I didn't realize it then! You've never met him, how would you know?!"

Megan visibly flinched at Joanne's tone, and it looked like she was about to retaliate. But instead, she stood silently as Joanne continued to search for her clothes, her breathing composed and methodical. For some reason, this irritated Joanne even more than her earlier wisecracks.

"What is your deal, anyway? Why are you suddenly treating this seriously the moment I try to leave?" Joanne scoffed, shooting daggers at the brunette. "I don't get you, Megan; I wake up hungover and you're trying to make a joke out of this whole thing, and now you're trying to comfort me? How about you just pick an attitude and stick with it?!"

Megan's eyes slowly narrowed. "*Because* it's my instinct to lighten heavy situations where I can... but I know that mindset can only go so far in matters like this. And right now, I need you to listen to me."

Before Joanne had a chance open her mouth, Megan had resumed talking; all remaining hints of sarcasm or snark were gone. Her words were deliberate, and stern, as she stared at Joanne unflinchingly. "When I first met you, hun... you were completely sober. We talked for nearly an hour before I ordered our first drinks of the night."

"*You ordered—*"

"And the only reason I did," Megan once more cut Joanne off, as she slowly began to approach the taller blonde, "was because you broke down crying after telling me everything this sadistic, miserable excuse for a man has done to you. And I know it goes *far* beyond just what he did last night. This wasn't just some failure to communicate, or one bad day. This man is manipulative, *abusive*; practically psychotic. And I don't know whether he was ever a good man, but he certainly hasn't been for a *long* time."

Megan was now standing in front of Joanne, starring right into her sea blue eyes. "No part of what he did was your fault, Joanne. And knowing that... piece of *shit* couldn't give you the Valentine's Day you wanted... I tried to give you someone who could. Just for one night; no questions asked, no consequences or drama in the morning. But... I see now that wasn't enough. You don't need a break. You need to hear the truth."

As the two women stared into each other's eyes, a warm smile formed on Megan's lips. Reaching up to put a hand on Joanne's cheek, Megan's emerald green irises almost seemed to burn with passion. "So here it is: You are a *wonderful* woman, Joanne. If Marcus doesn't love you, then that's his own damn loss, because you deserve someone better in your life. And even if that someone isn't me... I know for a *fact,* just from this one night, that you are a woman worth loving."

Staring down at Megan, Joanne tried to fight back her tears again. She tried to remain angry at the woman standing before her, and pretend that she was in control... but then, her walls finally crumbled. Without even realizing what she was doing, Joanne leaned down to envelope Megan in a tight embrace, her tears freely rolling down her cheeks and onto Megan's shoulder. The brunette returned the hug, resting her head lovingly against the blonde's neck.

"Thank you," was all Joanne could muster through her tears, even though she knew it could never convey the extent of what she was feeling. For the first time in years—maybe in her entire life—she truly felt like she wasn't alone in the world. She felt appreciated. *Loved.* Even as her face was soaked with tears, that warm feeling bloomed in her chest and spread throughout her body. In that moment, her years of living with Marcus fell away, and Joanne felt truly happy.

Finally, the two women broke the embrace. They stared at each other for a moment longer... before it finally dawned on them that Joanne still had yet to get fully dressed.

Fortunately, Megan seemingly read her mind, and before Joanne could voice her embarrassment, the brunette was already heading to the bedroom door. "The rest of your clothes should still be outside," she said matter-of-factly. "Stay here and relax. I'll bring them up, then start on breakfast for us."

Joanne's face immediately went red. *"O-outside?"*

Megan let out a hearty laugh in return. "Heh, yeah; guess you could say we started early. Count yourself lucky I remembered to bring your purse in before hitting the hay myself!"

There was that sass again... but judging from the laugh that escaped Joanne's lips, it was more than welcomed after the much more sobering conversation that came before.

Before Megan could depart, a thought suddenly occurred to Joanne. "Do... you have any bacon, by chance?"

Megan paused in the door before turning back to Joanne with a grin. "Yeah, of course! You want me to fry you up some along with the eggs?"

"If it's not too much trouble..." Joanne hesitated briefly. "I just... haven't really had any since I moved in with Marc. He says it'll ruin my figure."

"Well, girl, he can feel free to fuck himself! I'll whip up the whole pack for ya!" Megan gave Joanne a beaming smile—the very same she had when they first met, and the blonde felt that warm feeling come over her all over again. "I'll be right back with your clothes, hun. Don't go nowhere, alright?" And with that, Megan left the room, leaving Joanne with a bright smile on her face.

With a content sigh, the blonde sat down lightly on the mattress, sinking into the soft materiel. As she did so, her gaze drifted down to her phone, still laying on the bed from when she'd thrown it aside earlier. Taking it into her hands once more, Joanne starred down at the dark screen, smiling as she saw herself reflected in it.

God, her hair was a mess. It had been so long since she'd been able to let her hair go unbrushed without a teasing "joke" from Marc... in hindsight, a "joke" wasn't really the right word for it, Joanne realized. But at the same time, she also began to process that was behind her. Megan was right; she deserved better than what Marcus could give her. And when she got home, she'd tell him so. It wasn't up to Joanne to "fix" him. She'd done all she could time and time again to no avail, with no thanks or even acknowledgement on his part. Looking back, Joanne wondered if she'd known this all along... and just needed someone to repeat it aloud for her to truly believe it.

Staring at her reflecting, Joanne looked down at the device with rekindled hope. "It's time to leave this relationship behind me. It's time—"

Blip.

Joanne's body froze up. Almost immediately, her heart sank; there he was. There *it* was. That damned text notification he refused to let her change. Of *course*, it couldn't last.

Maybe he'd gone back out after their fight, maybe he'd drunk himself into passing out on couch, but it was only a matter of time before he learned she hadn't come home on time. And now, she'd have to explain where she'd been.

But then, Megan's words came back to her. A feeling of bravery filled Joanne's body; if she wanted to put this behind her, she had to confront him. Calming her mind, her thumb drifted to the home button on the phone, pressing it gently. The screen powered on...

...but there was nothing there.

The young woman stared, unblinking, at the small screen in her hand, until its power saving feature shut off the screen. "What?" As though in a trace, she pressed the home button again. Still no new messages.

Holding down the power button, she quickly reset the phone... to no avail. The notification field remained barren.

Then why had she just heard a text notification?

After a few seconds of confusion, Joanne stumbled upon the logical conclusion: It was *Megan's* phone getting a message. If she'd been able to remember to bring in Joanne's purse, then it wasn't that far fetched to assume she'd brought her phone in, as well.

But that possibility was quickly shot down as Joanne heard Megan returning, whistling a cheery tune. "Hooo *man*, blondie, are you lucky I grabbed your purse!" Megan laughed, coming into the room with her arms full of Joanne's clothes. "Last night I left my wallet and phone in my good jeans; checked the pockets just now, and both the lil' fuckers were gone! One of my douchebag neighbors must have swiped 'em."

Joanne gasped, almost forgetting the unidentified notification. "Oh my god—I'm so sorry!"

Megan shrugged nonchalantly in reply, lobbing Joanne's clothes onto the bed beside her. "Eh, don't worry about it. I've been meaning to get that brick replaced for a while now; those cheap bastards can have it. And between you and me, hun, this isn't the first time I've had to cancel my cards. When you go out as much as I do, you can get a little forgetful in the—"

Blip.

"—heat of the moment."

Megan punctuated her final words with a wink, but Joanne didn't even notice it. In one efficient movement she snatched her phone back up and turned on the screen... the notification feed was still empty.

"Hang on, what's wrong, hun?" Quickly noticing the woman's sudden onset of anxiety, Megan crossed the room to stand by her. "Did that son of a bitch start texting you after all? Because I'm more than willing to—"

Blip.

"S-stop! Could you hear that just now?" Joanne interrupted, turning to Megan with the hopes she could resolve the issue. Judging from the brunette's confused expression, however, that was quickly becoming unlikely.

"Joanne... can you tell me what's going on?" Megan inquired, her voice taking on a more neutral inflection as she sat down next to the increasingly distraught woman.

"I keep hearing my text notification." Joanne stated, holding up her smartphone as she spoke. "It's unmistakable— I'd know the sound anywhere. And it sounds like it's right in my ear... but when I check my phone, there's nothing there."

It was for the briefest of moments: Megan's concerned expression faltered, replaced by a sudden flash of fear. But almost the exact moment that Joanne could acknowledge it, Megan had moved forward and embraced her.

"Joanne... it's alright," Megan reassured the woman, whom was taken off guard by the gesture. "The alcohol must still be playing tricks on you; you're paranoid that this can't last. But it can... I promise you, it can." Joanne couldn't bring herself to return the hug, even as Megan pulled her closer. "Just for now, I want you to put Marcus out of your mind. Can you do that for me?"

"For... *you?*" Joanne's voice was very quiet, her arms remaining limp at her side until Megan pulled away; a strange feeling had started to come over her.

Getting to her feet, Megan paused to look down at the confused blonde. "I'm going to go make breakfast. After you get dressed, there's a bathroom just down the hall," Megan directed. "You're free to use anything in it if you need it; by the time you're through with your morning routine, I should have the bacon ready. I'm sure that'll be nice, right?"

"Yeah...." Joanne slowly nodded as she stared up at the brunette, before watching as she turned and walked back out into the hall. Absentmindedly, she retrieved her shirt from the pile of clothes, and tried to pull it on... but her mind's eye was taken over by the split-second image of Megan's fearful expression.

Joanne blinked, squinting her eyes; something blurry was in the corner of her vision. Was she seeing things? Had Megan's expression changed at all, or had she imagined it? She thought back to the still unknown texts. Could it be she be hallucinating? But she'd never had hallucinations before... and these felt too real.

What was happening to her?

"Rrrggh!" Shaking her head firmly, Joanne forcefully pulled her sleeves over her arms as she tried to clear her mind. "No. Megan's right: I'm just paranoid from last night. He can't hurt me anymore; I'm going to be fine," she reassured herself, buttoning up her shirt as she did so.

Really, the lack of texts really wasn't *that* hard to believe; Joanne had often come downstairs in the morning to find Marc passed out on the couch, and last night he'd been drunk out of his mind. The idea that he'd simply not woken up yet was incredibly plausible.

Yet, as Joanne continued to get dressed, the persistent feeling that something wasn't completely right remained in the back of her mind. The notifications sounded too *real* to just have been her mind playing tricks on her, as did Megan's sudden change in expression. While, in contrast, she couldn't shake the feeling that Megan's actual reaction to her concerns had seemed... faked.

Or, maybe "forced" was a better word? Stilted, perhaps? Joanne found she couldn't decide.

Now fully clothed in last night's white button-up shirt, black dress skirt and stockings (with only slight grass stains from the lawn), Joanne left the bedroom in favor of the restroom further down the hall. It was a pretty standard bathroom, all things considered; a small mirror over a sink built into the countertop, with a moderately sized bath beyond a basic toilet. Noticing a towel already hung up, Joanne considered taking a soak to clear her mind, but it occurred to her that the food would likely be cold by the time she got out.

Instead, she spotted a bottle of toothpaste and a frizzy toothbrush in a plastic cup on the counter, opting to simply brush her teeth and hair for the time being, and finish up later. As she reached for the brush, though—

Blip.

—the sound rang out again. At the same volume as before, as well; which should have been impossible, with her phone still discarded back on the bed.

But this time, Joanne tried to push the unidentified noise out of her head. "You're just stressed; it's not real." Joanne tried to convince herself, evenly dispensing toothpaste onto the bristles. "You're not in danger, you're okay... everything is going to be okay."

But what happened next, she couldn't ignore.

From outside the bathroom, a faint crackling noise began to play from back down the hall. What sounded like a ringtone cut in and out of the crackles, so faint Joanne almost thought it was the white noise playing tricks on her. It almost sounded like an old radio switching between stations, and for a moment Joanne wondered if the television was acting up... until she heard his voice.

"...that's what you did?! You stormed out... some brown haired cunt... a whorish lesbian fantasy?!"

The toothbrush clattered into the sink. Staring into the mirror, Joanne gripped the counter as she began to shake violently. It was Marcus. His messages finally came through, and he knew what happened. The knowledge that the absence of texts had been exactly what she'd feared drained Joanne's bravery down to her core, like an emotional drainage pipe had been impaled in her gut...

"No... that's not what I'm saying at—"

...and that was when the second voice broke through the interference.

It was hard to notice from a distance. Even harder to make out through the static... but what Joanne heard made her heart skip a beat. A painful stab of adrenaline shot through her body... what she'd thought she had heard was impossible. But it was unmistakable. She knew that voice. How could she not?

It sounded exactly like it did in her head.

Joanne came close to literally sprinting back into the bedroom, but promptly stopped herself; the heavily filtered exchange didn't seem to be ending, and something in the back of her mind told her that she shouldn't call attention to herself.

Cautiously, looking over her shoulder to make sure no one was coming upstairs, Joanne stepped back into the bedroom. And there was her phone on the bed, right where she'd left it, with a flickering image of Marcus from the torso up playing on the screen.

"...left me alone, black out drunk?! For all you... be *dead*, you inconsiderate... kind of whorish excuse for a girlfriend are you?"

Lifting the device as though it could literally explode in her hands, Joanne starred at the screen as Marcus continued to rant and scream, his words segmented by the skipping video and fluctuating audio clarity. But it wasn't her boyfriend's furious verbal barrage that made her heart begin beating out of her chest.

There, in the corner of the screen, was a small box showing what Joanne's phone camera was capturing, and what Marcus would be seeing on his screen... but it wasn't Joanne as she was now.

"...one to talk, Marcus! ...all these years, you still..."

In contrast to Joanne's complete bewilderment, the Joanne depicted on the screen was furious. She was buttoning her shirt on the fly, as though Marcus had messaged her while she was still undressed, all while trying to make a case for herself, to finally defend herself against Marcus's cruel words... while the real Joanne sat in dead silence.

"Well, look who... up for herself!" Marcus let out a spiteful cackle, lifting a bottle of cheap beer and flashing a sickening grin as he responded. "You wouldn't have... if it wasn't for me! Step to me, Joanne, and I'll make sure you... nothing but a useless, homeless tramp!"

Even with the video's fragmentation, the real Joanne felt a spark of anger at Marcus's words... and the Joanne on the screen seemed to feel the same way, the feedback lightening slightly as she retorted, "You know, Marcus, I'm honestly happy you feel that way! Because that means I don't have to stick around, *pretending* to love you anymore!"

Marcus's grin faded instantly. Lowering his beer mid-drink, he moved to look directly into the camera. "You think... that *you've* had to pretend?"

The interference became worse, and what the other Joanne said was lost. But Marcus's next response suddenly came through clear as day, *"You've been using me from the start, you goddamned inbred whore! I know it, all my friends know it, and especially your fucking parents know it!"*

The real Joanne literally flinched back as Marcus's voice roared through the speaker, the volume of his scream assaulting her ears, "Ever since high school, you've used me as your fucking beard to get the social stigma off your back, while the whole time you've just been *waiting* for an opportunity to run off and start your fairytale life with some braindead *dyke!* Well, guess what, Joanne: There isn't a fairytale in the world that ends with a fucking street whore like you leaving her Prince Charming for some penniless *lesbo!* You never even came out to your own fucking parents—you think those wrinkled old shitstains would approve of you dumping me for some inbred whore?! Don't you fucking say that *you've* had to put up with *me,* Joanne! I've been your motherfucking *savior!* And if you had a fucking brain cell left in your goddamn *degenerate head,* you'd realize what a good thing you could have with me if you didn't talk back like the *cunt* that you are! Now put on your fucking clothes, bring home the car *I* bought for you, and get your whore ass back into the fucking real world. Or else I will find you, *and* that cunt, and—" Marcus never finished his sentence.

"Die and go to hell, Marcus! Just fucking die!"

A rush of agony shot through Joanne's head as the scream of rage echoed throughout the house; her own voice was now ringing in her ears to a deafening extent. She dropped the phone into her lap as she grabbed her temples, clenching her teeth and shutting her eyes against the pain.

As the pain gradually began to subside, Joanne began shaking, frightened at the words that had come out of her mouth... or, from the Joanne on the phone? Even though all logic would state it would be obvious which "version" of her had spoken, Joanne honestly wasn't sure which of them had finally snapped. But even though she had no idea what was happening, she had *never* screamed at Marc like that! To hear those words said in her voice was incredibly frightening... but when the pain faded completely, what Joanne saw on the screen upon opening her eyes almost scared her more than her outburst.

The Joanne on the screen had broken down crying. She sat on the bed, her shirt hanging off her shoulder, as she cried into her hands. But the whole time, Marc was just... staring at her. Head tilted, his expression cold, his eyes dark... Joanne was dumbstruck. Had she just *screamed at Marcus to die*, and he was completely unfazed?!

Then, out of nowhere, his voice spoke up. "That's right, you little bitch. Let it out; you know I'm right." His mouth never moved as his voice spoke; it was like voice over on an edited film.

And that was when Joanne realized... Marcus was literally not moving, at *all.*

Not to talk. Not to blink. Not to *breath.* The Joanne on the screen kept crying, but Marcus remained still as a statue.

Up until now, the one thing Joanne thought she could tell for certain was that Marc didn't know the "real her" was there. But now, as he stared unblinking into the camera,

Joanne began to even doubt that. Marcus's dead eyes seemed to be looking directly into hers... and something dark was pooling on his shirt.

Red. Dark red, spilling out over Marcus's shirt, while his head slumped, limp, to the side. Joanne felt a twitch in her eye as the room began to spin, her peripheral vision during into a jumbled mess. A static-like haze began to set in over the image of Marcus, five gaping wounds across his chest suddenly splitting open as his skin became devoid of pigment. Joanne stared in horror... as her voice began to speak.

"I did this."

"He's gone."

"He can't hurt me anymore."

"And no one ever—"

A hand suddenly snatched the phone.

"Aahhh!" Joanne snapped back to reality with a jolt, looking up at the brunette now standing over her, phone in hand. "M-Megan... you startled me." Admittedly, as she said that, Joanne fully expected—almost wanted—the other woman to respond with a snarky quip... but Megan didn't answer.

With an unreadable expression, she stared at the phone screen, barely blinking. The minuscule relief Joanne had felt upon Megan's appearance was now lost, and a looming sense of unease came over her.

"Megan?" Joanne addressed her hesitantly... she was suddenly very afraid of what Megan might do from seeing Marc on the phone.

But, after a few seconds, Megan simply lowered the

phone, and moved to sit down on the bed. "Joanne. Can you tell me how you felt about Marc?"

Joanne was confused. "Huh? W-why do you ask?" Subconsciously, she shifted away from Megan. She still felt that something was off with her.

In response, Megan let out a somber sigh. "I know you've been thinking about him; you were just holding a dead phone. It's clear that you're having a hard time… letting go."

Joanne stared at Megan in silence. "A… dead phone? But, there was—"

Once again, a flicker of fear suddenly flashed across Megan's face. But this time, she recovered from it quickly. "Well… I've been thinking, and I really think that the alcohol may have been more than you could handle. I think that you're probably seeing things." She delicately set the—indeed dead—phone on the bed between them, before reaching out to take Joanne's hands in hers. "But Joanne, you don't need to worry; I can help you. I want to help you. So please, let me in: Was it only what Marcus did that pushed you to this? Or was there something more? Please… I'll listen to you. Tell me everything."

Joanne felt a lump begin to form in her throat once again. But this time, she refused to let herself cry. She pulled Megan into a tight embrace, her breathing strained and eyes shut as she held onto the brunette like she could disappear at any moment.

"Megan… I don't know what's happening to me." Joanne's voice was strained as she spoke, barely coherent as her heart raced in her chest. "I'm hearing things, and seeing things, and—God, M-Megan, please, don't let him hurt me. I'm so scared!"

Even through Joanne's slurred words, Megan understood her perfectly, returning the embrace as she gently began rubbing her back. "It's okay... it's okay," Megan told her, letting Joanne rest her weight on her. "You're going to be alright, Joanne. We can work this out. I promise."

"Okay, okay," Joanne repeated, tightening her grip; though Megan's words couldn't fully put Joanne's mind at ease, Megan's reassurance did make her feel safer, even if just by a bit. Swallowing hard, she rested her head on Megan's shoulder. "Oh, Megan... how do you always know what to say?"

Megan let out a friendly "hm" in response; the tone of her voice upon replying indicated she was smiling slightly. "In my line of work, I have to."

"Your line of..." Joanne's eyes opened as she broke away from their embrace, looking at Megan with confusion. "Wait, what do you mean? Earlier, you said you did MMA."

"Oh!" Megan seemed to startle at this claim. "D-did... she not get to tell you?"

A chill shot down Joanne's back as Megan trailed off. "W-what do you mean 'she?' Who are you talking—"

Megan promptly cut her off, not even seeming to acknowledge her question. "Well, yes: I do MMA, but... that's not my actual job. I actually work in town as a thera—" And then... she froze.

On the spot, all emotion drained from the woman's face. Her eyes stared ahead, her arms at her side, staring right through Joanne as though she wasn't there... as devoid of life as Marcus had been.

"M-Megan?" Joanne exclaimed. "What's wrong?"

There was no response.

"Megan! What's going on?!" Joanne moved to touch the brunette's shoulder, shaking her gently... her limbs were completely limp. Her eyes unblinking... and blood was dripping down her face

"Megan!? What's happening to you?!" Joanne was practically begging as she got to her feet, taking Megan by the shoulders and desperately shaking her unresponsive body, blood flying off into the air. "No, no, this can't be real! Megan, *say something!* You can't be! You couldn't— *I couldn't—!*"

"—therapist; it means a lot to me to be able to help other people."

Bewildered, Joanne blinked dumbly. Sunlight filled her vision, pouring in from large, rectangular windows to her right. Joanne was suddenly sitting downstairs, at a small, rectangular dining room table.

A steaming plate of bacon and eggs was in front of her; the hands that had held onto Megan's inanimate body now held a knife and fork. And Megan herself was sitting across the table, completely alive and face blood-free, continuing her last sentence as though nothing had happened.

Joanne set down her utensils. Propping her elbows on the table, she rested her head heavily on her interlinked hands, and stared blankly downwards. She felt like needles were burning in her skin. "You... y-you..."

Megan's casual tone faded. "Joanne? Is something wrong?" she asked, setting down her own utensils.

Though she felt on the verge of a heart attack, Joanne forced herself to take a slow, if shaky, breath. "Where were we thirty seconds ago, Megan?" she managed, not even looking up at the other woman.

The answer was exactly what she expected. "What do you mean, Jo—"

Before the brunette could finish talking, Joanne's face shot up with a deathly cold glare. "Megan! *Don't.*" Even Joanne was surprised at how harsh her voice became in that instant. Trying to collect herself, her head hanging once more, she repeated her request. "Just answer the question, please... Thirty seconds ago. Where were we." It wasn't a question.

A short pause. And then, in a shaky tone of voice: "We were... r-right here, at the table. We were... eating breakfast, and I was just telling you about my job as a therapist."

"No. You're wrong."

"What do you mean, Joanne?"

As she spoke, Joanne slowly raised her head. "We were upstairs, in your bedroom. I had seen Marcus, on my phone, speaking to another version of me. You took my phone, and told me it had been dead the whole time." Joanne stared directly at Megan, her face blank. "You said you wanted to help me... but then you started talking strangely. And when I questioned you, you froze up. I couldn't get you to respond, and your face started bleeding... it was like you had been murdered in front of me."

Joanne swallowed heavily at the image, her heart beating out of her chest. "And then... I was here. Eating breakfast with you, alive and well... acting like I'd lived an entirely different life."

Megan's eyes stared, unblinking, at Joanne as she responded. "Joanne... I thought we'd been over this..."

"Have we? Or was that in my other life? I don't know anymore!" Joanne exclaimed, her voice hysteric. "This isn't alcohol that's making these things happen, Megan! These memories are too vivid to be hallucinations! I held your *limp body* in my hands, blood streaming down your face—and just moments later, we were both in an entirely different location! What aren't you telling me?!"

"J-Joanne, please calm down!" Megan implored, trying to regain control of the situation. "Why do you think I'm hiding something from you?"

"You're... you just told me you're a *therapist!*" Joanne began to stumble over her words. "How can you not know what's happening to me?! Are you lying? Am I dreaming? I-is any of this even real at all?!"

"Of course it's—" Megan tried to reach out and take Joanne's hand, but the blonde pulled away.

"I. Don't. Need. Reassurance," Joanne punctuated, her breathing labored. "I need the truth. You said it yourself... so *why* won't you tell me what's happening to me?!"

"You..." Her form noticeably trembling, Megan looked aside, her voice barely audible. "They weren't supposed to...."

"What?" Joanne demanded, leaning closer.

Megan swallowed heavily, still looking away... and then, a visible calm came over her. Finally looking back up at Joanne, her voice began to stabilize as she responded, "I-I'm sorry, Joanne. You weren't supposed to remember."

The two watched each other from across the table. With that statement, Joanne realized that she wasn't speaking to the Megan she knew anymore... but she no longer knew what to say.

Fortunately, the other woman did. "Many people have gone through this procedure before you, Joanne. But I'm not omnipresent. This system is not without flaws. And each mind is not as—*cooperative*—as the last."
The stress Joanne had felt was snuffed out by confusion, as she struggled to address the woman across from her. "Who... what... are you?" Joanne finally got out.

"W-well... to start, I suppose: I'm not Megan. Though, with my many slip ups during this session... I guess that's obvious by now." The woman slowly smiled at Joanne. "My official designation is LH-201. But my personal creator and operator affectionately calls me 'Sylvia.' Usually, these proper introductions would be optional, and reserved for after your treatment has concluded... as things currently are, however, I believe getting to know the 'real me' may help expedite the process going forward."

Joanne blinked. "So you're... not real."

"Not by traditional definitions, I suppose. But really, even then that's not entirely accurate," Megan—or,Sylvia— set her jaw contemplatively. "Yes, my current form, and by extension your surroundings, are technically fabricated. But

I *do* exist as a being; my emotions and physical limitations as the same as yours within these digital worlds. And this world is as real as your mind allows it to be."

Lifting an arm in front of her, Joanne ran her fingers over it. She felt the sensation of her fingertips against her skin; she realized that this conversation had given rise to goosebumps.

The artificial "woman" noticed this with a small smile. "I apologize for any of my prior anxiety you may have perceived, Joanne. But right now, the best thing you can do is to remain calm. If you accept this world as your reality, then your mind will likewise follow."

"As... reality?" Joanne stared at the artificial human like a deer in the headlights. "Wh-why in God's name would I do that? How *could* I do that? You just told me none of this is real—why would I want to stay in this... fabrication you've put me in?"

At this, Sylvia looked down with a sigh, shaking her head sadly. "You really don't remember. I can't believe they had to block off so much."

At that moment, Joanne began to feel an ache in her head. "Block off... what?"

Megan looked her dead in the eyes. "The most I can tell you, Joanne, is this: You agreed to this. So we could help you."

The blonde's blood went cold. "Help me?" As she spoke, the minor aching feeling in Joanne's head increased slightly. "Meg— I-I mean, S-Sylvia... why can't you tell me more?"

Sylvia let out a calculating, slow breath. For not being human, she certainly had the mannerisms down. "I'm sadly not at liberty to say, Joanne. That knowledge could cause further mental damage... even what I'm telling you now would usually be restricted." The AI's voice was somber. "My job as a 'virtual therapist' in this facility is to restore your psyche to a stable condition. My creators aim to achieve this by reverting you to a state before your mental health began to decline. Or, in layman's terms: When you were last truly happy."

"And... what would I have to do during this treatment?"

Sylvia smiled warmly. "Nothing, Joanne. As long as you're able to mentally accept this world, we'll handle the rest."

It felt as though a weight had been lifted from Joanne's shoulders; the blonde literally slumped in her chair as she exhaled, a rush of relief coming over her. "Then... I'm okay. You don't want to harm me, and this is just some kind of... therapeutic VR. A treatment I agreed to... that I can leave whenever I want."

"No, Joanne."

"What?" Confused, Joanne shifted to sit upright. "I... started this session, right?" All of a sudden, the AI's voice became cold; a grim expression coming over Sylvia's face.

"You agreed to it. But you willingly relinquished control to us." Sylvia stated. "I'm sorry. But you're not permitted to cancel this treatment."

The mild ache in Joanne's head turned into a

pronounced throbbing, as a faint, electric hum began building in her ears. The room surrounding them began to blur, flickering as though Joanne was blinking rapidly.

"My head... wh-what's going on?" she asked, her eyes squinting as she looked around at the room in terror. "Sylvia, what are you doing?!"

Despite Joanne's worsening vision, Sylvia's form remained almost entirely unaffected, barely flickering as she answered her patient's inquiry. "In the time I've taken to set your mind at ease, my creators have begun to rewind this scenario. Upon its complete reset, we should ideally be able to follow through with your treatment."

The electric hum continued to build, now beginning to skip, as though it was being played on a broken record. "You and my creators both unanimously agreed that the procedure should continue indefinitely. Until your mind is cured of all problematic symptoms."

Joanne stared in horror as the plates of food set on the table, were suddenly replaced by two flat squares of static, before the table was left completely barren. The sunlight streaming in through the windows cut out like a switch had been flipped, but instead of going dark, the room took on an almost monochromatic shade.

"But, S-Sylvia," Joanne stammered; the pain in her head felt like something was slamming against the inside of her skull. "What happens if you can't... cure me?"

The details of Sylvia's surroundings slowly began to fade away, the dining area they were sitting in being replaced by blank walls and textureless models... as the world deteriorated more and more, Sylvia simply sat in silence. Joanne's heart pounded in her chest, her head feeling like it was on fire...

When Sylvia finally spoke, the world had almost gone completely black. But her words were crystal clear. "Then we'll take care of you, Joanne. I promise."

And that was all it took.

"*Aaaaagh!*" Joanne grabbed at her temples as stabbing pain shot through her body. "*No, no, no no no!*" The "room" she was in suddenly flashed back into existence before turned into an indiscernible haze. Squeezing her head in agony as her mind broke down, Joanne tumbled from what had once been a chair onto the ground, landing with what felt like a burst of static coursing through her body. "*Megan, help me! I don't want to be hurt anymore!*" She felt on the verge of a heart attack as needles of adrenaline stabbing into her as her mind was flooded by images and sentences that she couldn't describe. "*Don't let them hurt me! I don't want them to hurt me! I don't— I don't—*"

"Joanne?!" Joanne barely recognized Sylvia calling her name, as the AI tried to run to the fallen woman's side, speaking to an unseen third person as she did so. "Dr. Paxton, stop the system reset! Something's going wrong, she's—"

"Stay away from me."

The warped room solidified in a new form. Megan was gone, and Joanne was no longer on the floor. She was standing at the kitchen counter, in the third apartment Marcus had moved them into since that day. Beer bottles were broken on the floor. That single lightbulb flickered above them. Joanne's hand reached for a wooden handle.

"Excuse me? What the fuck are you trying to do?" A distorted body stood in front of her, speaking with Marcus's voice. "Let go of that and get over here, you insane cunt, or I'll punch your fucking face in!"

"No. I won't let you hurt me anymore."

The last ten years flashed before Joanne's eyes as she stared at the figure before her. The being shifted and morphed, her perception of its features shifting with it. Sometimes appearing as Marcus, bags under his eyes and a scowl on his face. Sometimes a faceless, grey figure, standing rigid before her completely barren of features. Or a snarling, bloody clawed monster, drooling bile onto a body—Joanne's own body clasped in its long fingers; the Joanne it held was bleeding, bruised and crying. Joanne's grip tightened as she pulled the cleaver from the knife rack.

It didn't matter who it was, or what would happen to her. All she knew, was that it had to die.

"You won't lay a goddamn hand on me! Not now, and not ever again! You... I'll... I'll—!"

"J-Joanne, what did I just fucking say—"

"*I'll kill you, Marcus!*"

"Sylvia, the patient is relapsing! You need to step away from her immediately, we're preparing the euthanization process!" The voice of an unknown man cut through Joanne's memories. But her shattered mind barely processed the meaning of his words. Finally, she remembered everything.

She was back in Megan's house, but the textures of the room were a mess of colors as her memories flooded into their walls, ceiling and floor. Images of her life were now the textures of the house that her own mind had constructed, keeping her imprisoned her in a virtual mental ward. But throughout it all, one thing remained clear: Sylvia. Megan, backing away in fear as Joanne slowly got to her feet. Clasped in Joanne's hand, the same cleaver, stained with Marcus's blood, now hung down at her side.

As the air was filled with a cacophony of distorted sound, Sylvia tried to get the first word in. "Joanne—" But her patient cut her off.

"You all want to hurt me," Joanne seethed through her teeth, lifting the butcher's knife towards the fake woman before her.

"Joanne, that's not—"

"But I can't be hurt anymore. No one can *ever* hurt me again!" Joanne practically spat out her words as she took a heavy step forward. "I remember everything now: I remember what Marcus did to me, when I went home to him. How my parents encouraged me to stay with him, thinking he was a provider for their talentless daughter! How he would lash out and attack me, *each and every time* his day went badly!" A low laugh escaped Joanne's throat. "But most of all... I remember that you never found me. I remember you never saved me. *I remember, that you promised to protect me, and then I never heard from you again!*"

The appearance of the room shifted again; the image of a stormy sky, pouring down rain, covered every surface.

Joanne's footsteps were wet as she moved towards the AI, her fingers tight on the cleaver.

"But I found you, Megan! I found you *so easily!* After all those years, you never moved—your office was barely thirty minutes into town!" Joanne didn't even process the tears streaming down her face, mixing with the rain coming from nowhere all around her. "Why didn't you stop him, Megan? Why wouldn't you help me?! *Tell me why!*"

"Sylvia, what's happening in there? Something's stopping my commands from going through!" The unidentified male voice was barely audible, as what sounded like deafening knocking boomed through the room.

"Joanne! Please, calm down!" Sylvia pleaded, stepping back and away from the taller woman trembling before her. "We can help you! We want to help you! If you—"

"*No!* He's trying to kill me! *You're* trying to kill me!" Joanne took a wide slice at the air with the cleaver. "I can't believe that this is how you would treat me, after everything he did to me! He wouldn't stop, Megan! *He wouldn't stop! I had to make him stop!*" Like a million skylights opening, the room was suddenly enveloped in blinding light.

"*Aaaahhh!*" Sylvia threw an arm over her face, staggering backwards blindly before knocking into her chair, toppling to the ground with it. The impact knocking her arm aside, Sylvia squinted her eyes open.

The entire room was overlaid with images of Megan. The *real* Megan. But these weren't the happy memories Sylvia had tried to recreate, and expand upon... these images showed Megan distraught, terrified. Tears in her eyes as a hand hoisted her up by the neck. A horrible, deep gash slashed across her face, splitting her head open, as Sylvia's own voice—*Megan's* voice—resonated through the room, sentences and screams overlapping into meaningless noise and calamity.

And the Joanne standing in the middle of it all was no longer the woman she'd been before. Her slightly messy hair was now completely unkept, and speckled with red. Dark bags were prominent under bloodshot eyes. Her white shirt was soaked in blood, as were her hands. And she stared down at Sylvia, the look on her face chilled the AI to her core.

"After everything he did, Megan... how did you think you could still help me?" Joanne approached the fallen Sylvia slowly, spreading her arms. "Look at me... I'm not the woman you knew anymore! He broke me down, and in response—I turned myself into *this!* You thought you could help me, save me... *now?!*"

"J-Joanne! You need to stop!" Sylvia slowly began crawling backwards. "I'm sorry, b-but you... you know that I'm not Megan!" A firm hand came down, painfully gripping the brunette's shoulder.

"No. You are." Kneeling down, Joanne looked Sylvia right in her eyes. "Because just like you, despite everything... the *real* Megan tried to save me. She wouldn't defend herself. Until her very last breath, she—" Joanne's grip lessened as she choked down a sob. "Sh-she *truly* wanted to help me...!"

The surrounding noise decreased, just the slightest bit. The disturbing images became faded, as Sylvia looked upon the broken woman kneeling before her.

"Joanne. Listen, please...." Ever so cautiously, Sylvia reached up to Joanne's arm, intending to lift it aside—

"And just like you..."

"Ooww!"

Joanne's grip tightened tenfold, causing Sylvia to scream in pain; the sound caused the blonde to bare her teeth in an insane smile. "Megan couldn't didn't realize her *existence* was what pained me." Joanne's smile widened as she lifted the cleaver. "Because she was the last thing to remind me of my old life... of what he had done to me. Everyone else was gone... but *her* voice remained. Anything she could have done, still wouldn't have solved the true problem."

Megan's wordless screams became almost deafening. The images of her were replaced by agonized, spasming faces and limbs, blood flowing from open wounds. The voice of the unseen man barely broke through the onslaught of sound as Joanne lifted the blade to Sylvia's throat.

"Sylvia! Sylvia, please, respond!" the man cried out. "The patient's mind is deteriorating at a rapid pace, the system is completely overloaded; if you can hear me, send me your information so I can retrieve you!"

"Doctor! I'm here, I'm here!" Sylvia screamed desperately. "Please, do something! I don't want her to kill me, I don't want to—" Her words died in her throat as Joanne pressed the blade against her skin.

"What kind of 'therapist' are you. I thought you said you'd help me," Joanne hissed, as a drop of blood trailed down Sylvia's neck.

"P-please... please, don't..." Sylvia begged tearfully, her voice slurred in her desperation to preserve her life. "This, this isn't you! You loved this woman... you couldn't... you wouldn't!"

Suddenly, the male voice spoke up, much clearer than before: "Joanne! This is Doctor Alfred Paxton! I don't know what you're doing in there, but I beseech you: Do *not* harm Sylvia!" The man's voiced was strained, the surrounding room flickering rapidly. "Applying trauma to an AI assigned to a VR session could cause a cataclysmic power surge; if you kill this form of my daughter, you and everyone in this facility could potentially perish! We are still willing to help you, but if you have a thread of sanity left, you *cannot* do this!"

Sylvia and Joanne stared at each other, reality tearing apart at the seams around them. Slowly, her grip lessened slightly, and the cleaver moved away from Sylvia's prone neck, leaving a thin, red line across it where it had split the top layers of skin.

And then, Joanne began to laugh.

"I can't believe it... even now, you still don't understand!" Joanne reaffirmed her grip on Sylvia's shoulder even harder than before, the room around them literally spinning as Joanne lifted the cleaver to right above Sylvia's head. "If you really want to help me—" The room's geometry bending and contorted in impossible angles, the roar of agonized screams drowned out Joanne's thoughts and filled her mind. "—if you truly want me to be happy—"

"Joanne, no!"

"—*then you'll let yourself die!*"

The blade swung downwards into a horrible ripping of flesh. And the AI's screams joined the chorus, as the world exploded around them.

"Joanne... Joanne, hun! I-I can't believe it, after ten years!"

Megan didn't even notice the torrential rain. When she had opened the door to find that gorgeous blonde standing on her doorstop, nothing else mattered as she pulled the woman into a tight embrace.

"I know you said not to look for you, but I couldn't stop thinking about you...." Megan spoke into the taller woman's neck as she nuzzling her head into her shoulder, still unable to believe this was happening. "I've tried to find you for so long... I tried *so damn hard,* but after you moved, I had so little to go on! I prayed, if I just stayed here, you'd find me... god, Joanne, I'm so sorry I couldn't do more!"

Joanne said nothing in response, remaining unresponsive as Megan separated from her, and stepped back to gaze at the tall, beautiful woman standing before her.

She just as beautiful as Megan remembered... though her hair was a complete mess, her eyes were bloodshot, and her clothes were soaked. But beyond it all, it was still the same Joanne that Megan had met so many years ago... and then she finally realized what the stains were. The front of Joanne's shirt wasn't just soaked from the rain. It was coated in the unmistakable dark red of blood.

"O-oh my god!" Megan cried out, clasping a hand over her mouth; a vision from her worst nightmares had suddenly come to life. "Joanne, what—what did that fucking bastard do to you?!"

Finally, Joanne spoke up. Barely a muscle in her body twitched, as she spoke with a monotone inflection. "He hurt me, Megan. And wanted to hurt me again last night... I killed him before he could."

"Oh my god," Megan repeated, leaning on the doorframe as her mind raced. "Wh-what happened to your parents? Why didn't they—"

"They refused to believe me," Joanne responded. "So I killed them, too."

A distant boom of lighting sounded as Megan's face went pale. After ten years of worrying, and countless nights she'd wake up in tears... the woman she'd loved, was standing at her door... as a mentally broken *murderer*.

"Megan."

The brunette looked up upon hearing her name, to see the taller blonde slowly tilting her head. "Are you afraid of me, Megan?"

For the first time in her life, Megan couldn't bring herself to speak. Even as her body was frozen in place, inside her emotions were completely running amuck.

Every logical part of her being was telling her to *run*. To lock the door, grab her cellphone and call the police. Joanne had admitted to killing both Marcus, *and* her own family, and was now staring at Megan like a shark looks at a wounded swimmer. Megan could tell: *She was next.*

But she couldn't do it. Megan had loved this woman with all her heart. From just one simple night, Joanne had become her entire world... for ten years, she'd failed to protect her. That changed, now.

"No. I'm not afraid of you, Joanne," Megan finally answered. "But I need you to listen to me."

Joanne almost looked... surprised, at the woman's answer. But Megan didn't waste time trying to gauge the blonde's emotional state.

"I know I never had a chance to tell you this, but... I actually work as a therapist in town. And a new type of treatment has recently become available to my office." Megan stepped forward, placing a reassuring hand on Joanne's arm. "I couldn't be there for you when you needed me; nothing will ever make up for that. But I know you never wanted this. And if you'll just let me make one call, these people can help you recover."

Joanne slowly blinked. "They can... help me?"

"They can, and they *will*. I promise." Stepping to the side, Megan motioned to the open door, the warm light of her home shining within. "Let's head inside, hun... from now on, I swear to you: You will *never* be hurt again."

Gently, Megan led Joanne inside, trying to tell herself it wasn't too late. That Doctor Paxton could save Joanne, and the two of them could start over. Looking up at the blonde as they crossed the threshold, Megan admittedly felt a twinge of fear... but she forced herself to ignore those thoughts.

Just one call... I just have to make one call, she repeated internally. *Alfred and his department have saved so many people... Joanne will be no different.*

Letting go of Joanne's arm, Megan stayed behind to close the door. Joanne drifted off towards the kitchen as

Megan pulled it shut against the rainstorm outside.

Just one extended session, and the woman I love will be saved, Megan told herself. *Joanne would never want to hurt me... I know it.*

"I'm sorry... I'm so sorry...."

MARCH

Wailing

Amber Rainey

We aren't speaking to each other. I watch you sitting on the other side of the table, glaring down into your mug as if it holds the answer to all our problems. The only indication you are even aware of your surroundings is the slight flinch when the sound of wailing starts up again. It's been like this for days. We sit at the table and you frown and we don't talk.

I look at you now, really concentrating on the details of your face. Your hair is graying at the temples and in the stubble on your cheeks and chin. I don't remember when that started to happen. Do I look just as old and tired? You are still the most handsome man I have ever known but the weariness makes your face look ashen. The bruising under your eyes has become a little too dark and it makes me feel like you are a shadow of the man I married. You haven't looked at me in days but I can imagine the dullness of your once bright blue eyes. I could get lost in those eyes forever and you would laugh at me when we were young and you caught me staring.

I try to remember the last time we were happy. I look around the small cabin and remember all the good times we have spent here. It used to be the most treasured place in the world to me. Now, it is a mess. Dirty mugs sit in and next to the sink. The couch is covered in tangled blankets and the pillow has fallen to the floor. It could use a good dusting and a vacuum. I start to say these things but the wailing just seems to get louder and you sigh, which distracts me as I look back at you and watch you run a shaky hand through your hair. It's a tell, your way of showing me your displeasure without actually saying anything.

The wind kicks up, carrying the wails to our ears even faster. I clamp my hands over my ears, so tired of the sounds. It has to be a banshee. I wince at that thought as if I've betrayed your trust just by believing in the superstition in my head. I've always believed in the magic of the old land—something you fought with me about time and again. *Be rational* you would say in the most disgusted tone. It was the only thing we ever fought about. I shake my head. I don't want to think of the bad things. I want to remember the good. I want to fix this.

When you asked me to marry you, I felt like I was the luckiest girl in all of the world. You cocked an eyebrow when I told you what I wanted for a honeymoon. I don't think you really believed me at the time. You loved me—no, you *love* me because I can't bear it if you no longer do.

"*Do you really want to spend our honeymoon driving*

around a wet island?" you'd asked.

"Yep! It's magical and beautiful and green."

You'd laughed at that. Then you studied me as if I had two heads and made a face at me to make me laugh. You kissed me breathless and then pulled back to look deep into my eyes.

"Our wedding is in March. It's going to be raining. You hate the rain."

I shrugged, "It's Ireland. It's magic rain."

You'd rolled your eyes at that, our argument on the topic not reaching the levels it did in later years when the magic of being a newlywed wears off and all the things you once hid come into the light. In the end, I got my wish and we came to Ireland in March in the bitterest winter storm the island had seen in a hundred years.

We took it all in stride. We visited all the places I'd always wanted to see. We stopped and ate at little pubs where we were the outcasts and we met interesting and lovely people. The land really is magical, if not for the beauty of it, but also for its people and their welcoming ways. It was the best vacation I had ever had, despite the bitter cold and rainier than normal weather, and it almost went off without a hitch.

We were traveling through the Gap of Dunloe in the late evening. The road was a one-lane, winding thing. It was a good thing the car was tiny as well. We'd laughed when we first rented it because you practically had to bend at the waist to get in and then getting out proved an even bigger problem. The cars are definitely not as spacious as the ones we are used to in America. Anyway, there were sheep on either side of the road—as usual—and I wanted to stop and take a picture of them. The sheep were bleating at us and coming towards me and you just kept reminding me to get in the car. There was a baby and I wanted a picture of it. I finally did get that picture but then when I showed it to you, the flash had made all of the sheep look like they had menacing, glowing eyes. You laughed it off but I could see it disturbed you just a little.

Anyway, we got through the Gap and were on the opposite side of where our bed and breakfast was located. I wanted to continue along—always moving forward instead of going backward. You let me be crazy like that sometimes and reluctantly agreed to let me keep driving forward. It gets dark fast in the winter in Ireland and we found out fairly quickly that the headlights were our only source of illumination in the dark countryside. I'd seen a map and figured that we would eventually find our way back to civilization but I didn't know the exact way.

When you heard me tell you that, you started freaking out. Did we have any food in the car? How would we stay warm? What if we broke down?

As if on cue, the car started to sputter and you started groaning and fretting. Neither of us is a mechanic and we were in the middle of the darkened Irish countryside with no flashlight. I let the car coast as far as I could before pulling off to the side as close to the stone wall as possible. The Irish roads are like that, no curbs, just stone walls lining the path. I thought it was to keep the sheep in at first, but a driver is most likely to encounter sheep in the road despite the walls. It's just another charming quirk of the country. You got out and looked under the hood, then scanned the road as if hoping a gas station would pop out of nowhere to rescue us. I pulled my jacket tighter around me and hopped up on the stone wall.

"There, it's a house," I called down to you.

"How far?"

I shrugged and then laughed at myself, knowing you couldn't see it in the dark.

"Not too far, I guess. It's up ahead on the road. I think…"

You checked the car and made sure we locked it up. You stopped me and zipped up my coat, always worried that I would catch a cold in the damp just like I did at home every time we got a winter storm. I think your pockets were stuffed with more things than I have ever seen you carry—a road flare, an umbrella, the half-drunk bottle of water you found under the seat, a bag of chips that were probably all crumbs by now. I laughed at you and you just raised your eyebrow to me and held out a hand.

I took your hand and we walked down the dark road. The house had seemed much closer when I was standing on the wall next to a car with headlights. In the dark, everything seemed much closer and more spooky. We walked in silence and you chuckled nervously when I jumped at a sound but you squeezed my hand and then put your arm around me. The unknown is often the thing people fear the most and I think it was no exception to us.

When we finally made it to the cottage, the owner and his wife were nothing short of lifesavers. They told us there was nothing that could be done about the car until the morning and they fed us tea and *biscuits*. It turned out, they had another cottage they rented out in the summer and offered it to us for the night. They drove us the short distance to the little place and made sure we were comfortable. I think it was the happiest night we ever spent together. We cuddled together for warmth, although the little peat fire did prove useful once it had been burning for a few hours. The smell that greeted us from the peat the next morning was heavenly. I smiled at you and you kissed me with the sun streaming in through the window.

"*Let's never leave.*"

I was surprised to hear you say those words. We had a schedule to keep and you'd always kept us moving. It made my heart soar to hear those words. To hear that you could be content with me in one place. Perhaps I had feared you would never be completely happy with me—even though we were now married.

"*We could buy this place and move here,*" *I replied overeagerly.*

It was like throwing cold water on you. You got up and we got dressed. I kept stealing little glances at you but I had doused our moment and it was lost to me forever. Our saviors supplied us with breakfast, helped us call a tow, and then waited with us while politely discussing our travels until it arrived. You talked with the owner but he refused payment and so we went on our way and continued the last of our trip.

You honestly surprised me when we returned to that same cabin the next March. I remember you keeping it a secret until we were at the airport and you could no longer hide the destination. The moment it was revealed, I couldn't contain the squeals of excitement and you turned red, scratching behind your ear and looking like you wished the floor would swallow you up whole. You were never used to so much attention.

After that year, it became a tradition for us to go to the cottage for a few weeks every March. It was our happy place. We would take long strolls through the fields. You'd spot me while I tried to balance as I walked along the stone walls and then I would fall dramatically into your arms when I was tired of the effort. You'd pick flowers and weave them into my hair as we sat next to the little stream, wishing it wasn't too cold to dip our toes into the crystal clear water. I'd once suggested maybe we should start visiting in the summer months but you had gasped and gone on a lecture about *tradition*.

We were happy. I don't quite remember when we stopped being happy. The last trip I remember in detail started out like every other trip. We'd flown into Dublin just before St. Patrick's Day. Normally, you would have avoided a party of that magnitude like it was the plague. However, I had convinced you to at least experience it this once and the dates lined up so we took the plunge. Dublin was absolutely spectacular. There is really nothing that beats being with the Irish on their holiday. We drank and laughed and reveled. We stayed up much later than we had ever done before and we overslept the next day with heavy hangovers. *Being* Irish for one day of the year was more than enough, despite the enjoyment.

We drove to our little cottage, newly cleaned and spruced up. The little peat fire was already warming up the main room and a welcoming plate of homemade bread was sitting on the table. Irish hospitality lacks for nothing. I was intrigued by the little note left by the plate and picked it up, reading aloud.

"Fáilte! If you need anything, you know where to find us. I baked this bread fresh for the holidays and hoped it might take off the edge until your supper. Be aware, the faeries have built up a new ring near the oak on the edge of your field. Best not to disturb them. May luck be with you."

You rolled your eyes when I looked up and I shrugged, grinning.

"What?"

"It seems they would give up that nonsense in this day and age."

I sighed, *"It's part of the magic."*

"It's a gimmick," you groused.

I shrugged and watched you take our things into the bedroom. I didn't want to cause another argument on the subject. I'd learned you were set in your black and white ways. It is just a part of who you are and I can respect it, even if I disagree with it. I've pointed out countless times my feelings—the belief in magic doesn't cause any harm and you've always countered with some rational objection. It isn't anything we are likely to ever change each other's minds about so we just try to agree to disagree.

The intrigue of a fairy ring would not stop swimming

around in my mind. I'd visited all the ancient and mystical places in Ireland but I wanted to feel closer to the magic of it. I'd listened raptly to people talking on videos on the internet and read many a novel on the subject. I was fascinated by the prospects of another world just beyond our reach. A world that knew of us but stayed hidden for obvious reasons. It seemed within my grasp when I was in the little cottage in the Irish countryside.

I begged you to go out with me that morning. I wanted to just look at the faery ring. The mention of it made you scoff and turn me down. You made some excuse about needing to check on something in town and I got mad at you, screaming at you for the first time ever in our little haven. We fought, the most we had ever fought before and it ended when you stomped out the door, getting awkwardly into the little car and driving away. I cried for who knows how long and then stubbornly pulled on my rain boots and grabbed an umbrella, heading out into the cold to make my visit.

With every step, I argued with you in my head. I finally found the little ring of mushrooms and plopped down next to it. I spilled all my worries out, talking to that faery ring as if the faeries themselves hung onto my every word. I was sure they could relate to my woes. The old ways had died off long ago and the newer generations had a healthy dose of skepticism. Perhaps the faeries felt neglected.

I don't know why I cling to my stubborn belief in magic. I had always been enraptured with the idea of magic and princesses and *somewhere else.* My childhood had not been a pleasant one and escaping into a fantasy world was the only thing that kept me sane. I could hear your rebuttal about my possible insanity. Even though it was usually meant as a joke, somehow hearing you say it in my head turned it into something ugly. I started crying again. I hated that we were fighting. No matter our differences, you are my best friend and I love you. I will always love you.

Somehow, I got it into my head that it was a good idea to climb the oak tree, in the rain, with heavy rainboots on. I tried to get a foothold a few times and my foot slipped off each time. I was still crying and it didn't make it easier because each new slip was an insult to my pride and it made the tears come faster. I finally got what I thought was a good foothold with the first foot and lifted myself using the branch to place my second foot. That is when it happened. I fell off the tree in a heap.

It took me a moment to catch my breath. I silently took stock of my body, trying to feel if I had broken anything. The rain started falling softly on my face and forced me to sit up before I drowned. I laughed a little to myself. It would be just like me to drown in a drizzle. You would have thought it apropos. I frowned at that, hoping that by the time I returned to the cottage, you will have cooled off and come back to me. Patience in that regard has never failed me before and you always come back with an apology and a kiss that can make me forget why we argued in the first place.

I stood up and began brushing myself off when it caught my eye. I looked down felt horror like I have never felt in my life. At my feet lie the remains of the faery ring, the little mushrooms crushed and some lying next to their stalks where

I decapitated them in my fall. My heart started beating loudly in my ears and I dropped to my knees, the sobs returning. I gingerly picked up one of the mushrooms and began apologizing profusely to the unseen faeries. I had destroyed their ring and now I had brought ruin and destruction upon us. You would have been equal parts horrified at my irrational behavior and consoling at my despair. I could hear you in my head again—*It's just a superstition.*

It wouldn't matter how much I argued with you on the topic, you would not have believed anything I said, chalking it up to nonsense and trying to distract me from my concerns. You don't believe in fate or destiny. You've always told me we make our own and no one can determine yours. You don't avoid superstitious things like other people. To you, they are just the old ways of scaring children into behaving as they should and keeping adults under some unseen control. To me, however, it doesn't hurt to avoid upsetting the natural order of things and having a healthy dose of reverence to the old beliefs. Maybe our ancestors just told stories to protect themselves and their children from the outside world but maybe there were also grains of truth in those stories.

Sheep bleating in the nearby field roused me to my senses and I looked around, realizing it was beginning to get very late and the sun would set soon. Once the sun was set, the darkness would surround me in no time. I hadn't thought to bring a flashlight and the trek back across the fields would not be quick in the dark. I looked down at the destroyed faery ring one last time, once again making my apologies, and then surveyed my surroundings. I got the bright idea of taking a shortcut, making my way towards the road and deciding to follow it home instead of picking my way through the fields.

By the time I reached the road, the rain had become a downpour and I could barely see a hand in front of my face. The umbrella did little to protect me from the onslaught and the road was beginning to flood in a few places. I decided to climb up onto the wall and try to balance on it as I continued towards the cottage. You'd always laughed at how bad my balance was and warned me not to try walking on the wall without a spotter. I'd stuck my tongue out at you the last time. You'd laughed and I remember how much I loved that laugh. My heart was aching for our fight to be over and yet, I knew, I had to tell you what I had done to the faery ring and my fear of their reprisal. It was a double-edged sword, wanting your comfort for something I knew would only increase your displeasure.

I saw the headlights of a car in the distance, coming towards me and I decided maybe I could ask the driver for a ride home. I pondered a way to get the driver's attention and waited until they were near before attempting to open and shut my bright green umbrella in a gesturing fashion. That was when the wind hit and knocked me into the road. I only remember the fleeting feeling of flying and then the rest went dark.

The wailing picks up in volume again and I jump and look up at you when you slam your fist into the wall of the cottage. You lean your head against the wall and I can tell you are sobbing when I see your back trembling. I want to go to you but I am rooted in my chair. I watch you turn and my heart hurts to see the tears streaming down your face. You look straight through me, the despair and heartache plainly written on your features as you slide down the wall and drop your head into your hands. The wailing mixes with your gulping sobs in an odd chorus of grief. I don't know how much more of your pain I can watch. I struggle to break free of the invisible holds keeping me in my chair and silent. I can't let you suffer. I would give anything to see you laugh again.

Talk to me! I scream it in my head, over and over again, trying to break through to you. Finally, you look up, straight at me as if seeing me for the first time in ages. I can see the shock on your face the moment your eyes lock with mine. I don't understand it and the moment fades as you look around the room, as if trying to find me again. The wailing had stopped in that instance but now it starts even louder. An odd look crosses your features and you stop searching. You seem to be having a silent conversation with yourself and I long to be a part of it. I can tell when you've made a decision. A strangely calm resolve crosses your features. It scares me.

I watch you gather up your things and walk out of the cottage. I don't follow and I don't understand why. I try to tell myself it is because we aren't speaking. We haven't spoken in so long and I don't remember why we stopped. I am helpless to break the impasse, the unseen force continuing to keep me in my place and the wailing increasing to unbearable volumes. I try to scream to the rafters but the wailing drowns me out. I don't know how long I continue struggling with myself and pleading for it to end. I can't live like this anymore. I can't let us grow apart and it be all my fault for my stupid beliefs in magic. Magic was supposed to be joyful, not sorrowful. I berate myself for being so foolish and lash out at myself, rocking back and forth in my chair with my hands over my ears in an attempt to drown out the wailing and cling to what little sanity I have left.

I am startled by a hand on my shoulder and nearly fall out of the chair. Suddenly, as if you'd never left, you kneel in front of me, taking my hands and wiping my cheeks dry with your thumbs. You smile at me, one full of love and sadness.

"You can stop now, my love," you say to me.

I'm confused, shaking my head at the first words he has spoken to me in a very long time. Then I realize what has happened. The wailing has stopped. I hold my breath, waiting for it to begin again and it seems you do as well. The patience in your eyes speaks volumes and for once I feel truly understood. We wait like that for an eternity before you squeeze my hands. I look down at you and smile with trepidation. I don't understand what has happened to make you look at me with such love again but I don't really care. As if understanding my needs, you lean up and kiss me, pouring out all of your pent up emotions. It's the best kiss we have ever shared. Reluctantly, I pull away and rest my forehead against yours. I wait for your eyes to open and meet mine before I ask the question burning in my head.

"How... how did you make it stop?"

"It was you, love. You could have made it stop but you didn't, so I helped you," you explain.

"I don't understand."

"Come with me."

You take my hand and we go out of the little cottage. It is cold, but I don't seem to feel it anymore. We walk through the fields towards the home of the owners of our little cottage. It is bustling with activity. Children are playing a game in the yard and they pay us no mind as we pass them and go inside. Once there, I notice adults milling about in various hushed conversations. The owner's wife is standing to one side, sniffling into her handkerchief while the woman who runs the grocery consoles her and conceals a sniffle of her own. I look at you, still not understanding and you just smile at me and lead me to a couple of empty chairs. A woman near us shudders, crosses herself, and moves to a different part of the room. I am about to call her out for her uncharacteristic rudeness when you put a hand in mine and squeeze.

We sit in the chairs and I am still confused but unwillingly to question your motivations. I just got you back and I am loathed to rock the boat and cause a scene that would embarrass you and push you away again. Everyone in the room avoids our little corner and I can observe them with unfettered curiosity. The owner's wife passes around a plate of biscuits and politely chats with her guests. All of her guests except us, who continue to cross themselves at periodic intervals in their conversations. I finally pick up on one of them.

"It's a tragedy, really, but probably for the best," a man says to the owner's wife.

"Yes, poor dears. Perhaps he would have recovered if not for the banshee. The faery folk themselves must have cursed her. I warned them about the faery ring but that young lady was wild and impulsive."

I look at you in horror, hoping you haven't heard them but you are staring at me with such intensity. Your eyes hold knowledge that I long to unravel and yet you aren't speaking again. I can see the pleading in them for understanding but I can't seem to grasp the point they are trying to make.

"I'm lost, help me," I beseech.

"You have to remember. I can't make you do it."

I want to run from the cottage, the air suddenly feeling stale and stuffy. I stand up and a draft blows through the room, all in attendance crossing themselves in unison. It is too much for me and I push past everyone, running outside. My head hurts and I feel like I am going to vomit. I know the moment you join me, I can feel your warmth. You make everything around me seem a little brighter.

"We can be together again if you only remember."

I look up into your eyes, full of love and trust. You believe in me. I am searching for the answers but I only see your patience. I close my eyes, hunting through my memories, trying to find the answer to the puzzle.

When did we stop speaking? When did we last fight? My brain reminds me of the fight about the faery ring and I scoff at it. Surely we'd fought since then. Our marriage was never perfect but we fought and made up dozens and dozens of times. What was the last thing we fought about? The more I try to remember, the more I only remember the faery ring. I remember the fall from the wall and then... nothing.

I start backing away from you, my hands held up in

defense and trying to ignore the conclusion my brain wants me to believe. I remember the car and falling from the wall and then I remember your despair. The wailing, constant and dreadful. How did you get so gray?

"That's it, my love. Remembering will set us free," you comfort me.

I don't want to remember this horror. I don't want any of it to be true. I always said I believed in magic and superstitions but it is too much for me to realize it might not have been a false belief. Not if it means you are here with me. If you are here with me, then all hope is lost. I shake my head at you, denying the facts flooding into my brain. You only come closer, gathering me in your arms. I almost succumb to you but I need the answer to the last piece of this twisted puzzle.

"What did you do?" I ask with horror.

You smile sadly and shrug, "I heard you in the cottage, you were screaming at me to talk to you."

"That was in my head!"

"I heard you, my love. Every March for the past five years, I have heard you. I couldn't bear to hear your misery any longer. I did what was needed so we could be together again."

"That… wailing…"

"It was my own personal banshee."

I gasp. All the memories come flooding into me at once and I see clearly the misery I have subjected upon you. I am mortified but you just take my hands again. You nod at me and I realize at that moment just what it means for you to be here, talking with me. Tears start sliding down my cheeks and you kiss them away.

"I love you and we are together. No more crying," you remind me.

I nod and you kiss my forehead. You smile at me the way that melts my heart, if I still had a beating one, and you hold out your hand. I take it and we walk back across the field to whatever the future may hold for our spirits.

aPRIL

Ashes to Ashes

J.W. Capek

The spring Hellebores hung their fading blossoms over the body bleeding out beneath them. The slugs were already appearing. They slimed toward the mouth, nose and eyes of the old man, fallen upon a lethal tote of gardening implements. It seemed obvious and fair—Ralph had tripped on a flagstone circling the Koi pond and was impaled on the gardening tools as he fell. Even now the blood drenched baby tears tried to crawl from beneath him.

Carolyn, his wife, calmly called 911 and spoke with an equally calm dispatcher. "There's been a terrible accident in my garden. My husband is dead." Following instructions, she circled the house, through the garden gate and watched the mansion driveway fill with vehicles. There was a police car, a County Sheriff's off road vehicle, a fire engine, a Fire Chief's red sedan, an ambulance, two more Sheriff's vehicles, a

Coroner's van, and eventually, a service van from the Acme Cremation Society. There were EMTs snapping on blue latex gloves, sheriff's pulling out writing pads, one policeman going ahead to the garden and making an all clear signal to the others, and a scurry of men and women trying to avoid falling in the pond as they accessed Ralph, the body.

It was soon clear to all that Ralph was beyond any assistance. One particular Hori Hori blade was thrust deep into the hemorrhaged mid-section while a stainless-steel cultivator was jammed into the chest. It was only guesswork where the grubber on the digging ax was buried. The EMT's rubber gloves were removed and a backboard, defibrillator, emergency cache, and IV tripod were repacked in the emergency vehicle and it, along with the firetruck, left the premises. The coroner's gloves stayed on through phone calls and moving Ralph about. The crematorium people waited on the sidelines. A woman officer guided Carolyn into the house and suggested a cup of tea for them both.

"Your garden is magnificent! Your husband must have tripped on the slippery flagstone," the officer offered.

"Yes, the moles dig under them, Ralph is always... was always... having to fix them." Carolyn was surprised by her own sense of resignation. "How appropriate that today is April Fool's Day," she said while thinking, 'Of all the cultivated plants on acres of garden, Ralph had been foolish enough to die beside the Koi pond. Drowning would have been less messy.'

By bedtime, Carolyn was at last alone in her house. Jennifer, her husband's niece, had rushed over but seemed to be more in the way than helpful. Carolyn was glad when the flighty woman with scraggly hair had finally left. The door to Ralph's bedroom remained closed as it always was. Her door was closed to him as well. How had it all come to this, she wondered. How had they grown so far apart that his death was just a relief, instead of a tragedy?

In college, they had attended very different schools. Carolyn's father sent her to Seattle University even though she was not Catholic. She was an English major because her elitist father felt it would develop eloquence and critical thinking for his shy daughter. Meanwhile Ralph was a Landscape Designer at the State University. They met at an intercollege mixer and both were drawn to the other. Ralph thought an English Major would enhance his plebian status in agriculture studies, and Carolyn was sure her father would approve of a Landscape Architect who could enhance the mansion's gardens. They married. Ralph was content to manage the Gardens. Carolyn was her father's daughter and her husband's wife. That was enough.

Jennifer insisted on accompanying Carolyn to the Crematorium the next day. She fidgeted and kept weeping as if she had really cared about her uncle. Carolyn had never liked her and now found her more irritating than ever. With Ralph gone, Carolyn saw no need to even be polite.

"Jennifer!" Carolyn said crisply, "If you can't act like a mature woman and stop this sniveling you should leave. I have business to attend to and your presence is not necessary!"

Jennifer caught her breath and held a tissue to her nose and stopped the crying but eyed Carolyn warily as a man in a black suit entered the office where they were seated. Non-descript background music came with the man as did a sweet smell of flowers.

"Madam, we are so sorry for you untimely loss," the man said simply, taking Carolyn's hand gently. "I am Quincey Toomes, your Service Director. We of the Blissfully Quiescent Crematory and Slumber Gardens are here to help serve you whatever way we can."

Carolyn withdrew her hand and spoke brusquely. "My husband made the arrangements with your company some time ago. I didn't care then, but now I must take everything into consideration. First, Quincey, what are you required by contract?"

The widow's address as "Quincey" caused the manager to sit at his desk and quickly open a portfolio, realizing this was not the time for solicitude but concise negotiations.

"Madam, your husband, may he rest in Peace, contracted for the Premier Package. That includes our oak casket to hold the body while it is in the retort for cremations, a display urn or cinerary urn for the cremated remains, a full memorial service in our chapel, and a memorial plaque. Also, there will be medallions with your husband's name and dates. These can be bronze or silver as mementos for the bereaved attending the memorial."

"*Nope!* Absolutely not!" stated Carolyn with such

certainty that the manager looked up from the contract.

"I'm sorry, Mrs. Greiner, I know this is a hard time for you, but your husband's wishes were quite clear."

"And my wishes are even clearer, and I'm alive to make them! I do not want all of this silliness surrounding an even sillier life and death. I believe my husband paid you a deposit on your Premier Package. Now, I expect you to bring the whole cremation into that price range." Carolyn folded her hands on her purse and looked directly into Quincey's eyes.

"Madam, let me assure you . . ."

"You can't assure me of anything! You already have my husband's body. You must have put him in a refrigerator overnight. Now, let's look at your *reduced* plans for him."

"Oh, Aunt Carolyn," Jennifer said nervously, "you are just too upset for this now." She looked pleadingly at the manager as if he could understand.

Carolyn reached across the desk, took the portfolio and started crossing off Premier services.

Quincey Toomes was flummoxed and almost in awe of the choices she made. She finished and glared at him and with all of his years of dealing with bereavement, he was at a loss for words. She designated the elaborate oak coffin be replaced by a cardboard box for the cremation. Return of the cremated remains should also be in a cardboard box as well within two days. There would be no urn, no service, no medallions. And, the entire process would be covered by Ralph's deposit.

Satisfied, Carolyn stood and ignored Quincey's shaky

hand held out to her. She demanded a copy of her altered contract and promptly left the office. With a glance over her shoulder, she said, "You can deliver the cremains to my house, personally."

The following morning, Carolyn dressed in a formal gray suit with a brightly colored mandala scarf—formal attire with no hint of mourning. She had an appointment with her family legal and accounting office. The firm had taken care of her father's business and hers and she wanted to be sure of her status, commitments, and responsibilities. Unfortunately, Jennifer had overheard her plans and met her in the office. Carolyn preferred she not be there but at least she wasn't sniveling. Ralph was her uncle after all, maybe there was a reason for her to be there.

"Mrs. Greiner, I am so sorry to hear about Mr. Greiner's death. Such a tragic accident. We just never know, do we?" The young attorney, Stephan Pullet, was appropriately dressed in a suit that fit with the legal office and its cases of legal books. He attempted to look older and more formal by growing a sparce mustache. His desk was neatly organized, with no computer to be seen.

"Do any of you ever read those law books?" Carolyn asked without acknowledging his condolences, just gesturing at the library.

"I beg your pardon," he said, his expression puzzled.

"I just thought lawyers and accountants did all their work on the Internet." Carolyn's sarcasm warned the upcoming meeting would not be an easy one. It wasn't. It was very difficult for both.

Carolyn was exhausted by the time she reached home. She hadn't noticed when Jennifer faded away, she didn't care. In between questions and exclamations, Carolyn had learned her state of affairs. Her mansion home had been left to her by her father but all of the land and gardens were left to Ralph. She thought it must have been her father's way of insuring their marriage. By law, half the land was hers, the land with the house. Unfortunately, there had been a pre-nuptial agreement signed years ago that all the land and gardens inherited by Ralph would go into a Garden Trust or Heritage Park or something or other. Carolyn didn't understand it all but knew her father was obsessed with the Gardens and that was his common interest with Ralph. 'Those *damn* plants!' Carolyn thought to herself.

The final result was there would be a legal tie-up if Carolyn tried to sell the gardens. Her father and Ralph's tendrils wound themselves tightly around Carolyn until she couldn't breathe. Daddy loved the garden best, Ralph loved the garden best. Exotic plants from around the world would hold onto her forever! She was legally bound to sustain the gardens until the "something or other" could take possession.

Preparing for bed, Carolyn saw an old lady in the mirror. Where had the time gone? Who was that woman with graying roots, stern creases on her face, and aged hands? She began to tremble and sat quickly on the bed. Still, no tears came. Intellectually, she knew there were stages of grief and now alone in her bedroom, she let herself think of them. There was no denial. The picture of Ralph laying in the mulch with implements of destruction piercing his body meant his death was real. Anger was the rage she felt dealing with the death mongers at the crematorium and legal office. Bargaining would come later as taxes, property distribution, and legal matters demanded she make compromises for expediency. Depression? Not really. The years of marriage to Ralph had numbed that emotion. Now there was just relief. Acceptance was a possible goal, whatever it meant. Never could Carolyn remember the inclusion of Complete Exhaustion in the stages. Her sixty-three year old body ached with bone weariness. Curling into a fetal position, she pulled a fleece comforter about her.

Carolyn hardly moved all night.

When the three death mongers appeared together at Carolyn's entrance door, she took it as a sign that Ralph was continuing his April Fool's Day joke on her. Mr. Toomes stood with a brown cardboard box in his hands. He had an impatient expression as if he just wanted this task to be over. The young lawyer stood protectively near Jennifer with a briefcase certifying his presence. Jennifer just fidgeted and kept avoiding her aunt's eye contact.

"Well, look at this, the Three Horsemen of the Apocalypse!" Carolyn said sarcastically. She reached out and took the box from Toome's hands. He didn't hesitate to let her take possession. "You may go now, Quincey. I'll take care of this." She raised the box slightly.

Quincy Toomes was both affronted by her dismissal, and relieved. He nodded to the two remaining and with a muffled consolatory comment, then retreated to his black limousine. He had to resist the temptation to peal out of the driveway. After all, Quincey was a professional.

"You two can go as well, the driveway is unblocked." Carolyn said while turning the box in her hands.

"But, Carolyn, what happens now? You've never talked about a memorial service or ashes dispersal. How can we help you in this sad hour?" Jennifer had never liked Carolyn but Ralph's death gave a purpose to her attentions. "Even Mr. Pullet is here to assist you." Jennifer nudged the attorney.

"Yes, Mrs. Greiner. What can I do?" Pullet asked.

"Can you dig a hole?" Carolyn looked directly at the young man.

"Why, yes. I suppose so."

"Follow me, both of you."

Reaching the garden, Carolyn gestured to a shovel for Pullet and immediately walked the flagstones to the Koi pond. "There. Just dig around there by the Hellebores."

"The soil is discolored and torn up," Pullet said in disbelief. He looked to Jennifer who just nodded and looked away.

"Of course, it's torn up. The coroner men did their jobs and left the dirt." Carolyn said disdainfully.

"But what do you want me to do?"

"Shovel up the clods and dig a hole."

"But... but..." young Pullet stammered.

"You were the one who wanted to help," Carolyn said pointedly. "So help!"

"But is this legal? I've never done this before." Pullet

was very nervous now.

"All I'm asking you to do is dig a hole in my garden, then you can leave. You can look up the something or other rules and torts at another time. I suggest you try the Internet." Carolyn never flinched as she looked at the young man with the shovel.

Exasperated, Steven Pullet simply dug a hole in a widow's garden. That was all. When finished, he gestured to Jennifer and the two of them circled the house to leave. Mr. Pullet kept wiping his hands on a handkerchief trying to get them clean.

Carolyn turned her attention to the box in hand. "That's it, Ralph! Ashes to ashes and all the other words someone who cared might say." Without further ceremony, Carolyn dropped the box in the hole. She didn't bother to remove the gritty fragments from the plastic bag inside. She shoved the dirt back in place with her foot. That evening, she watched the rain nurturing the garden. Her garden.

In the sunny morning, Carolyn took her coffee out to the Koi pond. "Stupid fish." She thought. "All they do is hover around with opening mouths waiting for someone to feed them." Then she remembered they had not been fed since Ralph died and turned to the garden shed to get some granules. Walking on the flagstones she noticed a mound of dirt near the Hellebores. She would have thought the rain would blend in the freshly turned soil. It wasn't until she returned with the fish food that she thought the soil mound looked larger. The top of the crust was beginning to crack. Carolyn made a mental note to check Ralph's garden papers, to confirm employment with the landscaping firm he always used seasonally.

Evening brought Carolyn back to the pond but the soil next to it had a strange mound growing out of it. It was off white and grainy. Its irregular shape reminded her of a candle melting from a point on top. It was definitely larger, and she wondered if it could be some unusual fungus growing from the remnants in the box beneath the soil disturbance. She called the landscape service that evening but they were already scheduled ahead for Ralph's summer prep. She would have to wait.

Curiosity drew Carolyn to the pond the following day and she gasped at the sight of a man's figure. Formed from the ashes and adjacent soil, it was Ralph's height. Although the facial features were still obscure, Carolyn would recognize the posture of a man contemplating his garden. Ridiculous! Carolyn thought. The strain was getting to her imagination!

She turned to escape to the house when she heard a familiar voice. "You know, Carolyn, those pants really make you look fat. With a butt as big as yours, you should be careful what you wear."

Carolyn stopped in shock. She began breathing rapidly as she turned to look at the form in the garden. It was just a lump of dirt, for God's sake. Just dirt, fungus, and... And... ashes! It couldn't talk in a snide voice to insult her. She turned again to the house and a glass of sherry to calm her.

Looking out of the living room window that April evening, Carolyn held her second glass of sherry and surveyed the gardens. Immediately, she saw that the night landscaping was turned off. The carefully placed lighting system, so planned by Ralph, had only one flood light illuminated. Highlighting the area of the Koi, shadows wove around the flora like fingers. Except for the statue. The earlier form was now a fully developed statue of a gargoyle. A man gargoyle. It stood as if spotlighted, the Ralph face looking directly at Carolyn.

With a gasp, Carolyn yanked the drapes closed and backed out of the room, stopping only to take a decanter of whiskey with her. In her bedroom, Carolyn sat shivering and holding another glass of comfort. Perhaps, she thought, all those ceremonies and traditions she had ignored did have a purpose. She had no faith the dead person was helped, but maybe the living survivor had need of them. Maybe, maybe, maybe. It was over now. Ralph was dead, his ashes in the garden, his legal manipulations being processed, and Carolyn was becoming delusional! Ha! What a conclusion to a long and boring marriage!

By the last glass of liquor, Carolyn was convinced everything would right itself when she sold the damnable garden. Her father had succeeded in his financial goals and like many wealthy people looked for a purpose to balance any guilt they might have developed in becoming rich. Donations to charities were just tax numbers, but developing the garden gave him a tangible connection to the earth. It was a leftover concept from the Hippie Stage of his life before he succumbed to the call of wealth. When Carolyn brought Ralph Greiner home, her father saw a live-in garden expert. By then, Carolyn's father saw the Pacific Northwest Gardens to be his legacy and he negotiated with Ralph that the Foundation would forever reflect the multi-millionaire's devotion to beauty. Or, so it said in the Foundation brochures.

With a terrible headache, Carolyn fortified herself to go to the garden in the bright sunlight. Near the house, everything was in order. Spring flowers were budding and beginning to bloom. There were birds chirping in the trees and somewhere a pileated woodpecker was drumming his territorial rights. The drumming matched a similar throbbing in her head. She approached the Koi pond with some hesitancy. It was still there. Her husband's gargoyle looked less ominous in the daylight and she stepped closer.

"Morning, Bitch!"

Carolyn jumped. Her head screamed, 'This isn't real, this isn't happening!'

"You know, Slag, I never did love you. You were such a mealy bitch, your father despaired of ever marrying you off. That's why he was so glad when I pretended interest. He and I used to laugh at you trying to be pretty for a social club." Ralph paused, then added, "We knew you would never fit in at the Country Club. Your father always resented you weren't the son he deserved!"

"No, no!" Carolyn cried and her heart sank as profanity continued to pour out of the gargoyle's mouth. It used words she had only heard on television, never from Ralph. Disgusting. Physically impossible sexual terms. Various names for perverted female genitalia. All offensive verbiage was thrown at Carolyn who stopped processing the words and focused on the hate in the face of her former husband.

"Fuck you!" was her only retaliation as she spun and ran towards the house. She almost tripped on a flagstone and grabbed at a thorny bush for balance. With a cry of pain, she let go of the branch and saw the garden shed door open to her. Rushing inside, her hand was bleeding as she saw an ax on the wall. She struggled to release it from its hook and hurried towards the pond carrying it as she had seen gardeners do.

"Damn you! Damn you! You are dead and will stay that way!" She lifted the ax and brought it down on the gargoyle head. She heard the crack as it entered and scattered the bone fragments. Again and again she pounded the statue. It offered no resistance just curses and epithets. Sweating, Carolyn's hands were slippery from her blood but she held tight and crushed the figure into a lump on the ground.

Crying, she dropped the ax and stumbled into the house. Carolyn wrapped a washcloth around her hand and fell to her bed, exhausted.

When Carolyn awoke it was dark. She went to the bathroom to get a drink of water. She grimaced at her tear stained face and gingerly tried to remove thorns pounded into her skin by holding the ax. There were bone particles as well, leftovers from the cremation process. Bits of pulverized fragments.

With a little composure she went to the living room, pulled back the drapes and looked at the partially lit garden. In the glow by the pond there was a whitish form growing without definition. It was quiet now, but for how long?

Startled by her phone ringing, Carolyn saw the ID of

Stephan Pullet from the Law and Accounting Firm. She answered, wanting to hear a human voice.

"Hello, Stephan," she answered. "I'm sorry if I was a bit brusque the other day, I'm just a bit overwhelmed, I guess."

"Oh, I understand, Mrs. Greiner. This has been a terrible time for you." His voice sounded a bit relieved. "I'm only calling you at this late hour to confirm our worries at the last meeting. I thought you would like to know."

"Know? What worries exactly?"

"Concerning your inheritance of the mansion and gardens." He rushed on. "Our initial reviews show some rather complicated contracts and agreements. It will take our accounting division to work out the details. Let us just say, there may be litigation over your Father's and Mr. Greiner's Wills in relation to the garden Foundation named as primary beneficiary. I'm sure the two of them wanted you assured of protection."

"What does this mean? Exactly?" Carolyn asked tensely.

"It means, that for the foreseeable future, you will continue to live in the mansion, your home. An allowance will be given for service help. Nothing can be sold, nothing. The gardens will fall under the supervision of the Foundation who will oversee maintenance and care of the flora. Again, nothing can be sold or changed while the litigation and probate is being conducted."

"And this is to *re-assure me*?" Carolyn heard the sarcasm in her own voice and hoped Mr. Pullet did as well.

"Well, everything is status quo for now, and you can be assured... certain, I mean... we will do everything we can for your best interests."

"Fuck you!" Carolyn exclaimed. Those words were becoming more comfortable to her every time she said them. She turned off the phone wishing she could slam it as in the old days of Ma Bell.

Week followed week. Carolyn could ignore the April 15 Income Tax Day because of Pullet's promise the estate was in compliance. She busied herself around the home taking up some knitting she had begun months earlier. Deciding she would not use a wool scarf for the summer, she let that drop. She tried to attend a Book Club meeting announced in the newspaper but found the women to be tedious and she hadn't had time to read the boring book they were discussing. Most of all, she avoided the garden and kept the drapes closed so she would not have to look at it. She knew the *Foundation*—whoever—were assessing the garden and wringing their grubby, dirty hands over the exotic plants her father had collected over a lifetime. Good riddance. Let them take the plants and the gargoyle with them.

"Oh, Carolyn, it's so dark in here, let the sunshine in!" exclaimed Jennifer as she pushed herself into the living room one day. She opened the drapes and light filled the room with dust flickerings and a view of the garden. "Oh, look. How beautiful everything is. It's too bad Uncle Ralph can't see it."

"Oh, he sees it all right," Carolyn said ruefully.

"Of course he does, he's watching from heaven right

now, I'm sure," Jennifer said in a little girl voice irritating to Carolyn.

"Or closer than that, I'd imagine," Carolyn almost whispered.

Jennifer looked at the older woman but hesitated to ask her what she meant. Instead, she linked her arm in Carolyn's and pulled her through the doors to the garden. "Let's get some fresh air."

Carolyn allowed herself to be drawn into the garden. Her curiosity had grown over the last days of not seeing the mound she had pummeled. She was oblivious to the new spring growth and concentrated on the Koi Pond.

"Oh, look, Carolyn," Jennifer said as she waved her hand over the water surface. "The fish must think we're going to feed them the way they are gathering."

Carolyn could not pay attention to the Koi. All she saw was the statue of a man standing near the fully-leaved Hellebores. The figure was looking at the garden with a rake and shovel held together in one hand while the other had a pointed digging tool. A garden hat topped the casual work clothes. It appeared to be concrete but on closer inspection, it was an amalgamation of bone fragments and ashes.

"Oh, Carolyn!" Jennifer exclaimed as she turned around and gave her attention to the sculpture. "What a beautiful garden statue, fantastic garden art! I didn't know you had commissioned it. No wonder you were so secretive about a memorial. This statue looks just like Uncle Ralph and is a testimony to the garden he loved so much." Jennifer was actually chortling as she hugged Carolyn's arm.

Carolyn couldn't answer Jennifer's babbling. She could only stare at the grotesque form. When Ralph's niece started walking toward the house, Caroline heard Ralph's voice, "That Jennifer is a stupid bimbo!" followed by profane words about the niece's lack of intelligence, money hungry greed, and lack of morality. For some reason, Carolyn did not find Ralph's remarks as offensive this time.

The first month of mourning was coming to a close. Carolyn occupied her time making lists of things she wanted to do, places she would visit, items from the house that she would take with her once the legal office put actual money in her hands. She even collected a few books she might read. She was surprised that she could tolerate Jennifer for brief periods of time. But then, Jennifer was a human being, at least. A "least human being" according to Ralph's remarks.

Carolyn went to the Koi pond occasionally if only to renew her knowledge the "garden art" was still there. Each visit, the gargoyle would escalate the vile remarks to Carolyn. She wanted to ignore the profanity but somehow the statue knew just the right words to hurt her. Childhood memories, bullying statements, remarks from her parents. Her father's disappointment in a daughter too ugly and too stupid to ever succeed at anything.

Carolyn became obsessed with the gargoyle in the garden like the evil creature looming on Cathedral walls. She hated it but could not get it destroyed yet, could not sell it, could not tolerate it any longer. Even when she could not see it she knew it was out there formatting words of pain for her.

When the lawyer called to tell Carolyn there had been

a delay in litigations and it might take years before the ownership of the gardens was resolved, Carolyn knew she could stand no more. Anger at her parents, anger at Ralph, and even anger at herself raged. Her breathing became a pant, her throat tightening. She spun around looking for a weapon. With a scream, she grabbed the metal poker from the fireplace and smashed the statuary on the mantle. She crashed the liquor server and heard the crystal clinking with delight and swung the poker higher to reach the chandelier overhead. Portraits were stabbed, vases were broken, she swirled in a circle like a dervish for the pure pleasure of dizziness. Then she stopped. This destruction was not enough.

Carolyn dropped the bent poker and ran to the garden shed. Yanking open the door, she grabbed the ax that had served her so well. Still dizzy, Carolyn carefully tread on the flagstone. She did not want to slip and deter her goal. The moonlight flickered through the foliage playing light on the stepping stones and creating shadows for night creatures. She stopped and tried to take a deep breath but her chest was so constricted, she could hardly breathe. All she could do was scream and scream and scream as she ran at the gargoyle statue.

Swinging the ax, Carolyn heard the sound of the metal blade connecting with the bone fragments. Again and again she swung her weapon. There was the scent of foliage being torn from the ground and the crack of branches when the ax connected. The metal twang of blade was balanced by the thud of the flat head hitting on a backswing. One swing broke the shovel and rake from the statue's hand. Carolyn could still hear herself shrieking as she spun in the mud to attack her enemy's other side.

The gargoyle started to teeter. Carolyn knew she was having her affect and she would not stop until that smirk on Ralph's face was cracked in half. With a mighty heave, Carolyn lifted the ax to swing at the grinning face and the splitting sound was sweet. With the force of her swing, she lost her balance and sprawled onto to broken shards. Beyond the pain, Carolyn rolled and looked up just as the statue started to topple onto her. Falling. Falling. The hand holding the digging tool came closer and closer to her supine body. She couldn't move but heard herself screaming as the fragment tool drove into her chest. The hated gargoyle face loomed inches from hers and grinned as the blood oozed around the digging tool, grinding into Carolyn.

It was Jennifer and Stephan who finally found Carolyn. She was impaled with a digging tool that had somehow broken off the hand of the garden art. The statue of Ralph remained standing over her and was unharmed in any other way. It was almost as if the husband, the gardener, stood watch over Carolyn.

Now, as the only living relative of Mr. & Mrs. Greiner, it would be up to Jennifer to make decisions. Then again, she would have Stephan Pullet of Frokt, Frokt, & Wylie to help her, along with Quincy Toomes of the Blissfully Quiescent Crematory and Slumber Gardens.

Jennifer thought it would be fitting to have a memorial when she requested Carolyn's cremated remains be delivered in a Cloisonné urn. It could be interred beneath the garden statue of Uncle Ralph. They could be in the garden together.

Forever.

May

Dance of the Spring Flowers
Mark Robijn

Nebraska, 1927

elilah sat amongst the brightly colored flowers in her flowing white cotton dress. Her long black hair, normally combed so pretty by her mother and tied with a bow, was now tangled and messy and stuck up in the air. The bright sun warmed her face, and a breeze blew over the white, yellow and pink flowers, making them dance. The May Dance, Delilah thought, that's what her momma always called it. How Delilah loved flowers!

She gazed at the calm, blue lake in front of her. She loved sitting by the lake and just looking at it, but her belly ached. The sensation told her it was time for Mama to call her to eat. Why wasn't Mama coming? It didn't make sense, and Delilah tried to think it out, but the effort tired her so after a few minutes she gave up.

She looked down at the dark red spots on her pretty white dress and frowned with dismay. Mama was gonna be so mad she would surely beat Delilah with the broomstick again. Where did the spots come from? She tried hard to think again. She remembered vaguely she was planning on doing something about them but couldn't recall what. After a few minutes, she gave up thinking about that, too, for her head hurt once more.

She lifted her hands, palms up and stared at them. More red. She touched her face. And there was some there too. She moved her tongue in her mouth and tasted an unpleasant metallic. Did she drink something bad, like that time she drank the stuff from the red can and Mama had to take her all the way to town to the doctor who gave her that yucky stuff that made her throw up? No, she was sure she hadn't been drinking out of a can. She vaguely recalled it was the same stuff as the spots on her dress and face, and it had flown through the air to land in her mouth. Now what made it do that? She couldn't remember.

She looked down at the dead mouse in the grass. She had caught it running through the flowers. She like to catch mice, they were so pretty and soft, but they never seemed to move long. Each time she caught one and held them in her hand, they stopped moving after a few minutes. That always made her angry and sad, so angry that she ate them, chewing them up, making sure to mash them into a mess before swallowing them. She picked up this mouse and popped it in her mouth and started chewing. Maybe it would make her tummy stop hurting.

She tried to remember what had happened in the past and why she was sitting there. The only thing she could really remember was that all the bad things started when that man come to the Farm. That's when bad things started to happen.

Leonard shuffled down the dusty, dirty road staring down, looking at nothing. His mouth was as dry and dusty as the road. Even though it was only May, it was already hot. He walked in stilted steps, each one only after a mental battle of wills with his body and a decision whether it was worth going on or better to just lay down, close his eyes and die, decay and finally become part of the road.

His threadbare corduroy suit was so cached with dirt it felt like he wore cardboard. He couldn't remember the last time he'd had a bath. The soles of his shoes were more holes that shoe, and the ends were loose so they flapped when he walked.

As he shuffled along, he glared through red, rheumy eyes at the corn fields on either side. His stomach felt like an empty potato sack, but one with a little man inside stabbing him with a knife. If only the corn was ripe, he could eat that, but there was nothing but raw stubs. He would fall soon and lay in the dust rotting in the sun. People would drive by, glance at his corpse with distaste and move on. Just another nameless dead tramp, with no name or person to care.

He cursed for the hundredth time for being so stupid. He had a good in Missouri working at a sawmill, until stupidity and greed made him steal fifty dollars from the boss's wallet. Fifty lousy dollars! The man caught him. In a panic, Leonard hit him with a pickaxe. The man died, and now Leonard was a wanted man, with a noose waiting for him, and the small amount of money was long ago spent.

He spotted a farm ahead, like a shimmering mirage. A white house with a big porch floating on a sea of green grass beckoned. Behind it sat a red barn and a silo, just like a picture in a farm magazine. The scene looked so warm and inviting, peaceful and happy, he almost wept, for he knew he wouldn't be welcome there. He would have to pass it by, continue on the dusty road, longing and jealousy eating him alive.

Anger rose up inside him like boiling lava. He didn't know the people in that farmhouse, but he hated them anyway. Why should they be happy and well fed, sleep in warm, soft beds and have a bath every night and good clothes, while he had nothing and lived like an animal? He should burst into their house, kill them all, bury them in one of the infernal cornfields and claim the farm for his own.

As he grew near, he saw someone watching him from the side of the house. It was a young girl in her twenties with long black hair tied in a ponytail wearing a long white dress with grass stains at the knees and elbows.

She was very attractive, with nice round breasts and full hips and lust instantly filled Leonard's mind, an erection growing in his pants. A desperate longing filled him, momentarily taking the place of his ravenous hunger. He could tell right away there was something wrong with her. Her face—she was blank. She was simple-minded. The realization put bad thoughts in Leonard's head. If he could grab her before the owners of the house knew, he could drag her into the corn fields. Then he'd rip that pretty white dress off of her. He could take his time, use her up, then choke the life out of her, taking all his anger and frustration for his treatment out on her, knowing and enjoying the thought of the sorrow and pain he would cause her parents in the farm house. He would leave her lifeless body in the cornfield for the crows to feast on. Maybe he had a reason to live, after all.

Leonard glanced around, but then disappointment filled him. A woman on the front porch had already seen him. Still, maybe this farm held possibilities.

Lydia saw him through the kitchen window where she kneaded the dough for bread on the counter. She scowled, deepening the wrinkles on her lined face. She wiped a strand of her graying hair, tied up in a bun, out of her eyes. Another tramp begging for food or a place to stay. That meant another day of fear for Lydia, worrying about Delilah and whether the tramp would hang around to rob or kill them.

When the Depression started, they had tried to help the poor who came by, but soon there were so many they began to run out of food, and some began to turn violent. One had even threatened Abraham with a knife, and he had to shoot the man with his shotgun. The man was buried across the road where Abraham said his rotting corpse wouldn't affect the crops or pollute the lake.

She'd have to find out where Delilah was. The silly girl would walk right up and talk to anyone who wandered by. Evil, dirty men, filthy animals, willing to prey on a simple girl.

Lydia wiped the flour on her hands off on her apron and hurried to the kitchen door to intercept the man before Delilah could do anything foolish. She pushed the screen door open with a rush and it banged on the side of the house. She stomped outside as the screen door swung around again and slammed closed with a loud noise.

Lydia gazed around. Sure enough, there was Delilah at the side of the house, staring at the man, transfixed. Lydia swore, it was a miracle she was still untouched.

"Delilah!"

Delilah's head spun to look at Lydia. She pointed at the man.

"Man, Ma!"

"Barn, now! Go! No lake!"

Delilah turned and ran.

Lydia frowned and looked back at the road. The man wasn't far now, and she could see he watched her, looking disappointed. She wondered if he'd seen Delilah. She hoped not, but by the look on his face she suspected he had, and just like the others, already had evil plans in his mind. How she hated all these tramps coming by. She spent most of her days in a fright, worrying about Delilah.

The man stopped at the fence and looked at Lydia, his eyes full of hopelessness, as if knowing already she wasn't going to give him anything. He smiled anyway and spoke in a friendly voice. "Afternoon, Ma'm. Is the man of the house home?"

Lydia didn't smile back but just stared, stone-faced. "We ain't got nothing for ya here. Times is hard for us too."

The man shifted his feet and his smile disappeared, as if expecting the response.

"I ain't looking for a handout, Ma'm. I was wonderin' if

you had some work. I'm a good mechanic and been working farms all over. All I ask is room and board. I'll do whatever chores need doin'."

Lydia opened her mouth and was about to tell him no when she got a mild surprise. From behind her, a strong man's voice replied. It was Abraham. "You fix tractors?"

The man's eyes lit up with a glimmer of hope.

"Yes sir, been fixin' 'em since I was knee-high to a grasshopper. Stood at my daddy's knee while he fixed everything from balers to plows."

Lydia looked at Abraham crossly. Dressed as always in his faded blue coveralls and white shirt with his long graying beard draped down the front, he held his pipe in his right hand and gazed back at her with steady eyes.

Lydia turned back and studied the tramp. He had brown hair that jutted out from an old, dirty derby cap. His eyes were dark, beady and small, like a crow's. He was a handsome man, maybe German or Dutch, but sometime before his nose had been broken for it was crooked and he was missing two lower teeth. He looked like an old boxer. Even though he wore a pleasant enough smile, Lydia could tell he spelled trouble.

She turned bodily around to face Abraham. "Father, may we discuss this?"

Abraham kept his gaze on the man, purposely ignoring Lydia.

"You ain't afraid of hard work?"

"Been doin' it since I was a young'un."

Abraham nodded. "Come around back."

Lydia frowned, angry at being ignored. "Abraham!"

Abraham had already turned and started walking away. Lydia seethed, but knew when Abraham had made a decision, his word was law. He would never answer her. She might as well accept it.

"'Scuse me, sir."

Abraham stopped and looked at Leonard.

Leonard held his cap in his hands, kneading it, and his face showed angst and shame.

"I ain't ett in a long time. Do you think maybe first—"

Abraham nodded. He started walking again. "Feed him, Mama. Then send him back."

Leonard smiled, and Lydia scowled. His smile turned on her with a glint of victory and smugness in his eyes. Lydia decided she would hate this man. He was a bad one, and both her and Abraham would rue the day he walked into their house.

She walked over to the stove and with her teeth clamped tight began ladling soup into a bowl with angry, fast motions. With a stiff jaw she barked, "Sit down at the table. Don't touch nothing."

"Yes, Ma'm."

Leonard laughed inside, knowing the old lady had lost the argument, and enjoying watching her squirm. He felt his insides tighten and his hand shook at the thought of actually eating again. He felt pee fill his penis, whether in excitement or nervousness he couldn't tell, but he squeezed it off. The last thing he needed now was to make a puddle on her kitchen floor. That would be the end of things real quick.

He watched the soup pour into the bowl with fascination, unable to take his eyes off of it, as if he did it would suddenly disappear. Big chunks of beef and delicious orange carrots dropped from the ladle into the bowl. He hand clamped and unclamped in fetid excitement. Despite his best efforts, he did pee his pants a little, creating a small dark stain in his crotch. He didn't care anymore, just give him the soup already! His mouth was so dry and full of dust and his lips so parched, he hoped he could open it to eat.

After what seemed an eternity the old lady finally set the bowl in front of him. The heavenly aroma wafted up and filled his nostrils, making his head swim. He couldn't remember smelling anything so wonderful before.

She set a spoon in front of him and he grabbed it eagerly and dove into the soup.

"Wait just one minute, MIster."

Leonard stopped and looked up to see Lydia staring at him sternly.

"We say Grace before we eat here."

Leonard put the spoon down, nodded and tried to look contrite, cursing her in his mind. "Oh, yes Ma'm, sorry Ma'm." He closed his eyes and folded his hands reverently.

Lydia smiled primly with no real joy in it. She closed her eyes and folded her hands.

"Dear Lord, we thank thee for this bounty thou hast provided for us. We are profoundly grateful for all thy blessings and kindness in these dark days. We now humbly ask thee for guidance and wisdom as we fight the evil desires of our flesh. Lead us not into temptation but deliver us from evil.

For thine is the kingdom, the power and the glory forever. Only thou can lead us on the path to Glory through the sacrifice of your son Jesus Christ and our obedience to they Holy Word..."

Leonard grumbled to himself and his stomach twisted. Was she gonna preach a whole sermon? She was doing it on purpose, to pay him back for losing the argument. He wanted to take the ladle and bash her head in. He vowed someday he'd pay her back. She'd go to Glory all right, when her lifeless body lay on the floor of her rotten kitchen. It took all the restraint he could muster not to pick up the spoon and start eating or simply grab the bowl and gulp the soup down.

Finally, after ten more minutes of spouting nonsense, she said, "Amen." They both opened their eyes. She turned back to the stove, and finally he was able to eat. He picked up the spoon slowly and dipped it in the stew, capturing a big piece of meat and some tasty broth. He raised it to his mouth and sipped the broth. It was heavenly. As he started to eat, he thought of how someday he hoped it would be him standing at the stove, and the old bitch and her husband would be in unmarked graves in the corn field. The worms would eat her, and her flesh would rot into dust.

She sat next to him as he ate, eyeing him suspiciously. He tried to act polite, taking his time. After he'd taken a few bites, he'd had enough food he could finally relax and eat slower, though he still wanted to devour the whole bowl in one gulp.

She stared so hard he felt sure she was going to bore holes into him. "Where you from?"

He smiled at her humbly. "From Missouri ma'm." *Where I killed a man*, he thought. *And someday I'll kill you.*

"Missouri." She said it like she suspected it, and it was a bad place. She sat back and sipped her coffee, looking suspicious. "Hurry up, Father's waiting."

He wanted to ask her about the girl but knew better. He decided he had to stop such thoughts, for his member grew hard again under the table. Though he enjoyed the sensation, he suspected if the old lady noticed it, his new employment would be over before it began. Still, he had to find a way to get that pretty girl alone.

He finished the bowl, stood up and nodded to the old lady. "Thank you, Ma'm."

She didn't reply, just stared at him crossly. He grinned and walked out the back door.

He found Abraham waiting for him by the barn doors, leaning on a pitchfork. Leonard studied the man. Tall, six feet and something, Abraham looked strong, but he also looked old, turning gray with a fair-sized belly. Lydia fed him good, and from what Leonard saw in the kitchen, he like he liked the beer. Still, he looked tough and ornery. Leonard would have to pick his moment to kill the man carefully, or it would be Leonard lying in the cornfield. Leonard walked up and stood a few feet away.

Abraham stared at Leonard his face hard to read. "Ten cents an hour. You work from sunup to sundown. Sleep in the hayloft." Did he have any idea what Leonard was thinking? Leonard couldn't tell.

Leonard nodded contritely, trying to look humble. "Yes sir, yes sir."

"You take your meals in the barn. You never go in the house. There's an outhouse behind the barn. You wash in the lake. And you ain't got no need to talk to Mama or Delilah."

Delilah, so that was her name. *Oh, I'll speak to Delilah all right,* Leonard thought darkly.

"Get somethin' straight right now."

Abraham's dangerous tone brought Leonard out of his reverie quick. He looked to see Abraham staring at him with a dark gaze under bushy white eyebrows.

"Yes sir?"

"Mama's against me hiring you, but I need help, and you're as good as any other. But you cause me any trouble, I catch you stealin' or plannin' mischief, and I won't think twice before planting you in the ground."

Leonard was right; Abraham wasn't going to be an easy man to fool or get the jump on. He'd have to play his cards tight to his chest. He nodded and said, "No trouble from me, Sir. All I want is an honest job."

Abraham didn't look any more convinced, but simply continued to stare at Leonard suspiciously.

"And hear this. Delilah's simple, been that way since she fell off a horse when she was a young'un. She may talk to you. You just ignore her, don't talk back and she'll go away. I see you trying talking to her or trying anything, as God is my judge, I willl break your arm. You touch her, and I'll bury you out in the field, and no one will say a thing 'bout it. Nobody cares about another bum dying'."

Leonard tried hard not to show his hatred. "I won't even go near her, I promise." *Not until you're dead,* Leonard thought.

Abraham looked satisfied. He turned and led the way into the barn, and Leonard followed. Over his shoulder, he kept talking. "No liquor. We're good Baptists here. If you got to smoke, do it by the lake. I don't need you burning my barn down."

"Yes sir," Leonard said.

"Now let's get to work."

And work they did, or really Leonard did. Abraham stood by, watching. It must have been a long time since anything had been worked on, for all the farm equipment needed repair. The barn needed new slats, Lydia's garden plot was full of weeds, and chicken coop door was broken. And Leonard had to fix it all, while Abraham smoked his pipe and watched, making it hard for Leonard to stop for a second. It was the first day, and Leonard already hated the job. He'd never worked so hard in his life.

After four steady hours of work, Leonard hoped for a break, but was disappointed. He was sent out into the cornfields pick grass that had grown up between the stalks. The sun beat down on him mercilessly and he grew close to passing out more than a few times, but he pushed himself onwards. He almost wished he had stayed on the road and kept going. But he couldn't afford to look like he couldn't handle the job, not on the first day, or he'd be canned, and that would ruin any plans he had for Delilah.

Once he walked out of the field to get some water

from the pump. He saw Abraham sitting in a chair under a tree in the shade, snoozing. Hatred for him filled Leonard's heart. Now that he had Leonard to do all his work, he could take it easy. Leonard couldn't wait until he could pay the old man back.

Dinner was the same stew, and she didn't even bother to heat it up. Then it was back to work until sundown. A fear gripped him. Was he going to be the old couple's slave, working until he dropped? Maybe that was their plan all along, use a tramp until he died then bury him in the corn field. Well, Leonard would make sure that didn't happen. He'd find his chance and take care of Abraham and Lydia, as God was his judge.

Leonard lay in the dirt between two rows of corn, staring up at the twilight sky. The stars shown through the darkening sky as night fell.

He heard a sound and raised his head. There stood Delilah, watching him. Leonard sat up and grinned at her. "Hello, Delilah."

Delilah's expression didn't change, she just kept staring, a look of curiosity on her face. She wore the same white dress, only it was even more stained by grass and dirt.

"I'm Leonard. Can you say Leonard?"

"Leonard," Delilah repeated, her voice without inflection.

"That's right." Leonard patted the ground next to him. "Come sit down and talk to me, Delilah."

"Bath time."

Leonard's eyes lit up. "Bath time? Why don't you come tell me about bath time?"

"Mama—lake. Clothes off, water cold."

Leonard's gaze was dark and unreadable. "Why don't you take your clothes off now, Delilah? After all, it's bath time."

Delilah looked confused. Then as Leonard watched with joyful anticipation, she moved her hand towards the buttons on the side of her dress.

"That's right, Delilah. Unbutton." Delilah undid one button, and Leonard gulped. "Keep going, that's right."

Delilah undid two more buttons, and the top of her dress fell forward, exposing the tops of her breasts. She didn't wear undergarments.

His eyes wide, he leaned forward. "Let me help you, Delilah."

Lydia called from somewhere. "Delilah!"

Leonard's heart skipped a beat as fear gripped him. He looked at Delilah. "Don't tell Mama about this. No tell, you hear?"

Delilah just stared as Leonard took off into the corn, and just in time, for he heard Lydia talking to Delilah behind him.

Leonard made his way down to the lake and tried to find a spot where he could watch the bathing.

He finally spotted them, but he was too late. Delilah was already dressed, wearing a set of pink pajamas, and Lydia was leading her back towards the house. Leonard pulled down his pants—his need too great—and masturbated. Then he followed Lydia and Delilah at a discreet distance, having nothing better to do.

As they walked, Lydia held Delilah's arm tight and pulled her along.

"Bedtime."

"No bedtime, Mama."

"Be quiet."

"NO BED!"

Delilah grew angry and thrashed about in Lydia's grasp. As Leonard watched Lydia slapped Delilah's face hard. Delilah stopped thrashing about and sobbed, touching her cheek with her hand.

"Settle down and it's the broom handle!" They walked again, and Leonard followed, intrigued. He watched as the two entered the house. Looking around but not seeing Abraham anywhere, he walked up and peeked in the kitchen window.

He couldn't see them, but the cellar door was open. He could hear them tramping down the stairs, Delilah crying and Lydia yelling at her.

Then the tramping stopped. And he heard the distinct rattle of chains!

"No Mama! No chains!" Delilah wailed.

He heard a slap as Lydia hit Delilah again.

"Hush! And don't pull, you'll bleed again."

Leonard sat down on the stoop and thought about what he'd just seen. Of all the strange things he'd ever seen, it had to be the most bizarre. Abraham and Lydia kept Delilah locked up in the basement like an animal. And Delilah didn't like it, not one bit. He wondered if he'd just found the key to a plan.

The next day was just like before, but even harder. At lunch Lydia brought Abraham a thick juicy steak and potatoes. Leonard smiled, anticipating the same for him. However, when Lydia brought him his meal, it was the same cold stew. Then with disgust and hatred he saw her take the rest and pour it in the pig's trough. So, he got fed the same slop as the pigs, while Abraham ate steak. His hatred for them grew even hotter as he ate.

Later Abraham had him digging a ditch for a cow trough. A few hours before sunset he walked up to the water pump near the barn and heard a strange grunting sound coming from the barn. Looking at the house, he didn't see anyone. Slowly he made his way over to the barn and peeked in through a gap in the boards.

What he saw almost knocked him over. Leaning over the wooden railing was Delilah. Her dress was up over her back, and behind her, his pants at his ankles, stood Abraham. Delilah looked confused, staring at the ground, her hands gripping the railing.

"You dirty old hypocrite," he thought. "Some faithful Baptist you are." Did Lydia know that Delilah was no longer a virgin and why? Did she know what Abraham was doing to her precious daughter while she was in the house baking cookies?

"Ow!" Delilah yelled.

"Quiet!" Abraham whispered in an angry tone. Finally,

Abraham finished.

"Messy," Delilah said, her voice neutral.

Abraham glared at her in anger. "What do you do?"

Delilah looked down, clearly frightened of him. "Not tell Mama."

Abraham nodded again woodenly then waved towards the outside. "Go play. No lake!"

Delilah hurried out of the barn as Abraham took out a handkerchief and wiped his forehead. Then he lay down in the hay. In a few seconds, Leonard heard him snoring.

Leonard ran and hid behind the chicken coop just in time to see Delilah run out of the barn. She headed towards the lake.

Leonard smiled. This was his chance. Silently he followed her, careful to keep an eye on the kitchen window to make sure Lydia didn't see him.

Down at the lake, he saw her waist deep in the water. She was walking out, further, towards the middle. Leonard saw why they didn't want her at the lake, for it looked like she was going to keep going until she drowned.

Leonard smiled and walked up behind her. "Delilah!"

She turned and saw him, and her eyes went wide with fear. "Lake—messy."

Leonard smiled at her with his warmest smile and motioned towards the shore. "Come here. Come here."

Delilah hesitated, then walked towards him.

"That's right. Back here. Come here, Delilah, let's talk."

"Delilah, Papa made you messy. He's going to beat

you. Make you hurt bad. Big hurt."

Delilah looked terrified, biting her lip.

"That's right. But you can stop Papa. He not hit you. He never make you messy again."

Delilah cocked her head, curious.

Leonard motioned. "Follow me. Before Papa comes!"

Delilah looked panicked and hurried towards Leonard. Leonard led Delilah into the barn. He pointed to the sleeping Abraham. Delilah looked at Abraham with terror in her eyes.

"Hurry!"

Delilah looked at Leonard, confused and unsure. Leonard walked over and picked up the pitchfork. He walked back to Delilah.

He made a stabbing motion with it towards the ground. "Like this." He pointed to Abraham. "Right here." He pointed to Abraham's throat. "Hurry! He's going to beat you!"

Delilah looked blank as Leonard thrust the pitchfork into her hands and led her over to Abraham.

She looked at Leonard then down at her father.

Leonard pantomimed again. "Hurry!"

Delilah stood over Abraham, looking down at him. Then she looked at Leonard again.

"Now! Stab! Stab, Delilah!"

Delilah hesitated, unsure. She looked at Leonard again and he pantomimed frantically.

Delilah raised the pitchfork and pointed the sharp tongs at Abraham's throat.

"Hurry Papa mad!"

As Leonard watched with grim satisfaction and with

one swift motion, Delilah stabbed the pitchfork down into Abraham's neck. The tines went deep in and blood spurted out, making rivers in the hay.

Abraham's eyes opened wide with shock, pain and surprise. He grabbed at the pitchfork with his right hand, his throat gurgling.

Delilah stared down, not sure what was happening.

Leonard, his eyes full of evil, stared at Abraham, enjoying his death. "Good girl! You did it!"

Abraham looked at Delilah, his face full of hurt and shock. Blood dribbled out of his mouth and down onto his beard.

"Again, Delilah! He's waking up! He's mad!"

Delilah stabbed again, sobbing with fear and confusion. And then again and again, shredding Abraham's throat until it resembled hamburger.

Abraham gurgled and lay his head down. He closed his eyes and died.

"Papa?" Delilah stared at Abraham, not sure what just happened. She turned to Leonard. "Papa?"

Leonard smiled but quickly hid it and frowned with shock.

"Delilah, what did you do? You hurt Papa!"

Delilah looked at Abraham and then at Leonard with a look of terror.

"You killed Papa!"

Delilah shook her head, not understanding. "Papa?"

Leonard pointed. "Look at him! You killed him! He's dead!"

Delilah dropped the pitchfork. "Papa messy."

"Now Mama mad! Cops come! Beat you real bad and lock you up!

Delilah started crying, shaking her head. "No chains."

Leonard looked even more serious. "Mama now!"

Delilah wiped her eyes. "Mama?"

Leonard pointed towards the house. "Mama too! Then no more chains!"

Delilah smiled at the thought. "No more chains!"

Leonard couldn't believe how well everything was going. Soon the old couple would both be dead. And then, it would only be him and Delilah. And she would finally be his.

He motioned for Delilah to follow him.

Leonard led Delilah to the kitchen. Inside, they could hear Lydia preparing lunch.

Leonard picked up a scythe.

"Like this!" Leonard made a slicing motion at his neck, "Hurry! Like this!" He showed Delilah again. "Cops coming! Mama angry! Do it quick, then no more chains!"

Leonard pushed the scythe towards Delilah. She looked down at it like it was a snake, then back at Leonard.

"Mama?"

Leonard placed the scythe in Delilah's hand and wrapped her fingers around it. He put an arm on her back and pushed her forward. "Like I showed you." He pantomimed it again.

"Hurry! Cops coming!"

Delilah looked at the scythe, unsure.

"Quick!"

Inside, Lydia pushed little indents into the edges of a pie. She heard the screen door open. She didn't look up.

"Delilah, is that you?"

She felt a presence next to her and saw a shadow block the sun through the window. She looked up then.

Delilah stood, eyes wild, holding a scythe in her hand. Lydia's eyes went wide with confusion and alarm.

"Delilah, what in the world—"

In one quick motion, Delilah swung the scythe and it dug into Lydia's neck. She screamed and grabbed for it as blood spurted out, all over the scythe and Delilah's arm.

Pain shot through Lydia's body and she instantly felt woozy. Her legs crumpled beneath her and she fell to the floor, the scythe still embedded in her neck.

Delilah knelt next to her and stared. "Mama?"

Lydia gazed at Delilah with pity and sorrow. "Delilah," she choked out. "Bad man. Do like I taught. Go—" Lydia's voice caught, her eyes going wide and she exhaled, her final breath leaving her body before she could finish.

Leonard saw Delilah kill Lydia through the window. He chortled and hopped up and down, happier than he'd been in his whole life. He couldn't believe fortune had finally smiled on him. Now he had a farm of his own. He'd bury the two on the back forty, and nobody would be the wiser.

He looked at the kitchen again and smiled darkly. Then he'd have some fun with Delilah, lots and lots of fun. If she thought Abraham was mean to her, just wait until Leonard had his way. He'd do what he wanted all right, and she'd be in chains every night. And he'd beat her, just for fun, and then tell her things just to confuse her for his amusement. Oh yes, he was going to make Delilah's life a living Hell, and enjoy every minute of it. Payment for a lifetime of people treating him like dirt, like he was nothing but a roach they needed to smash with their foot. He was a farm owner now, with his own slave.

The kitchen door slammed open. Leonard looked up, ready to congratulate Delilah and then give her the first beating. Out she came, but she had something in her hands. Leonard looked and his elation disappeared.

Delilah walked up to him, Daddy's shotgun in her hands.

Leonard raised a hand in defense, his eyes wide with panic and fear gripping his insides.

"Now, now, Delilah, put that thing down! Bad girl! I'll lock you up! Chains!"

Delilah leveled the shotgun at Leonard. "Bad man! Papa's gun!"

Delilah fired the shotgun, hitting Leonard square in the chest. The blood splattered back and landed all over her dress, on her face, and in her mouth. Leonard fell backwards, trying to speak but blood erupted from his mouth and he shook, his body twitching as it processed the damage of the shotgun shell. Delilah shot him a second time and he fell to the floor, finally still.

Delilah dropped the shotgun. "No. More. Chains."

She looked down at her dress, seeing the blood for the first time. She should run down to the lake and wash it off.

"Need bath," she said to herself. Delilah ran towards the lake, trying to keep in her mind what she had to do.

On the way, she spied the pretty flowers. How they danced in the morning breeze! They didn't yell or put her in chains. And they never told her what to do. She sat down and watched the flowers dance. Mama always liked it when Delilah brought her flowers. She started to pick a bunch. Then she saw the mouse.

The sun began to set, again. It had been a long time. Her tummy ached. Then she remembered. *Mama. Papa. The bad man and so much blood.*

"No more messy. No more chains. No more hurt," she reminded herself. She had to wash the blood off her dress. She stood up and walked slowly into the lake.

"No more."

JUNE

Song of the Night
Michelle Lee

I woke up as the nightmare shattered around me, reality setting in slowly as I recognized my bedroom, the crazy whispers fading to the back of my mind. An ominous feeling settled in my bones and I shivered. I was struggling to even remember what the nightmare had been about, but I had been sure someone was talking to me.

That feeling remained, even as I woke up fully and threw my feet over the side of the bed and stepped on the cold floor to pull the blackout curtains open to look outside. It was already light out and there was a mist that hung over the trees in random rivers of fog. The tops of the trees poked out in some places, and in others, it completely swallowed them giving the mountainside an eerie feeling that mirrored the ominous one.

I shook it off. I didn't even remember the nightmare, so there was no reason to let the odd feeling follow me around all day. I did find it strange that I could hear the echo of a voice in my mind that I couldn't place. Too bad. I didn't have time to dwell on it.

I hopped in the shower without looking in the mirror, I already knew I looked frightening. Not enough sleep and bad eating habits tend to do that. I'd been taking care of my dad lately who had been exhibiting odd behavior, and we finally learned he had dementia.

While we were searching for the medication that would help get him somewhat stabilized, I'd moved him in with me. I was thirty-eight and single, so it wasn't like he was cramping my style. My job as a coder let me work from home, all in all, it was a best-case scenario. I couldn't just leave my dad alone to fend for himself. He was my dad and I loved him.

The disease also seemed to be progressing rapidly in him, causing wild personality changes. This new medication seemed to be stabilizing it a bit, but there were times I found myself shaking my head as I watched my normally reserved and straight-laced dad become a teenager. More often, lately, he'd been having mood swings that bordered on aggressive when he realized what was happening to him and he got angry about it.

The anger I understood perfectly. I'd felt it myself. My dad was only sixty-seven, hardly seemed old enough to have this happening to him. My mom had died about ten years ago from a blood clot in her lung, devastating him. When I think back, it seems likely that the change in him had started happening then, but in my ignorance, I discounted it as grief.

I got out of the shower in a cloud of steam and dressed, wondering what state he would be in today. It was flag day, a day we usually went to the local national cemetery to put little flags on the graves of the soldiers. His dad, my grandpa, had been a veteran and he liked doing it to honor his dad. When I left the Air Force, he wanted to keep doing it to honor me, because I had served too.

It's true that I had, but I also picked the path of least resistance. Serving would get me an education I wouldn't have to pay for or strap my parents financially. I chose the Air Force because it was the easiest to get into physically, or so I had been told. It hadn't been easy.

It had gotten me in shape and paid for my schooling, which made it a fair trade. It had also introduced me to my best friend, Bryan. He was a pilot, he could pretty much fly anything. Sadly, he'd been killed while home on leave. He had been out on a run and was struck by a drunk driver. That had been eight years ago.

I visited his grave on Flag Day, Memorial Day, Veterans Day, and his birthday. Easy enough to do since it was where my grandpa was buried too. Multi-purpose visits to the cemetery became my norm.

"Dad?" I called out. "It's Flag Day. Want to come to the cemetery and put flags on graves with me?"

"Are you crazy?" he stepped out into the hallway looking a little unhinged. Not a good day for him then.

"Debatable. Is that a yes or a no? I'm going to put one on Pop's grave. You usually like stopping by and leaving a penny. It's foggy right now, but it will clear up," I tried again.

He glanced out the window behind him. "The fog looks like fingers that are trying to reach me, sink their cold claws in my skin. That place is haunted. There's ghosts all over that cemetery and something else there, too."

"Something other than ghosts?" I went along with the conversation to see where it would go. I agreed on the fog though. It did kind of look like fingers that were reaching down through the trees. "It's a cemetery, that there is ghosts there doesn't surprise me."

"Mark my words, girl, there's something bad there. I can hear it calling for you. That's not wind out there, those are screams," my dad's face transformed into something terrifying for a moment before going blank.

I looked back outside, "There's no wind, Dad. Just fog." A chill crept down my spine at the look on his face and the tone of his voice.

"What? Of course, there's no wind out there, Jonie. Why did you think there was?" he gave me a confused look. "What are you doing today?"

A wave of sadness hit me at the changes happening with my dad and I fought to keep my face neutral. "Going to put flags on the graves, it's Flag Day today. Want to come with?"

"It would be nice to get out for a little bit. Think that fog will burn off? The cemetery is creepy enough without that," he trudged after me to the kitchen.

"It's June, it will burn off. What do you want for breakfast?" I stopped in front of the fridge knowing he'd want an omelet. He always wanted an omelet, that was one of the few things that hadn't changed with him.

"I'm losing my mind, Jonie. I swear I could hear someone calling my name while you were in the shower. This low scratchy voice drawing it out, Steeeeeve," he mimicked. "I'll have an omelet if you are making one."

There it was. I pulled out the eggs, mushrooms, peppers, and cheese. I didn't know what to say about the name thing. The past couple of weeks he'd veered to the unexplainable things in life. "Maybe the pipes were groaning," I said casually.

Bryan and I had spent hours pondering on life's mysteries more than once. We each had a mindset geared towards scientific evidence and even given that, we had to admit that there were things that were just not able to be answered with science. We did believe in ghosts, and Bryan believed in bigfoot and other legendary creatures.

I agreed with the *possibility* of them because I hadn't seen scientific proof that they *didn't* exist. I was open-minded in that manner, but that didn't mean I was a diehard enthusiast about it. The universe was too vast to be confined to what we saw with our own eyes, any logical person could concede that.

My dad's sudden foray to this side of thinking was uncomfortable though. There was a lot about the brain that science didn't know or hadn't figured out yet, and when he got like this, some of the things he said made me think a little too hard about if what he was seeing or hearing was real. What if dementia had opened something within his mind that allowed him to see what others couldn't?

"I have the flags in my office, and we can grab a jar of pennies to bring with us too," I told him as I diced up the vegetables he liked in his omelet and whipped up the eggs. I tried to keep to routine with him to help him stay on an even keel.

"Okay, Jonie. I'm sorry I'm a burden to you," the sad side of him came out again, breaking my heart.

"Never a burden, Dad. Stop thinking that. I like hanging out with you," I took a stab at reassuring him. It worked sometimes. "Want some juice?"

"Tomato juice sounds good, do we have any of that?" There was a cold sneer to his voice that hadn't been there before and I stiffened, not knowing what to expect. My dad hated tomatoes.

"No. We have orange juice. Should I pick up some tomato juice today?" I kept making the omelet with no reason I could find to not turn around, other than I was suddenly afraid.

"Why? Neither of us drinks that," my dad's normal tone returned.

I wasn't following his rollercoaster today, so I stopped talking and finished his omelet, sliding it onto a plate and pouring him a glass of juice. The same breakfast he'd eaten for the past forty-two years.

"Aren't you going to eat, Jonie?" my dad asked, digging in.

"Not hungry today, Dad," I cleaned up the mess, choosing to handwash the pan today. "What do you want for dinner?"

"Meatloaf," he answered quickly. "And those little roasted potatoes." That was his answer at least three times a week. Luckily, I had some leftover from two nights ago, and

I'd just reheat it for him.

"Done deal. Finish up, I'm going to go get the flags and pennies. I have a little bottle of Jack to leave for Bryan too, he's probably thirsty," I said offhandedly knowing he wasn't listening to me.

"He's not, but the one watching you is," my dad replied. I blinked slowly, not sure what to say to that. "He's very thirsty."

A flicker of the nightmare pressed against my memory, but I couldn't grab a hold of it. "Who's watching me, Dad?"

"He won't tell me his name," he looked up at me, and I didn't see a hint of dementia in his eyes. "He's not good, Jonie. I know that much."

"Have you been watching horror movies at night?" I crossed my arms and frowned, watching his reaction carefully.

"I don't like that garbage. I watched a good show on the nature channel about carbon gases and the effects on the ozone," he told me. *That* was exactly the dad I knew.

"Finish up. I'm going to go start a load of laundry while I remember and grab some stuff. We can stop at the store on the way home for groceries for the week. Think of anything you might need," I instructed him and walked back down the hallway, fighting the urge to shine lights in all the shadowed corners.

I made a mental note to ask his doctor more questions at our appointment this week and see if this was a side effect of the medications he was on. It was starting to creep me out. It was something more than just the disease eating away at his mind. That's what my gut was telling me.

My room was unnaturally cold as I went in to grab my laundry basket and I crossed over to the window to see if I had left it open, but it was shut and locked. I shook myself again, my dad was making me paranoid. I grabbed the basket and stopped by his room to grab his and got the laundry started.

When I went to my office to grab the flags, I noticed how silent the house had gotten. It wasn't the good kind of silent either. It was almost lifeless silent. I sighed and was only beginning to realize that this is what it was like to be a parent. It was humorous in a very dark sort of way.

I grabbed the two boxes of flags and on my way back to the kitchen I found the garage door open. I flipped on the light and saw my dad huddled in the front seat of my car, shaking uncontrollably. I dropped the flags and bolted to the car door, flinging it open.

"Dad! What's wrong?" I cried, checking him for injuries.

"It's not the wind!" he said, his voice almost a whisper. He was in a closed garage, there was no wind in here. There wasn't any noise.

That tug on my memory came again, and the chill that seemed to take up residence in the base of my spine spread across my back. I stepped away and turned to grab the flags and found them two steps behind me when I was sure I had dropped them on the house side in the doorway.

Theme for the day: shrugging off the weird stuff. They probably just fell as I ran. I grabbed them and threw them in the back seat and went back inside for the jar of pennies, making sure to grab a dime and the bottle of Jack.

As an afterthought I grabbed light jackets for both my dad and me and went back to the car to find him holding the two boxes of flags, looking bright and eager. "Oh good! I was hoping you wouldn't forget the pennies."

I was tempted to roll my eyes and barely managed to refrain. I set the pennies on the floor of the backseat and went back for my purse and keys, having forgotten those in the morning's mental chaos. When I came back out this time, my dad was humming. He never hums. He doesn't even listen to music really.

"Dad, are you feeling okay?" I asked him cautiously as I climbed in the car and opened the garage door.

"Never better, Jonie. Flag Day is fun, and look the fog is lifting. No more fingers trying to pull me off the bed." He went back to humming. I took a deep breath.

It wasn't even ten in the morning, and this was already the weirdest day yet. It was starting to feel like my dad had several personalities brewing in his fragmenting brain, and I couldn't keep up. I wanted to cry or laugh, and I couldn't do either because explaining it would hurt his feelings.

I drove and listened to him hum. "What is that song, Dad?"

"The Song of the Night," he answered dreamily.

I'd never heard of it and made another mental note to look it up later. "Where did you hear it?"

"It's the song the one who watches you hums. Sometimes it sounds like the trees are playing it, but that's just ridiculous. Trees don't play music. If I listen closely to the screams, I can usually hear it there too. Remember Jonie, it's not wind," came the cryptic words that about had me careening off the road. I couldn't even find humor in his statement that trees don't play music.

We'd gone beyond weird to flat out scary. I didn't know what was happening to my dad. "Got it. Not the wind," I repeated.

"Don't miss the turn," he pointed out to the upcoming cemetery.

"I won't, Dad," I promised. It felt like the air in the car was closing in on me, pressing me down into my car seat and as soon as I jammed the car into park, I flew out the car door, bent over gasping for air.

"Get the pennies," he said, oblivious to my turmoil, over the roof of the car. "I've got the flags."

"Yep," I muttered, "getting the pennies." I thought about chugging the small bottle of Jack in my pocket, and through superhuman strength, managed to hold off.

I grabbed the pennies, took a large handful before handing him the jar, and took one of the boxes of flags from him. He went one way, and I went the other, keeping him in sight while we sought out the soldier's headstones and left flags and pennies there. My dad said the pennies told the ghost that we had visited them.

I made it to Bryan's headstone before he did and set the dime on top, and the bottle of Jack on the ground in front of it. "Bry, if you are watching out for me, help me, man. He's so far out there I have no idea what to do. He's talking about something watching me, ghosts, humming songs, and talking about screams that isn't wind. I'm having nightmares I can't remember, and pretty much feeling totally insane."

"He's not there, Jonie," my dad said from behind me. "He's over there," I looked up to see him pointing to a bench in a little flowered garden spot.

"What, Dad?" I asked, stupefied.

"Bryan, your friend. You are talking to him like he's in the ground, but he's over there," he repeated.

It was getting harder and harder to maintain my cool. "Okay. Should I go sit on the bench then?"

"No. Stay here by me. It's safer. The other one is around here somewhere. I told you this place is haunted. There's dark stuff lingering here that wants you," he glanced around nervously. "Let's go see Pop's."

I bit my lip hard to keep from crying, and followed him as he started humming again. "See, Bry? Not normal, even for dementia. This is out of this realm weird," I whispered.

"You should have married that boy, Jonie. He loved you, and you wouldn't be in this predicament." My dad turned and stopped in front of my Pop's grave.

"I loved him too, Dad. I wasn't his type, though," I told him for the thousandth time. "Bryan was gay. It wouldn't have worked as you think it would have, and even if he wasn't, he's still dead."

"Hi Pops." My dad ignored me and placed a flag in the little flower holder. "Keep that thing away from Jonie, would you? I don't think she's taking me seriously, and she needs to. Maybe you should have a word with her tonight when she's asleep. I think that's the only time she hears anything."

My blood chilled then, and it felt like everything around me was moving in super-slow motion, like it was underwater. It felt like the earth pulsed beneath my feet several times, and my vision went completely black for no more than two or three seconds, but it was enough to scare the hell out of me.

I'd never felt anything here other than peace, until today. Now it felt alive, and I wasn't sure if that was because of whatever was happening with my dad, or if there really was something here watching me other than the ghosts he clearly saw. I mean really, the earth just pulsed like something was trying to push its way out.

What was normally a fun tradition for us, had turned dark and creepy, and I just wanted to leave. When he was finally finished talking, I kissed my fingertips and pressed them to the headstone. "Love you, Pops. See you next weekend."

I followed my dad back past Bryan's grave and saw the empty bottle of Jack sitting on top next to the dime I had put there. There was no one else here but us. Thoroughly creeped out and not in my right mind, I set it back down in front of the tombstone and kept walking behind my once again humming father.

To make matters worse, while we were grocery shopping, he insisted we buy some tomato juice. I was done questioning anything, I just put it in the cart and into the fridge when we got home. I made him dinner, ate a peanut butter and jelly sandwich myself, finished the laundry, and went to bed.

I looked up Song of the Night while I was laying there

and listened to every one of them that came up in the search bar before landing on a classical piece by Mahler, which was the one he had been humming. Overwhelmed, I turned my laptop off and tried to sleep.

Sleep came in the form of twisted nightmares, fog that had fingers that was combing my hair, whispered instructions, and a piece of classical music I had never heard of before looking it up. In the morning, it all disappeared. I tried to complete my work as each day brought a new development with my dad and the one who was watching me.

By Wednesday, I was ready to start drinking heavily. I had a list of questions for the doctor, written out of course, so I didn't have to ask them out loud and hear my dad decline farther into the madness that had taken over him.

"Hi Steve, how are you doing?" Dr. Cline asked when he walked in.

"Great! I feel fantastic. I think the medications are helping, I have had less episodes than normal, and I see things a lot clearer now. Worried about Jonie, but it's a father's job, right?" my dad said jovially.

I handed Dr. Cline the list I had made and watched his eyebrows furrow as he read it. The look he gave me had me questioning my sanity again. "None of this is side effects of the medication he is on, and no, I don't think he has a dissociative disorder," Dr. Cline said softly to me. "The mood swings, yes. That's normal."

"Dr. Cline," I glanced at my dad to see him watching us. "I've never in my life heard my dad hum before. He's never listened to classical music around me, nor has he ever believed in what people call paranormal things. He's seeing ghosts, and whatever else he's seeing. None of this is normal for him, and it's scaring the hell out of me."

"Understandably so. You are also under a lot of pressure between your own life, work, and now taking care of your father. It's quite possible you are reading too much into something. He might have listened to classical music when he was a kid and you wouldn't know about it. His memory is a moving target, and he could be confusing past and present, you know this. We've talked about it before. It's very possible what is happening is a mixture of memories that are blurring into reality for him. My advice is to keep doing what you are doing, and if it gets worse, call for an appointment and bring him back. We'll do another scan and some blood work. He's only been on this regimen for three weeks, so there's still some adjusting for him to do."

It was a frustrating answer, but I did understand his position. It didn't quite ring true to me because of what I knew of my father on a personal level, but I'd watch and see what happens. Maybe he was right, and my emotions were so tied up in this because he was my dad that I wasn't seeing it objectively. Unlikely, because it's not how I operated. I couldn't discount the theory either, however.

As we got home that evening, the air outside felt heavy and thick. Like there was extra gravity to it, and it was humid. Both my dad and I didn't do well with humidity, so we turned the fans on inside and cracked the windows open.

I sat him down and put on one of the old comedy

movies he liked to watch and went to get some more work done, because I had a deadline approaching and was behind. I lost track of time scrolling through lines of script and fixing errors, and before I knew it, it was close to eleven. I stretched and stood up as thunder cracked, making me jump and knock my chair back into the wall.

A gust of wind tore through the house like we were in the middle of a tornado and I ran to shut the windows while my dad bolted off the couch screaming about the wind again. Frazzled, I got all the windows closed and tried to calm my dad down.

"It's just a storm, Dad. It really is the wind, look outside, see the trees in the yard? They are bent in half," I pointed out to him.

"No, Jonie, it's him. He's here, he's trying to get to you. He needs you. It's not time yet. Drink some tomato juice," my dad insisted, frantically wringing his hands.

"What does tomato juice have to do with anything?" I snapped, instantly feeling awful for my tone.

"It protects your heart," he said as if everyone alive knew that.

"Fine. If it will make you happy, I'll drink some tomato juice," I huffed. I didn't like it, but if it would stop the insanity, I'd do it. I poured a small glass, drank it down and watched him smile.

"Good girl. Time for bed. I'll see you in the morning," he started humming again and walked off to his bedroom.

I bit back a scream and did my best to not slam my bedroom door like a child. Maybe moving him here wasn't the best idea. I just wanted more time with my dad before he lost who he was to this stupid disease. Was it selfish of me? Should he be in a home?

For the first time, I fell asleep quickly and had no nightmares. At least I didn't think I did. I wasn't about to give credence to the thought that tomato juice was the cause of that. It was probably my brain just flat out shutting down because this was all too much. I noticed blades of grass in my sheets though when I made my bed, and I found that disturbing.

We got through the next couple of days with minimal weirdness, but I was beginning to hate that song he kept humming. That and the sound of wind, which he insisted wasn't wind, but screams. Tormented screams that he could hear that song in.

Summer solstice was on Saturday, and Father's Day was on Sunday. Which meant another trip to the cemetery to put flowers down on Pop's grave. When I woke up Saturday morning, I felt off. An odd sensation lingered in my chest, an ache almost. When I stopped to think about it, it felt like something was being pulled from me. I kept rubbing at it as I did the chores, as if rubbing it would stop it.

It was a beautiful first day of summer, and I had the windows open; the fresh air was scented with summer breeze and blooms from the yard. My dad was sitting out in the front, weeding the flower beds, but he kept staring at the mountain of trees and I could hear him mumbling. Each time he spoke, the ache in my chest increased.

I had ordered my dad a set of DVDs about the creation of earth and it's mysteries, something I knew he would watch over and over and pick out different things each time he watched it. He loved the science of earth.

While he weeded and mumbled, I wrapped it up for tomorrow and made out a grocery list. When the chores were done, I looked back outside and almost fell over through the screened window. My dad was dancing. He hadn't even danced at his wedding. A story I had heard countless times over the years and a point of contention between my parents when my mother had been alive.

"Dad." I opened the front door. "What're you doing?"

"Bryan told me I had to dance to keep you safe, so I'm dancing. Am I doing it right?" he paused to look back at me.

I let out a string of curse words under my breath that he couldn't hear and went to bring him back inside. Since when did my dad talk to Bryan and why would Bryan tell him dancing would keep me safe? "We need to go to the store, and you've got to pick out flowers for Pops. Tomorrow is Father's Day, remember?"

"Of course, I remember. I want chicken, rice, and peas for dinner," he informed me. I was happy it wasn't meatloaf so I wasn't going to argue.

"Perfect, that's what we'll get then. Want to have a fire out back tonight? We can make s'mores?" I asked, hoping for something normal.

"That sounds fun, let's do that," my dad agreed happily, seemingly childlike.

An ominous feeling like I had felt last week pressed

down on me when we got back from the store and I closed my eyes. "What is happening?"

"He's trying to break through," my dad said, carrying the graham crackers, chocolate, and marshmallows outside to set on the table. His tone matter of fact like I should have known that information.

I wasn't going to ask. I didn't want to know. Whatever was happening to my dad was something science couldn't explain. I fully believed that now. I didn't know if he was possessed, haunted, been probed by aliens, channeling demons, had been taken over by body snatchers or what, but it wasn't scientific. I had no explanations, and nothing I had researched thoroughly about dementia, covered any of this.

"Jonie, sometimes you have to take a leap of faith," my dad said from behind me, making me jump.

"About what, Dad?" I asked warily, unable to help myself.

"Life," he shrugged. "I can't stop it now any more than you can, so we just enjoy what time we have." He could have been referring to dementia, but I doubted it.

I slid the pizza we had picked up into the oven, a rare treat he allowed himself, and I poured myself a shot of whiskey and downed it. Then I did another. It was even rarer that I drank, but at this point, I needed it.

The burn made its way to my belly and I started to feel the numbing effects. When the pizza was done, I carried it out and set it on the table, enjoying the fading day. We roasted marshmallow's and made sloppy s'mores while my dad hummed that damn song. I drank two more shots before we went to bed. I felt weak for doing it, too.

I ran a bath, dumping a ton of bath salts into the water, and shaved my legs. I cut myself twice, one of them a pretty good-sized slice that bled profusely, and I blamed the whiskey for it. I didn't even drain the tub, I just crawled out, dried off and fell into bed.

Nightmares plagued me again, and when I woke up choking on a scream, the memories faded to nothing. I noticed my bed was covered with grass, dirt and blood, and I stunk. I was beyond caring at this point. Explanations weren't happening. Exhausted, a little hung over, and with no idea what had happened after I went to bed, I got up to shower the funk off me.

Bloody water filled the tub, along with bloody footsteps leading out to my bedroom. I shook my head and swore I wouldn't drink again, drained the tub and showered, feeling marginally better afterwards. I threw my damp towel on the floor and cleaned up the footprints, stripped the bed and got dressed to make my dad breakfast.

He was already sitting at the kitchen table waiting for me, a forlorn look on his face. He shook his head at me and stared down at his hands clasped in front of him. I had no clue if this was because I had drank or not, something he didn't approve of at all. I wasn't going to ask either.

"Happy Father's Day, Dad," I said quietly, gathering the stuff to make breakfast.

"Thank you, Jonie," was all he said in a soft and sad voice.

I put his gift down in front of him with his breakfast plate and let him know that we would go visit Pops after he was done. He shrugged and ate silently while I washed the pan and put stuff away. Unable to stand the uncomfortable silence anymore, I asked.

"What's wrong, Dad?" I leaned back against the counter.

"It's too late, Jonie. It's done. I tried to stop it, but he's too powerful. I still love you, though," was his reply that had me raising my eyebrows wondering just what I had done last night.

He wasn't forthcoming with an answer, and I didn't want to know bad enough that I was going to ask. Some things were better left unsaid. He cheered up after he opened his gift and was suddenly all smiles and ready to go wish Pops a happy Father's Day and drop off the flowers.

I opened the front door to bring the paper in for him for when we got back and saw a note pinned to the porch with a shard of metal. On top of the note was a handful of pennies, the dime I had left for Bryan along with the empty bottle of Jack and a flag.

"Dad, were you out here this morning?" I asked, my voice thick with apprehension. I didn't open the screen door yet.

"No. I already know what's out there. I heard him before you woke up."

Frustrated once again at the lack of understanding, I shoved the door open and looked down at the pinned note. "The ritual worked beautifully. Thanks for releasing me," I read. "See you at our wedding." What looked like splotches of blood were in a weird pattern over the note and part of the porch.

What the hell was this? I stepped back inside not touching anything and closed and locked the door. "Grab the flowers, Dad. Let's go," I said, my voice shaking.

"You can't change it now, Jonie," he said quietly. He grabbed the flowers and headed out to the garage.

Nothing felt right. Not the ache in my chest, the cut on my leg, the air, my dad. It was all wrong. Wedding? I wasn't even dating anyone. What ritual? Released? I drove to the cemetery and I drove fast. My dad didn't say anything else which I was grateful for, but as we walked up to Pops' headstone, a movement caught my eye. Hanging on a branch of the tree over that little garden area Dad had said Bryan was in, was a wedding veil fluttering in the breeze.

JULY

The Clique
Angela Faro

July 1st, 2020

endrils of steam rose from the blazing hot water of the jacuzzi as Justine soaked her troubles away with the aroma of scented oils and incense filling her senses. She stood up after a nice long soak and wrung out her long brown hair and then she heard the sound of her cell phone buzzing on the bathroom counter. She carefully stepped out of the tub and tiptoed across the room to see who was messaging her.

Justine? I know it's been forever since we've been in touch so I hope this is the right number

Justine read the text message from a number she recognized from long ago, Amanda. An old friend who then cast her aside.

I'm not sure if you already heard the news, it's pretty gruesome.

Well that certainly piqued her attention. *This is Justine.*

What news?

Greg and Valerie were found brutally stabbed to death in a murder suicide

Justine's eyes widened in shock. Those two had always been madly in love. She couldn't imagine either of them purposely hurting the other. There had to be more to it.

Valerie stabbed Greg repeatedly and then turned the knife on herself. They found a suicide note covered in blood. They say the writing didn't make a lot of sense but at the end of the note it clearly said 'Polly, please forgive us'

Huh, that's another name she hadn't heard in ages, in fact Justine never did hear from Polly again after the night she skipped town.

July 1st, 2010

Justine heard the buzz of a text message on her cell phone, it was Amanda.

Oh my god, Justine, you have to come to the party with me on the fourth. Greg and Valerie got the mother lode of fireworks to set off and you know they have all the best ones from their big boom stand. This is going to be epic

Justine didn't even want to go after seeing their new friend, Polly being mistreated by the other girls. She was no stranger to the effects of bullying so she wasn't cool with it. *Yeah I don't know if I'm going to be free that night or what, we'll see*

Bitch, don't make me put down my phone and come drag you along kicking and screaming, because you know I would. What the hell else do you have going on that night? You going on a hot date or something?

Justine couldn't help but laugh incredulously at that comment. Amanda knew better. *Yeah right! After the last few dates I went on, no thank you, I have removed myself from the dating market for the foreseeable future and I am far happier for it, thank you very much*

Oh come on, Emily wasn't that bad

This too made Justine chuckle in disbelief. *Not that bad? How drunk were you when I told you about that one?*

Um. Not gonna lie, I was pretty fucked up, why?

She was freaking married, omg Amanda lol

Oh yeah, my bad. Well, what about David?

Justine sighed heavily. *Needy as fuck. No thanks. We'd only had one date when he started calling me his girlfriend, saying I love you, and he already seemed to be getting jealous. Ew, gross.*

Okay but you have to admit that was kind of hilarious because that guy is normally a total player so that was basically his karma and I am so happy that it was you who got to hand it to him lolz

Justine rolled her eyes, Amanda often causes that reaction. *Anyway, I'm just thinking about staying home for the night. You could always come hang out over here you know. We could invite Polly since the other girls don't seem to like her much. I don't know why.*

What do you mean they don't like Polly?

How could she not notice? *Girl just pay attention to the way they talk to her. Anyway, let me know if you might want to hang with me instead on the fourth, we can do our own fireworks show and I've got tons of good weed. Edibles too!*

Hmm I don't know, everybody is already expecting me at the party so I don't want to just bail out on them like that. You know how bad that shit pisses Sonya off

Justine most certainly knew. *Yeah I get it, but if you change your mind the invite is still open. I'll be doing a Supernatural marathon that night too if that helps to entice you. Also Amanda, please be careful on the drinking if you do go to the party, I worry about you when Sonya encourages you to go overboard*

Justine wished she could get Amanda to see how negative this group was to be involved with. She wasn't like them. Sonya was the worst, she brought out the bad in everyone and she liked to talk down to people every chance she got. Justine had a hard time standing by and seeing anyone treated that way. She had been there herself too many times. It wasn't easy on her growing up. She was tormented by everyone, most of all by her own mother.

Justine had pushed those thoughts from her mind and carefully chosen a place to start anew, free of the demons of her past that had haunted her for so long.

July 2nd, 2020

he glow from the computer screen lit up the otherwise dark room, she had been researching into the deaths of Greg and Valerie. How had Amanda known the details when the information wasn't even out there for the general public to know about yet? She only found an article that didn't mention names about two people found dead in Ravens Hollow, where they lived but no details.

She was dying to hear more news about Valerie and Greg. *Amanda? How did you know so much about what happened to them?*

She waited for a response but none followed for some time. Since it clearly wasn't happening any time soon she went back to searching the web when a chat icon popped up on her computer screen from someone with the user id Dorothy.

Hi

Justine didn't know anyone named Dorothy. She responded cautiously. *Who is this?*

Just someone you once knew

She tried to remember anyone she had ever known named Dorothy and she was coming up blank. *What do you want?*

I want to talk to you, I need your help and you need my help

Justine frowned in confusion. *I'm sorry I don't believe I*

know you

You don't know me anymore but you did once. Please help me help you

Justine shook her head, frustrated. *Help you help me how?*

Let's just say I've been—stuck in Oz and I need to get back over the rainbow.

Justine was not amused. *Oh haha. Very funny. Who are you? Is this Amanda? Are you fucking with me right now?*

No. But I've been in contact with Amanda as well.

Okay, so this *Dorothy* knows Amanda and seems to be trying to play games with her mind. She thinks she knows now exactly who is behind this screen name. *Sonya?*

Ha. No. Try again

Justine had zero patience for games. *Polly?*

Justine waited but there was no response. Dorothy was no longer online, but all of a sudden Justine's phone was buzzing again, a message from Amanda.

I heard it from someone with inside information.

Why couldn't anyone give her a straight answer? And who is that someone?

I'm not supposed to tell you that. But I'm so sorry Justine, for disappearing on you, for all of it.

Amanda wasn't getting forgiven that easily after she completely bailed on her ten years before. *Oh yeah? Why did you disappear, Amanda? And why can't you tell me who told you about Greg and Valerie? Why did you tell me anything at all in the first place?*

I had to tell you. I had to warn you.

Justine was ready to just throw her hands up with all of it. *Warn me? What the hell does that mean? Amanda you are freaking me out.*

She's coming for you, Justine. She's coming for all of us.

Now Justine was terrified. *She? She who? Who is coming for us and for what? I haven't even talked to any of you people in ten years so why now?*

It's the ten year anniversary

Justine was fuming now. *The anniversary of what? Our friendship ending? Well happy fucking anniversary and screw you very much.* With an exasperated groan, she tossed her phone aside but it immediately buzzed again. Once again she was shocked by the words on her screen.

I've just been informed that Brian and Lonnie were in a rollover accident. Lonnie's dead and Brian is in a coma. Before he was unconscious, Brian was ranting and raving about Sonya. They haven't been together in years. Be careful, Justine

July 2nd, 2010

Justine was worried about Amanda, her binge drinking was becoming troublesome so she dropped by her apartment for a visit to check up on her. She was hoping to help her friend to talk it out, whatever it was that was bothering her.

Seated on the couch they chatted for hours until Justine discovered what was going on. She comforted her friend as best as she knew how. "Oh my god, Amanda, I'm so sorry," she said, "No wonder you haven't been yourself. How long ago did this happen?"

Amanda was sobbing heavily and pulled herself together just enough to choke out a response, "I had the miscarriage about two weeks ago. I swear I didn't know I was pregnant or I wouldn't have been drinking." She broke down into another sobbing episode.

Feeling so at a loss for what to do for her friend, all she could do was just be there for Amanda to have someone to talk to about it since she had been keeping it completely to herself until now, feeling too ashamed to share with anyone.

Regaining her composure once more Amanda continued, "I must have been a few weeks along and at first I couldn't even remember having sex, like at all. I was confused and scared and then I remembered, it was almost like it was in a dream." She started to lose it again a little bit then pulled it back together again and continued, "I was so hammered, Justine. If I were sober I would have never ever." With that Amanda was fully back in tears as Justine hugged her close and Amanda cried into her shoulder, "I don't even like Brian or Lonnie that way, I don't know how it happened."

Justine was quick to respond reassuringly, "They took advantage of you, that's how. You couldn't possibly have given proper consent in the state of mind you were in. Oh Amanda I'm so sorry."

Mortified, Amanda looked up at Justine and said, "I don't even want to go to the stupid party on the fourth, but I don't want to let on that anything is wrong. I know Sonya too well and she would just blame me. She's done that before to others." Tears falling from her eyes she cried, "Oh Justine, she scares me. You don't ever want to cross Sonya."

July 3rd, 2020

Paranoid and panicky, Justine couldn't stop looking over her shoulder at every little sound. She hadn't heard any more from Amanda since the day before but Dorothy had been trying to chat all day. She was too scared to open the chat or read any messages because she didn't know who Dorothy was or if she could be trusted. She tried messaging Amanda to ask if she knew about this Dorothy but she hadn't gotten a response. She was at her wits end. Finally her cell phone buzzed with an incoming text message from Amanda. It was not an answer to her questions about Dorothy.

Justine, I just got off the phone with Tara. She was hysterical, I could barely understand her but I'm pretty sure she said that Katie's dead. Suicide, supposedly

Although she felt like she should be getting use to this by now, nevertheless Justine was floored once again. *What?! How?*

I don't know. I couldn't make out what she said other than she thinks she's next

This was becoming more frustrating and frightening by the moment. *Amanda what is going on? Why is someone picking off all of our old friends and who is doing it?*

I don't know for certain quite yet, but I have some ideas.

I just can't tell you over the phone. Can you meet me tomorrow night around nine?

Against her better judgment, Justine knew she was going to have to agree if she wanted to get to the bottom of all of this. *Where do you want to meet up?*

Remember the party ten years ago?

Justine had to think about that one. She hadn't been in that area for many years now but it came back to her when she focused on it for a moment or two. *Uh, yeah sure, but why there?*

I can't tell you why but it needs to be there. Please just trust me.

She wasn't too keen on that whole trust thing thanks to past experiences but she remembered she still had an unanswered question. *Amanda, how do you know Dorothy?*

I've gotta go now. I'll see you tomorrow night. Be safe, Justine

Flabbergasted, Justine tried messaging her again about Dorothy but she wasn't answering any more tonight. She contemplated checking the online messages she had been ignoring all day but decided not to, for now at least.

July 3rd, 2010

Justine could hear her doorbell ringing repeatedly and had ignored it until she could no longer stand the racket, at which point she dipped her head under the bathroom faucet then wrapped her hair in a towel and threw on a bathrobe, swathing herself in it. I'm coming," Justine shouted. "Just a minute."

When she opened the door there stood Katie and Tara, smiling their fake smiles. "Justine," said Katie, saccharine sweetness dripping from each syllable. "We were knocking forever."

Smiling cordially although she was not pleased with them dropping in on her, Justine apologized insincerely, "Sorry you guys," pointing to the towel on her head she continued, "I was in the shower."

Tara then quipped, "We have also been calling and texting." The look on her face made it clear that they weren't buying it and they knew they were being ignored.

At this point, Justine didn't really care anymore. She'd had enough of the fake sweetness and sometimes downright rudeness from all of them. "Yeah I'm taking a sabbatical from technology right now, it's good for the soul," she asserted. "Anyway, to what do I owe this delightful visit?"

Katie and Tara glanced at each other with matching snobbishly smug grins on their faces then back at Justine. Katie replied, "Sonya has been trying to reach Amanda all week and she isn't returning her calls or messages."

They both stared at Justine as if urging her to give up some information on Amanda, knowing that Justine was her closest friend. She didn't offer anything.

Tara added, "Sonya hates being ignored, but me and Katie have been trying to reach her too. Have you heard from her at all?"

With a perfectly straight face, Justine stared right back at them and replied, "Nope I haven't heard from her this week, but I've also been really busy and it didn't seem out of the ordinary to me. Maybe she's out of town." As an afterthought she added, "Whenever I do hear from her I will let her know you are trying to reach her. Right now I've got to go however, so thank you for stopping by. Good day, ladies." Without another moment's pause she then closed the door in their faces.

No sooner than she got back inside to where her cell phone was laying on the counter charging, she grabbed it and immediately texted Amanda. *Whatever you do, I would not answer your door and make sure to lock it too if you haven't already*

Already on it. Don't tell me the goon squad showed up at your door too?

Relieved to hear from her friend, Justine messaged back quickly. *Yeah they showed up here for information on you. What's up with that?*

Oh I guess Sonya has some vendetta against Polly all of a sudden

Justine sighed loudly, she had been trying to tell Amanda for the longest time that Polly was being mistreated but she couldn't see it. *Girl I'm telling you, Sonya never liked Polly, there's nothing sudden about this*

Well I don't know what the deal is but she wants to confront her at the party with whatever it is she is pissed off at her for, in front of everyone.

Justine snorted defiantly at the gall of that

woman. *Well isn't that just Sonya's style. Make it as humiliating and demeaning as possible.* Anyway, does this mean you are ditching out on the party and hanging out with me then?

I'm honestly thinking I might just stay locked up at home watching movies and going through a million boxes of tissues like I've been doing lately

She felt bad that there was nothing she could do to help her friend feel better about what happened to her. Justine knew the best thing she could do was just be there for her when she was ready to talk more or to vent to. *Aww girl, okay if that's what you need to do, then you do you, boo. Hit me up if you change your mind, I'll just be hanging with the Winchesters*

July 4th, 2020

eelings of anxiety were crippling for Justine today and she was nervous and scared about meeting up with Amanda, just as she was about to message her a text came in from Amanda. Maybe she was finally going to tell her how she knows this Dorothy.

Tara is dead. Drowned in her bathtub. See you tonight

Justine was barely surprised this time, even with Amanda's no fanfare way of sharing the news. *So that leaves just you, me, Polly and Sonya huh? Oh and Dorothy*

But Amanda wasn't responding once again. Justine was always irritated by her way of doing that. She had several hours to kill before it was time to meet with Amanda at nine and she needed something to do because her thoughts were driving her mad. She eyed her computer, did she want to read those messages or didn't she? Just as she was staring at the screen contemplating, a new message popped up.

Justine, come over here

She was quite taken aback by this message. *Excuse me? Are you watching me?!*

Don't feel too flattered, I'm watching everyone everywhere I go

All the creepy vibes were coming on really strong now for Justine. *Not funny dammit, who are you?*

I thought it was pretty funny. Okay sorry, I don't mean to tease. It's just been so long since I've talked to anyone, I guess you could say my communication skills are a little rusty.

This Dorothy was more and more curious to Justine all the time. *Why have you not been in communication with anyone for so long?*

I didn't have the means, it takes a lot of energy and that doesn't come cheap

Speaking of energy, Justine was feeling pretty low on that herself. *Energy? I mean I get being tired but how much energy does it take to send an instant message?*

Well I suppose that depends on your physical form. Listen, enough with the small talk. I need you to promise you will be there tonight. This is important and it will help you and Amanda. I know you care about Amanda. Can you do that?

Justine wasn't a big fan of promises since they were so often broken, but she did plan on being there. *Okay I'll be there, but I want you to know that I know martial arts and I do carry mace and I know how to use it.*

That's good. You should probably also think about bringing a weapon of some kind for protection tonight. See you there

The messenger icon for Dorothy went dark again and Justine was back to being stuck with herself and her own anxious thoughts and still with several hours to kill. This was going to be a long day.

July 4th, 2010

Justine hadn't heard from Amanda all day although she had been messaging her non stop. Sonya, Tara, Katie and Valerie had all been messaging Justine all day. They still couldn't reach Amanda and didn't believe that Justine hadn't heard from her either. They sounded pissed off big time and as if they were out for blood but once Justine answered them they stopped trying to contact her.

Justine tried contacting Polly to invite her over to her place and warn her about Sonya's plans for the party but she got no answer from Polly either. She wasn't even sure if she had the right number for her.

It bothered her so badly that she still hadn't heard from Amanda. She figured she wouldn't want to come over most likely but she just had a hunch something was off. Justine decided it would be a good idea to just go over to

Amanda's and make sure she sees all is well with her own two eyes.

As soon as she arrived out front of Amanda's place she knew something was wrong. The front door was wide open but Amanda's car was still there. Her beloved cat, Termite, was roaming around outside and Amanda never lets him out. Justine rounded him back up into the apartment and went in to check things out. Amanda's phone was left behind on the counter and so was her purse. She didn't even bring her keys with her.

Justine then quickly left Amanda's place, shutting the door behind her and immediately began calling Sonya, Valerie, Tara and Katie continually. None of the ladies answered and no calls were returned. There was only one more thing left to do, head to the party spot. Thankfully she knew where it was because initially she was planning on being there until everyone started getting so hostile with Polly. Even though Justine didn't know Polly very well she could tell she was a decent person and from the little they had gotten to know each other Polly had confided in Justine how she had always been bullied and so they shared that common ground.

When Justine arrived at the party it appeared as though a bomb had gone off. Being Independence Day she supposed there had been several large explosives set off already that night. The group had multiple tents set up near the wooded area back a ways from where the fireworks were being lit up. On the beach they had a bunch of folding chairs set up around a roaring bonfire, flames flickering high into the air. You could hear the hiss and pop of crackling embers coming out of the flames. It was a giant mess and everyone looked like they had been through the ringer. Amanda was passed out cold in a folding chair but she didn't appear to be harmed, perhaps a little worse for the wear and surely inebriated. That made her feel much better to see. Seated around her were Sonya, Katie, Tara and Lonnie. Brian was up stoking the fire with a long stick. Greg and Valerie were standing in the distance, holding hands and deep in conversation. They appeared to be talking about something stressful. Everyone else except Sonya seemed a bit uneasy.

As she walked up to the campsite she could see everyone turn their eyes to her, faces switching from uneasy to curious, Sonya was the very last one to look her way. With her signature mischievous smile and evil glint in her eyes she said snarkily, "Justine, you decided to grace us with your presence after all. Too bad you already missed all the fun."

Justine retorted back, "That's alright, this isn't really my kind of fun anyway. I just came to make sure Amanda was okay. I went to her apartment and it looked like she'd been kidnapped."

Sonya laughed mockingly and the others feebly joined her. "Kidnapped? Don't be ridiculous, we simply lured her with alcohol," she paused briefly before adding, "After all that is her own personal kryptonite." Then she and the others all laughed heartily at Amanda's expense. Lonnie and Brian exchanged a conspiratorial glance and Justine glared daggers back at them. When they noticed the severity of the look on her face it quickly knocked the evil looks off of their faces.

At the sound of all the commotion Amanda began

stirring awake just in time to see Justine glaring at the guys. When she saw this she immediately got irritated and defensive and with slurred speech she spat, "What are you doing here? I thought you didn't want to hang out with everyone anymore?" Amanda was worried that Justine might say something about her incident with Brian and Lonnie, but there was something else Justine could easily sense. Amanda did not want her there. Sonya must have turned Amanda against her.

Justine was hurt and she somberly stated, "I thought you might be in danger. Termite was out in the street, I put him back inside and shut the door." She turned her head to hide her tears until she could regain her composure. "I guess I'll be going now."

She turned and began to walk away, then remembered she also came for Polly as well but she was nowhere to be found. Justine turned back and questioned the group, "Oh yeah, where's Polly tonight?" Valerie and Greg looked her way in surprise, abruptly ending their important conversation they had been having, now with concerned looks on their faces. She could see a strange look come across everyone else's faces that they each quickly tried to hide but not before it registered in Justine's mind as being odd. Everyone except for Amanda who seemed to be a bit confused by everyone else's behavior.

Sonya took the opportunity to quickly speak up, her voice unwavering, "Polly informed us that she was leaving town." The rest of the group looked nervously at Sonya and around at each other, before awkwardly nodding in agreement, if Sonya said it was true then it was pretty much gospel within the group. Amanda looked around cautiously trying to read the faces of the people around her.

Sonya grinned maliciously and stated, "She said she'd be sure to keep in touch."

Justine felt some kind of uneasy tension but she wasn't sure why so she replied, "Alright then, so long." She caught Amanda's stare for a moment, hoping she would decide to go with her and leave this horrible group behind but Amanda only stared back for a moment and then looked uncomfortably away. That was Justine's cue to quietly leave.

July 4th, 2020

Justine arrived, ax in hand, at nine o'clock on the same muddy shores where her closest friendship had ended ten years ago that night. There was nothing and no one all around her as far as the eye could see. She was beginning to wonder if it was all just an elaborate prank being played on her.

Just as she was about to leave, feeling defeated she saw Amanda walking towards her, off in the distance. Justine raised her hand to wave hello but then she saw another figure creeping up behind Amanda with a giant spiked club raised up above her head ready to bring it down on Amanda at any moment. Justine screamed at her old friend to move before she could get injured or worse, "Amanda, look out!"

Amanda turned and ducked out of the way just in time and now Justine could see it was a woman threatening to kill Amanda in the distance but she couldn't make out who. Justine began running towards them as Amanda ran away from her would be killer. She had managed to create a wide gap between herself and the club yielding woman chasing after her, as she reached Justine she looked apologetically at her old friend.

Justine was anxious to find out who was behind all of this. She stopped running and faced off against the woman who had also came to a halt. The woman was masked so Justine couldn't tell who she was looking at. "Who are you and why are you doing this? Take off your mask you coward," Justine spat her words angrily at the woman. She could only see her eyes, there was something familiar in them, that evil malicious glint. And in that moment she knew, "Sonya," stated with disgust so strong just saying it made her feel sick to her stomach. "You killed everyone," she continued horrified, "I always knew you were bad news, but murder?"

Sonya burst out into a maniacal laugh that echoed through the night, "Justine, so good to see you again, it's been too long," she paused to laugh some more, her mind was gone, "I'd love to catch up on old times. Too bad I have to," Sonya lurched herself forward, club raised in the air, "Kill you now," with that she brought it down so fast Justine barely managed to get out of the way, the club hitting the dirt and rocks on the ground where Justine had been standing. Sonya was fast though and she had it back up and swinging in no time. She also had no fear because she was completely out of her mind so that made her even more dangerous. Sonya swung again at Justine who hit the club with her ax knocking the club from Sonya's hand as she fell to the ground.

Justine stood above her, valiantly wielding her ax in front of her as she leaned closer to her enemy. "Who is Dorothy?" Justine queried through teeth clenched in anger and defiance.

Sonya just looked back at Justine confused. "Dorothy? What are you talking about? I don't know any Dorothy, unless you're talking Wizard of Oz." She appeared to be telling the truth on this one.

Justine turned her attention to Amanda, she had her in person to question about it finally and she wasn't getting away with brushing it off this time, "I need to know who Dorothy is and why she was watching me."

Just as Amanda was about to respond, with Sonya unguarded she managed to get up and grab her club but right as she was about to swing at Justine again a blinding brilliant flash of light burst out of the water, shooting up in to the sky like a firework and coming back down all around them. When it died down enough for them to see again, there was a beautiful ghostly woman who was also strangely familiar, standing—floating before them. "I am Dorothy." The ethereal figure spoke with authority.

Justine, Amanda and Sonya were all stunned silent in that moment and then the spirit began to morph into her previous humanly form, it was Polly. Simultaneously the three women's jaws dropped. Sonya's surprise immediately changed to fear when she realized who it was. She knew her gig was up and she was frozen in place, unable to move, bound by invisible bonds.

Realizing what so many others already suspected Justine queried, "So you didn't actually skip town ten years ago?"

Amanda was inconsolable. "I didn't want to believe it was true but I always had a gut feeling something bad happened to you that night while I was passed out." Amanda began crying, the guilt tearing her up inside. "After I woke up and you were gone, everyone was acting kind of weird but I didn't dare question it or Sonya would've just as easily gotten rid of me too."

Amanda turned to Justine, looking at her with appreciation and sorrow, "I only wanted you to stay away for your own protection. Because if my assumption was correct I didn't want to get you tied up into it any further. You are the best friend I ever had and I love you." Justine and Amanda were now both in tears.

Justine was still a little confused however so she questioned further, "But why did we have to come here tonight?"

Polly chimed in, "My energy is strongest here because this is where my body lies, down at the bottom of the river." Justine and Amanda still looked perplexed. "I had to protect you both from Sonya. I could only do that here."

Sonya, looking morose, whined, "What happens to me now?"

Polly beamed proudly, "Well, Sonya, the authorities are on their way and when they get here, they are going to lock you up and throw away the key. I've been watching you and let's just say I have ways with technology that have allowed me to gather evidence of all the bad things you've been doing." Polly winked at Sonya then continued, "You've been a very busy girl this week haven't you?"

Sonya tried protesting until Polly began holographically playing clips of the video and audio evidence she had been collecting against her. That shut her up real quick.

Justine had one more question for Polly: "Why now? Why wait ten years after the fact?"

Polly smiled broadly. "Well I've been going through some other worldly training. Energy building. See, the way it works on the other side, energy has to be built or earned, it doesn't come cheap or easy, you've gotta work for it." She paused, reflecting on how hard she had worked over the past ten years to be able to build the energy needed tonight. "It took me until now to be sure my energy was strong enough to do all that needed to be done. Being the anniversary of my death also made my energy more powerful tonight than it has ever been, I wanted to harness that extra energy and I did." Polly added as an afterthought, "As for why did Sonya snap just now? Valerie and Greg finally questioned her about my disappearance the other day, they were digging..." She paused for effect, then continued: "...their own graves, as it turned out."

Justine was content now, she had all the answers she sought, she had her best friend back in her life with an understanding of why she had been pushed away, and she could hear the police sirens in the distance coming for the villain.

She turned and looked at Polly and Amanda with a satisfied smile then she turned to Sonya and cackled, imitating Sonya's own famous malicious laughter. With a gleaming smile and glint in her eye, Justine said to her with glee, "Paybacks are a bitch."

august

Balance of Nature

Lauren Patzer

"Just get in the car," John said. "Your friends will be fine without you."

Becky stood outside the car glaring at her father with her striking blue eyes. John ran his fingers through his thinning blonde hair and thrummed his fingers on the steering wheel.

"This is our last summer together!" Becky screamed.

Becky's mother, Christina, with matching blue eyes and dark curly hair, sighed out loud. The fight had been going on for a week now and she was tired of the drama.

"Everything seems that way when you're young," Christina said. "Just get in so we can go."

"This is so stupid!" Becky shouted and climbed in the car. She quickly put on her seatbelt, crossed her arms and stared out the window.

John started the car and they backed out of the driveway. He glanced through the back window, forgetting it was blocked by everything they'd packed. He caught a glimpse of sleeping bags piled high on top of coolers before he returned his attention to the backup camera. It was all clear as he completed his maneuver and pulled onto the street, slowly accelerating. He glanced at the clock on the dash and winced. They were way behind schedule. They wouldn't get to the campsite until well after dark. Maybe he could find something on the way.

Becky remained stubbornly silent all the way through town, even as they pulled onto the highway heading out of town.

"Look, you're going to have another three weeks before school starts to hang out with your friends," John said as he accelerated to change lanes.

"Really, dad? Think they'll go to Cancun again next year?" Becky said, still seething.

"They might and next year you'll be eighteen; you can do whatever you like next summer."

"Well, I won't be spending it with you two," Becky grumbled.

"When you get older, you'll find you miss the opportunities you had to spend with family. You never know when fate will change your circumstances and someone will be gone," John said.

"You're not dying, dad," Becky sighed.

"People you love can be gone in an instant," Christina said sadly. There was silence for several minutes as Becky looked at the floor.

"This won't bring him back," Becky mumbled.

"I know sometimes it seems like we're smothering

you," John replied. "Your mother and I have been talking. We're going to be concentrating very hard over the next year on giving you some space. How about we plan on talking all about that over the weekend?"

"Sure," Becky replied. "But only if there's s'mores."

Christina chuckled for a moment.

"National S'Mores Day was Monday," John replied. "Do you really think I'd miss this opportunity to celebrate?"

"Okay," Becky sighed. John glanced in the rear view and caught her smiling for the first time that week. It faded away, but at least there was a glimmer of happiness.

A few minutes later, they hit some unexpected construction. The line went on for miles with no exit in sight.

"We might have to alter our destination," John said. "The camping grounds close at ten p.m. and we're running way behind. I'm going to get off at our next exit and check the map."

Forty-five minutes later, they reached the next exit and John pulled off. He turned right at the corner and stopped by the side of the road. John checked the navigation on the console of the SUV and chuckled.

"Well, I'll be. I haven't been here in years," John said and pulled back onto the road.

"Where?" Christina asked.

"When I was younger, there was this little piece of land off the road about ten miles outside of Nettles. My dad used to take us there and we'd make camp, roast hot dogs on sticks and just enjoy nature," John said as they sped along. "We should be there in just under an hour. Plenty of time to setup the tent, make a fire and get some s'mores going!"

"You ever take Bryan there?" Becky asked.

"I did," John replied and sniffed. "Before you were born, when he was five."

Christina reached over and touched John's arm.

"Are you sure you want to do this, honey?" She asked quietly.

"Yeah," John replied as he put on a brave smile. "It's a place of happiness. It'll be fine."

Less than an hour later, they passed the sign that read "Nettles 10 miles." John slowed down so he could spot the dirt road off to the right. He found it about half a mile past the sign and turned onto it. The rutted dirt road looked overgrown like it hadn't been used in years.

"You sure this is it?" Christina asked.

"Yes. It doesn't look like it's used much. We might have a little bit of work ahead of us to clear some brush."

"So much better than Cancun," Becky said snidely.

"No need for sunscreen under the tree canopy," John replied, smiling brightly.

"Ugh," Becky folded her arms and closed her eyes.

Minutes later, they reached a bend in the road that headed into the forest. John turned the vehicle around and backed in until they'd gone in about a hundred feet. An old picnic table sat a few yards behind the car. The forest floor was thick with leaves. Just a few feet beyond the trees was a small clearing with an old fire pit outlined by some haphazard rocks.

"Twenty minutes and we'll have this site in tip top

shape ready for the tent," John said. He got out of the car and Christina did, too. Becky grumbled, huffed and got out as well.

Using the rake and shovel John always brought along, they cleared the area of leaves and reassembled the fire pit. Christina and John continued clearing the tent area while Becky found plenty of kindling on the forest floor. Despite herself, Becky enjoyed the smell of the forest and the calm quiet of their surroundings.

When they got the fire pit going, Christina cooked up the hot dogs they'd brought and they enjoyed the roasted corn wrapped in foil that they put over a little metal rack on top of the fire. Finally, they broke out the chocolate, graham crackers and marshmallows and cooked up a wonderful couple of desserts. As they cleaned up the food and trash, Becky noticed the moon rising through the trees.

"That was Bryan's favorite part," John said as he walked up next to her. "He loved watching the moon rise up into the sky."

"He would've loved this trip," Christina said as she folded up the tablecloth and tucked it away in the crate they stored the lighter stuff in. "He also would've loved the tent up by now."

"Oh." John jumped up, ran over to the SUV and started pulling the tent out. Becky stood watching the moon for a few more moments.

"It's almost like he's here with us," she whispered. She shook her head and blinked her eyes. She cleared the lump in her throat and went to help her dad setup the tent.

By the time John and Becky had gotten the five-man

tent erected, Christina had packed up everything in the SUV so they wouldn't have to worry about animals getting into anything overnight. Raccoons were tricky, but they hadn't managed to figure out how to open up car doors.

They laid out the sleeping bags with pads underneath them and then sat at the table again watching the moon continue its ascent. John turned the lamp on the table down to almost dark.

"You ever think he's watching over us?" Becky asked.

"I sure hope so," Christina answered. "When it's quiet and everything is still, I can almost feel him sitting with us, enjoying our company again."

"He can worry about you when you're driving yourself to your extracurricular events next year," John said.

"Really?" Becky almost jumped off the bench.

"And you can go to the after parties as long as you're home by 2am," Christina added. "But you have to come and let us know you made it home okay."

"I will," Becky smiled.

"Well, let's get this after party started!" A gruff voice announced from the darkness around them.

"Who's there?" John said as he turned the lamp up on the table. Two men holding rifles walked into the edge of the light. One was older, a rough looking man with a scar running across his face from the left temple down through his lips. He wore a dirty white shirt and a dingy pair of overalls caked with dirt. His eyes seemed crueler as he sneered at the family. He raised his rifle.

"You're trespassing on my land," he said. "My name's

Zeke and this is my cousin Danny Boy."

Zeke inclined his head toward a younger man, with dirt dusting his black shirt and blue jeans. He was wiry and had a ginger tuft of whiskers on his chin matching his curly red hair; he didn't look much older than Becky. He raised his rifle at the family as well with a nervous giggle.

"Now we don't want any trouble," John said. "We can just pack up and leave. I was here years ago and we never had a problem with the owner."

"Well," Zeke said and spit out some tobacco at his feet. "It looks like you're gonna get something you didn't plan for tonight. You've been using my land, burning my wood and messing with my picnic table. That's gonna cost ya."

John stood up with his hands out.

"We can pay you money; we're awfully sorry for any trouble," John said.

Zeke walked up closer to John and lowered his rifle.

"Oh, it's gonna cost you something besides money," Zeke said. He looked at the women and smiled. "We'll be taking it out in trade."

John looked at his family and then back at the men.

"You can't—"

Zeke swung his rifle butt at John's head and knocked him to the ground unconscious.

"John!" Christina cried out as she jumped to her feet. Zeke flipped the rifle back into his hands and pointed it at her.

"Think we've had enough violence for one night, miss," Zeke said. Christina stopped moving as the gun pointed at her.

"Danny Boy, you tie up pops here and drag him into the tent." Zeke stepped across John's inert body and Christina backed up, tears in her eyes.

"This is illegal!" Becky shouted as Danny Boy got down on the ground and tied John's hands in front of him with some twine and then did the same thing with his feet.

"I could just shoot you!" Zeke screamed and Becky gasped. "Ya wanna die tonight or just have a little exchange of pleasantries and be on your way?"

Danny Boy dragged John into the tent and came back to pick up his own rifle.

"We was just out huntin' bear on our property when we happened upon a bunch of trespassers. Way I see it," Zeke said as he spit out more tobacco. "We can make tonight real bloody or just have some fun. Truth be told, I'd have fun either way."

"Can't you just let us go?" Christina asked.

"We're gonna get our payment or we'll use you as bear bait. You're choice," Zeke smiled, showing teeth darkened by his chewing tobacco habit. "Now get in that tent!"

Zeke waved his rifle at the two of them and Danny Boy moved aside, blocking them from running off away from the tent.

Christina swallowed deep and held her hand out to her daughter. Becky got up from the table and walked over to her mother, taking her outstretched hand. Their hands were shaking when they touched, but the combined strength of them both together calmed them somewhat.

"Come on!" Zeke shouted, waving the rifle at them. The two women moved slowly into the tent.

"Get the lantern, Danny Boy, so we can see our prizes real good," Zeke said as he followed the women to the tent. Danny Boy retrieved the lantern and joined Zeke at the tent opening. He held the lantern out, lighting up the women now cowering at the back wall of the tent.

Christina gasped as she saw blood oozing slowly from the gash on John's head. The look of fear was mixed with concern on Becky's face as well.

"Get naked ladies," Zeke said. "Time for the fun to start."

"Please, my husband needs a doctor," Christina said weakly.

"You want more of the same, you just keep protesting. Now get those clothes off, both of ya," Zeke said.

"Which one's mine, Zeke," Danny Boy said, his voice quick with excitement.

"I get momma, she knows how to please a man. She's got years of experience. You can fumble around with the girl. Figure you'll lose your seed before you even get your pants off!" Zeke laughed and Danny Boy's face got red.

"I know what to do with a woman!" Danny Boy said defensively.

"I ain't talking about kissing your cousin in the closet, ya idiot!" Zeke said. "All right, ladies, let's get going. We got all night, but I ain't that patient."

Christina stood tall and shook her head. Zeke could see her jaw clench and he lost his smile.

"Guess we're gonna do this the hard way," Zeke said. "That's alright; I like a little fight in my women!"

Zeke and Danny set their weapons down on the ground. They both rushed the women and everyone fell to the ground. Sounds of ripped clothing and screams echoed into the darkness. Then, there was a ruckus outside the tent. To Zeke, it sounded like someone moving the picnic table around.

"Dammit, Danny Boy! I thought you said there was only three of them!" Zeke hissed as he stopped and got off Christina.

"There was, Zeke! Honest!" Danny Boy whispered back. Christina sat up and pushed Danny Boy off Becky. Zeke turned and smacked Christina across the face and she fell back to the ground with the blow. Zeke quickly grabbed his rifle.

"Get up here and cover them while I go check out our visitor," Zeke whispered.

Danny Boy got off Becky and grabbed his weapon. His eyes darted back and forth between the two women nervously as he covered them. His hands shook as the rifle swung slowly between them.

Zeke exited the tent and could be heard as he stormed around the camp looking for the clamorous intruder. Inside the tent, everyone listened quietly as Zeke hunted for the source of the ruckus. Suddenly they heard a shot and a scream. An otherworldly roar echoed through the camp accompanied by the bloodcurdling sounds of a person screaming in anguish and then suddenly going silent.

"What the fuck?" Danny Boy whispered. "Zeke?"

Christina and Becky hugged each other, no longer

worried about Danny Boy and his shotgun.

"Zeke? This ain't funny!" Danny Boy whispered at the tent flap. He looked back at the women.

"We'll be back and we're gonna fuck you up!" Danny Boy growled. He exited the tent.

"Zeke!" Danny shouted. The women continued to be silent.

Christina looked at John and realized his feet were hanging out the tent flap, visible to whatever was out there.

"Help me pull Dad into the tent," Christina whispered to Becky. The women grabbed his shoulders but then they heard Danny Boy.

"What the hell is that? Oh shit, Zeke... that fucking bear," Danny Boy said with a mix of sorrow and anger.

Christina and Becky were still frozen, not sure if they should be more afraid of Danny or whatever kind of creature was out there with him.

"Come on out, ya mangy beast! I'll fucking kill ya where ya stand!" Danny Boy's voice was high pitched with a mixture of fear, anger and adrenaline. "Ya got the goats last night, but you're gonna meet your maker tonight!"

"They were really hunting a bear?" Becky whispered.

An unholy growl rumbled through the trees, a mix between a bear and a wolf. They heard a gunshot go off and then Danny Boy cursed.

"I got more bullets, ya rat bastard! I can fire this gun all damn night!" Danny Boy hollered into the night air.

The women gasped as they felt something large shaking the ground near them as it galloped past the tent.

Danny Boy screamed in anger and then screamed in fright. His screams seemed to float away from the tent accompanied by a frenzy of gunfire followed by a dull thud.

"Grab Dad," Christina whispered as she got up. "We're dragging him to the car, putting him inside and getting out of here."

"But Mom, it's out there!" Becky hissed, not moving.

"If we don't move now, we're all as good as dead!" Christina replied angrily. "We have to move while whatever that is occupies itself with those fucking hillbillies!"

Becky gasped as she'd never heard her mother cuss before. It was enough to shake her out of her fear. She got up and the two of them grabbed John's shoulders and drug him out of the tent. They continued their activity even as they passed something wet and slick to the right of them that smelled of warm blood and tobacco.

"Back seat," Christina whispered. "You get the door and then get his feet as I pull him inside."

"OK," Becky whispered back and she ran to the door and opened it quickly. She heard the wet smacking of jaws on flesh beyond the car and realized the beast was busy consuming Danny Boy while they moved her father about. She ran back as quietly as possible and helped Christina move John into the car. Christina pulled him in and was under John in the back seat.

"Climb over the seat and drive us out of here as fast as you can," Christina said to Becky. Without a thought, Becky scrambled up and over into the driver's seat.

"Keys!" Becky hissed.

"Get them from Dad's pocket," Christina said as she ripped her sleeve off what was left of her shirt. "I'm trying to stop the bleeding on his head."

Becky hung over the back of the seat and dug frantically through her father's pockets and eventually found the keys. Tears streamed from her eyes and she sniffled. She turned back around and started up the car. When the headlights came on, she gasped.

Up ahead of the SUV, lit up and hanging on to the bloody torso of Danny Boy, a large hairy creature was gnawing on Danny Boy's skull. With a sickening crack, the skull cracked open and a long tongue dipped into the brain cavity and slurped out the warm flesh. The beast then turned to look at Becky who was frozen in fear.

It opened its mouth and screamed a foul cry, blood and brains spewing forth from its gaping maw. It dropped Danny Boy's torso and turned toward the car. It towered above the SUV at what must have been ten feet or more. It threw its head back and howled into the night air, steam pouring forth from its jaws.

"Just drive," a voice whispered in Becky's ear. She recognized the voice in an instant. The last time she'd heard that voice was the night Bryan had left for the college party where he'd died from alcohol poisoning six years ago. It was her brother's voice and it snapped her out of her fear. She slammed her foot on the gas and drove right at the beast.

The beast leaped out of the way of the speeding car, but not before the driver's side headlight collided with what must've been its foot. The creature spun around in midair and its hideous face slammed into the driver's side window, smearing it with blood, saliva and orange brown hair. Becky screamed as she struggled to keep the car going straight.

She side swiped a tree, but managed to get the vehicle back under control. She drove onto the dirt road, turned back toward the paved road and floored the accelerator. Another unholy howl rang out through the night, but it faded in the distance behind the car and Becky hoped that meant it wasn't pursuing them in their flight from the forest.

As they approached the main road, Becky slowed down.

"Go right towards town," Christina said. "They have a small emergency clinic there, I think."

"Is Dad going to be okay?" Becky asked as she pulled out onto the main road.

"I think so, but he might have a concussion," Christina said. "Head injuries are tricky sometimes."

As Becky drove, her eyes kept darting to the sides of the road expecting the creature to jump from cover and attack them. Her pulse continued to race for the next couple of miles until they started passing homes at the edge of town. Another mile in, they reached main street as Becky saw the sign for the emergency clinic. She followed the signs and pulled up in the driveway of a small two story building lit up with medical signs.

She parked the car and jumped out. As she ran inside, she couldn't help but glance around looking for a hairy claw to knock her off her feet. She reached the automatic doors and ran inside.

"My dad's been hurt!" she cried out when she got in the building. A nurse looked up from behind the desk.

"What's happened?" she asked calmly.

"Some people jumped my dad in the woods and knocked him out! His head's bleeding."

The woman bent her head down and spoke into what Becky assumed was an intercom of some sort.

"Jim, possible head trauma emergency entrance," she said. As the nurse stood, she pulled on some gloves and then walked to Becky.

"Where is he?" she asked.

Becky led her out to the car and opened the back door. Christina sat in the back cradling John's head with a section of torn, blood soaked shirt pressed against his head. Becky's hands went to her mouth when she saw the amount of blood and she started crying hysterically.

A man in a white coat came running out of the clinic followed by another man in scrubs pushing a wheelchair.

"Gurney!" the nurse shouted at them and the orderly in the scrubs turned around and pushed the wheelchair back inside. The doctor went around to the other side of the car and opened the door.

"Just stay there holding him while I check him out, please," he said to Christina. The doctor quickly checked his pupils.

"Helen, get a head CT scan ready," the doctor said. He turned his head to Christina. "Hi, I'm Doctor Evans. Can you tell me what happened?"

"There were two men who approached us in the

forest where we were camping. John stepped in front of us to protect us and they hit him in the forehead with the butt of a rifle," Christina said. She spoke as calmly as she could, but her voice was shaking from the adrenaline.

"They just hit him once?" Doctor Evans asked.

"Yes," Christina said.

"OK, we're going to get him on a backboard and put a neck brace on just as a precaution. Can you sit here and hold him for a moment while we get that ready?"

Christina nodded. The doctor stepped back and between him and the orderly, they got the equipment ready. The nurse came out and handed Becky a cup.

"Drink this," the nurse said. "You're suffering from a little bit of shock and need some fluids."

Becky nodded and took the drink. With her shaking hands, she managed to get a few gulps down as they loaded her father onto the gurney. When her mom walked to her, she held out the cup. Christina took it and swallowed down the rest of the water.

Hours later, Christina and Becky sat in a small hospital room as John rested comfortably in a bed. There was a knock on the door and a sheriff stuck his head in the door.

"Hey, could I talk to you two about what happened earlier?" The man with dark brown hair flashed his badge and the two women nodded. He entered and they saw his full uniform in the dull lights of the hospital room.

"I heard there was an attack and I was kind of hoping you could provide me some details so we could get someone to look into it," he said with a smile as he got out a notepad and began writing on it. "I'm Sheriff Nick Daniels, but you can just call me Nick. Everyone around here does."

"Hi Nick," Christina said. "We were out at a camping place we'd used years ago and we were accosted by two men in the woods there."

"Where did you say this took place?"

"There's a dirt road just past the sign coming into town," Becky said.

"From the highway?" Nick asked and stopped writing waiting for an answer. "I didn't think anybody went back there anymore."

"That's right," Christina said. She yawned. "Do we have to do this right now? We're exhausted."

"It's best to do it when it's fresh in your mind," Nick replied. "So, it sounds like you were out on the old dirt road on the back side of the Jenkins' property."

"I guess," Becky replied. "My dad said he'd been there years ago, like twenty I think?"

Nick nodded and closed the notepad.

"I don't think anyone's been out there in over five years," Nick said.

"The locals weren't very friendly," Becky said.

"They said their names were Zeke and Danny Boy," Christina said.

Nick looked at them dumbstruck. He put the notepad and pen back in his pocket.

"Mind if I sit down?" Nick asked. Christina and Becky sat on the far side of John's bed. There was another chair at the foot of the bed. Christina waved at it.

Nick walked to the chair and Becky noticed he walked with a slight limp, favoring his left leg.

"Did you get injured?" Becky asked.

"Oh yeah," Nick smiled and patted his leg. "When you work in law enforcement, there are a great many hazards on the road."

He groaned as he sat down.

"Was helping one of our farmers change a tire when someone sideswiped the tractor. Put me in a cast for a couple weeks. Poor old man Jenkins wasn't so fortunate," Nick looked down at the ground. "Six years ago now."

"I'm sorry," Christina said.

"That's all right. Time heals all wounds," Nick said and then patted his left leg. "Mostly. It just flares up now and then. Humidity, I think."

"Did you say Jenkins?" Becky asked.

"Yeah, after old man Jenkins died, his son and nephew took over running the farm. Not very well, I might add. They weren't much for doing things the right way."

"Zeke and Danny Boy?" Christina asked. "I'd be upset if you went light on them, but I don't think they survived the bear attack."

"How'd you know about the bear attack?" Nick asked as he sat forward in the chair.

"That's how we escaped," Becky said. "After they knocked my dad on the head they were about to rape us when the bear they were hunting showed up. But, I don't think it was a bear."

"Look, Zeke and Danny Boy weren't the best guys in

the world, but I won't have you sullying their memory like this," Nick said firmly.

"What are you talking about? They just tried to rape us!" Christina shouted. "I'm sorry they're dead, but we're not doing anything but telling the truth."

"Zeke and Danny Boy died five years ago in a bear attack," Nick said sitting back in the chair. "Care to revise your story?"

Becky stood up.

"I hit the bear with my car! Their dead bodies are out there right now! Let's go and I'll show you!" Becky walked up to Nick.

Nick raised his hands and chuckled.

"Now, just calm down. You said you hit the bear with your car?"

"Front driver side. Broke the headlight," Becky said and crossed her arms.

"Well, I'll just go out and verify that if you don't mind," Nick replied as he stood up. "Any other damage to the car?"

"I think I hit a tree on the passenger side. We were driving out so quick, I didn't completely see the tree."

"OK," Nick scratched his head. "You two wait here. Anything happens to your father and you'll both be prime suspects. I'm going to have someone sit outside the room while I check your story."

"We're not lying," Christina said.

"Yeah, well then, you two got attacked by ghosts," Nick said. He limped out the door and shut it firmly behind him.

"What the hell, mom?" Becky said as she turned to Christina.

"I don't know, Becky," Christina said as she sat back in her chair. "That doesn't make any sense."

Hours later, Becky and Christina were sleeping uncomfortably in the chairs when Nick returned.

"Hey, sorry to wake you to up, but I need someone to go out to the crime scene to verify what's happened," Nick said.

"Sure thing," Becky said as she yawned.

"Becky," Christina said as she groaned and repositioned herself in the chair. Her left cheek showed the bruise from where Zeke struck her.

"I got it, Mom," Becky said, resting her hand on Christina's shoulder. "You need to be here when Dad wakes up and maybe get an ice pack for your cheek."

Nick inclined his head toward the door and Becky walked out the door. As Nick walked with his slight limp, the nurse from the evening before greeted him in the hallway.

"Are you sure you don't want us to look at that, Nick? Crazy how that acts up every year," she said. Nick just shook his head and continued walking.

"Could you get my mom an ice pack?" Becky asked.

"Sure thing," the nurse replied.

Nick stepped out of the hospital and Becky looked around for their car. There was nothing in the patient parking lot but Nick's sheriff SUV. Nick pointed to it and Becky climbed in. As he climbed in and started the car, Becky squinted at him. In the morning light, his dark hair had a slight reddish hue.

"Where's our car?" Becky asked.

"I had it towed to the shop so they could repair the damage," Nick said. "Free of charge."

"Why?"

"Your family alerted us to the need for a fence across that dirt road," Nick said.

"What? But I thought you said we were lying!" Becky growled.

"Just wait until we get to camp," Nick said.

Becky swallowed hard and stared straight ahead. Danger ran through her mind as she imagined a local sheriff who killed tourists for fun. As if sensing her thoughts, Nick chuckled.

"You're not in danger," Nick assured her. "Your family will be returning home soon. I'm just sorry your Dad was injured."

Becky just stared at the broken yellow line in the center of the road ahead. Trying to figure out when she could make a break for it and how she was going to outrun a cop. Would he kill her parents too? She realized she didn't have a lot of options available.

When they pulled onto the dirt road, Nick didn't slow down enough to where she felt safe jumping out of the car. She wondered if that was his plan all along.

When they reached the end of the overgrown road and pulled into the forest, Becky gasped. The campground looked exactly as it had when they first arrived yesterday, with the exception of the remnants of a tent that seemed like it was theirs but had been out in the elements for years.

"What's happening?" Becky whispered. She looked at the tree she struck last night and, while there was damage there, it looked years old.

"The Jenkins come back every year in some kind of time loop from the night they were killed," Nick said. "Ghosts really, but the original night they were killed, they did rape two women before they were killed by a bear."

"Bear?" Becky said and folded her arms across her chest. She looked at Nick and raised her eyebrows.

"All right, something more than a bear," Nick looked at the steering wheel. "It was my family camping here that night. They knocked me out and raped my wife and daughter. When I came to, they were howling at the moon. I made a deal that night with a force I can't identify, but it gave me the power to transform into something otherworldly and dispatch the vermin quickly with plenty of malice. I simply called out to the world around me for the power to wreak vengeance."

"Why did they do it?" Becky asked.

"I think they blamed me for their father's death. Invited us out here to the camp site, away from prying eyes. I never suspected them of the evils they would visit upon my family. Some trick of nature created a time loop. The brothers return every year and wreak havoc if anyone happens to be here. I came back last night to get you out of here, but they'd already attacked. That's when everything went fuzzy. I woke up back home in bed. Thought it was a nightmare."

"How did you know we were here?" Becky asked.

"A young man's voice awoke me from my sleep," Nick said. "Telling me his family was in danger at the camp site."

"Bryan," Becky whispered.

"Whoever that is, he must care a lot about you."

"He did," Becky said. "Does, I guess."

"Well, you answered a few questions I had anyway," Nick said.

"Like what?"

"That leg injury was from the night of the attack, when I was hit by a car that wasn't there the night of the attack. I've had the injury for five years."

"But Old Man Jenkins," Becky said.

"Old Man Jenkins actually died driving drunk on his tractor. Drove into a ditch and was crushed by the rust bucket falling on top of him. I found him, but he was already dead. Zeke and Danny Boy never believed it was an accident."

"That doesn't explain the time thing," Becky said.

"I suspect those boys made a deal of their own to get my family there and at their mercy," Nick said. "Two cosmic forces battling it out at the edge of a forest forever will do strange things to time and space."

SEPTEMBER

The Recovery of Mister Smith

David Martyn

The receptionist took the clipboard I handed her and returned my ID and insurance card. She picked up a wrist band and asked, "Left or right?"

"Left," I said, and she snapped the band loosely around my wrist.

A side door opened, and a nurse said, "We're ready for you now, Mister Smith."

I took a deep breath and turned to my wife, Hope. "I love you," she said as she kissed me.

"This is one Labor Day I'll remember," I replied, trying to smile.

I walked to the door. The nurse smiled professionally and said, "Are you ready?"

She turned to Hope and said, "It should be about an hour, Mrs. Smith. Why don't you go and have a cup of coffee? We'll call you when he goes into the recovery room."

This was not my first time in surgery, but the thought of general anesthesia still made me nervous. I tried to relax as my gurney made its way down the corridor towards the operating room. The door swung open, and they wheeled me under the large bright light in the center of the room. *Why are operating rooms always so cold?*

Four, no, five doctors and nurses were waiting, each hidden behind masks, surgical gowns, and caps. One of the green gowned team walked to the IV bag hung beside me. I recognized the same smile through the mask of one as she said, "This will put you to sleep. Please count down from five to zero." And she painlessly injected the drug.

I looked up at the bright light over me. It was so bright. Staring at it, I could see nothing else. "Five, four, three…"

My eyes opened, and there was the light—only the light. My eyes could not move from its intensity. *I feel it is searching my very soul.*

Sound. I could hear the sound of my gurney rolling along. Breathing—not me. Someone else was beside me. I listened to their breath. "Are you're back with us, Mister Smith?" a voice asked.

The voice, now reassuring continued, "Rest, Mister Smith. You need to recover."

"I can't see—I mean, I only see a bright light."

"You are on your way to recovery. Your condition is normal. My name is Gabriel. I will be with you through recovery."

"It's strange. I don't feel anything. I can hear you—but the light…"

"Close your eyes and rest. I will be here to take care of you—just rest until its time. And I will take you through."

"Take me through? Where? I am tired. Yes—tired. The light is so bright."

"Close your eyes. You can close them."

I closed my eyes, and the burning stopped. I opened them again, and I was overwhelmed by darkness—darkness I have only heard about but never experienced—only blackness. My eyes were of no use to me.

I screamed, "I can't see! I'm blind!"

I heard the soft voice of Gabriel penetrate the still darkness. "Which shall it be? Light or darkness?"

"The light is too bright and the darkness too dark! I wish to see, but not be overwhelmed."

Gabriel replied, "You choose a world of gray, neither light nor dark. It is a compromised world where you do not see the truth of the light and hide from the despair of darkness. You have made yourself comfortable in your gray world, yet you remain truly blind. But I will show you even in your world of gray a vision of the truth."

I blinked once, and I could see the curtain surrounding my hospital bed. I saw the blanket neatly folded and tucked over me. A subdued light shone over my bed. I scanned all about and saw a young man sitting in a chair in the far corner against the blue curtain. "Gabriel? I asked.

The young man smiled and nodded.

"It's just not right. I must be dreaming."

Gabriel asked, "What's not right, Mister Smith?"

I tried to sit up but only managed to lift my head. "The light, the darkness, this room, and you. You are not right, Gabriel. You don't look like a nurse."

Gabriel kept smiling. "What's wrong with the room?"

"Well, for one thing, I should be hooked up to a monitor…"

Before I finished the sentence, a monitor appeared beside me, beeping softly in time with my pulse. I could only wince and shudder as I stared at the machine. I was sure it wasn't there before.

I looked closely at Gabriel. "You aren't a nurse! You have no mask or hair cover and your clothes, they are very bright white but not like hospital scrubs."

Gabriel folded his arms. "You mentioned a dream. Do you dream, Mister Smith?"

"Everyone dreams—of course, I dream. But not like this."

Gabriel took a breath and asked, "Do you find that your dreams can be a patchwork—a quilt of your life joining past events and future fears into one fabric? In your dream, it all makes sense only to fall apart when you wake? Why is that? Do you control your dreams, Mister Smith? Did you place the hospital bed beneath you, the curtains around you, and the monitor beside you?"

Exasperated, I sighed. "You're confusing me."

"The dream was your explanation, not mine. Try sitting up for me. You must be able to walk before you leave."

I sat up and took a breath. I was neither dizzy nor sore. I lifted the blanket from across me and swung my feet down. "Let me sit here on the edge of the bed for a moment."

"Don't forget your slippers."

I looked down and saw soft slippers now on my feet.

"If this is a dream, I guess I just go along with it."

Gabriel stood up and walked beside me. "Stand up and take hold of my arm. We are going to walk. You were right about one thing, Mister Smith. I am not a nurse, really more of a guide. Before we start, let me check your wristband."

Gabriel smiled. "Just protocol," and took my left wrist. He read aloud, "Name, John Smith, correct date of birth, and religion—hmm—atheist. Tell me; you have never been baptized?"

"No—not something done in my family."

"No confirmation?"

"No."

"Never prayed? Never worshipped God?"

"No. That's my wife's department. She's religious enough for both of us. Oh, I've been to church for weddings and funerals, but never felt any need to worship what doesn't exist."

Gabriel looked into my eyes. "It never seemed arrogant of you to deny the existence of God? How could you know? Have you searched the universe? Yet you say you know? And if God were outside the universe, then what?"

I stammered, "Well, it not that it's just..."

Gabriel replied, "Not an agnostic—someone who says they honestly do not know—but this says 'atheist' you have declared there is no God."

Gabriel asked, "Are you a betting man, Mister Smith? Have you never been awed by the beauty of the earth—the resilience, the balance? What are the odds?"

I mumbled, "Well, no, I am not a gambler and the

odds?—again, it just happened."

"It just happened? Really? You say you are not a gambler, yet you stake your very soul on what you could never prove!"

We both stood in silence. Gabriel looked into my eyes. I could only see tenderness. He smiled and held out his arm. I linked my arms through his. He glanced at my face and said, "Pay attention—you will find this very enlightening," and Gabriel brushed the curtain open.

The late afternoon sun burned hot on the back of my neck. I stood outside the door of a stone villa. It reminded me of the villas of Pompeii I once visited, but everything appeared new. Bright paint and mosaics made it welcoming and luxurious. Inside I could see a fountain and a garden. I could hear the gentle splashing of the water and smell its sweetness mingled with the pleasant scent of lilies. At the far end under a portico, a group of men reclined on cushions around trays of food. One man, sitting in the center, was speaking softly.

Gabriel whispered, "We will wait here for Master Luke. You have chosen a gray world. You only see what your weakness allows."

A man in a white robe with a gold sash and gold crown walked out of the garden. Gabriel bowed to him and said, "Master Luke, I brought a dead soul, one who has denied God."

Luke looked at me and said, "You have refused the Master's invitation?"

My heart sank when Gabriel called me a dead soul, and I pleaded, "What invitation—I never..."

Just then, I heard the man seated in the garden say, "Blessed is everyone who shall eat bread in the Kingdom of God."

Luke put his hand on my shoulder and said, "You are given sight and hearing to a living simile of what is too bright for you to see."

Confused, I asked, "Is this real?"

"Not all that is real is physical."

Luke clasped my arm and said, "Come with me. See chapter fourteen."

Instantly I was inside the great hall of a mansion, filled with tables and decorated with flowers. Servants were setting golden goblets, golden bowls of wine, and silver plates. The aroma of roasting meats, sweet and savory foods enticed me away from the visual. My senses were overwhelmed. I closed my eyes and breathed deeply. Spoken words broke my bliss. Opening my eyes, a saw a richly robed lord speak to a servant. "Gather the invited. Tell them to come, for everything is ready now."

I don't remember blinking, but I was no longer in the mansion. I was above the servant at the door of a country villa. A man was at the door, speaking to the servant: "I have bought a piece of land, and I need to go out and look at it; please consider me excused."

Instantly, the servant was at another door. A different man was speaking: "I have bought five yoke of oxen, and I am going to try them out; please consider me excused."

Again the servant was at the door of a compound in the city, and I heard a man say, "I have married a wife, and for that reason, I cannot come."

I was transported back to the banquet room in the mansion. The servant reported what he heard from those invited. The master became very angry and told his servant, "Go out at once into the streets and lanes of the city and bring in here the poor and crippled and blind and lame."

The servant said, "Master, what you have said has been done, and still there is room."

I watched the servant as he went out onto the highways, and along the hedged roads and fields and compelled all who he found to come to the banquet of the great lord. But few came.

When the servant reported to his master that there were no more to be found, the master replied, "I tell you, none of those who were invited will taste of my dinner."

At once, I was standing in the garden of the villa watching the man seated at the dinner. Gabriel took my arm and said, "Not yet."

Bright light blinded me. I closed my eyes for a moment and slowly opened them again. I was in the operating room. I was at the ceiling looking down. I could hear the steady, unbroken beeeeeeeeep of the heart monitor. The doctor and nurses were beside me, intent on their work. A nurse shouted, "I have no pulse!"

I think it was the doctor who grabbed two paddles and held them against my chest, who called out loudly, "Clear!"

I saw my body jolt up from the bed. The doctor looked at the monitor and the faces of the nurses. He lifted the paddles and placed them against my chest once more. Again, he shouted, "Clear!"

Again the shock sent my body up off the bed.

I blinked, and I opened my eyes to the bright light. *So bright! So very, very, bright!*

But slowly, the brightness began to fade. I could make out the overhead lights of the corridor. I could see where the yellow walls intersected with the drop ceiling. I could hear the wheels as they rolled softly against the polished floor. I bent my fingers and wiggled my toes. I breathed a sigh of relief and closed my eyes. *It's over. Thank God. Was it all a dream? A warning? Not now—I can't think about it now—just rest. Hope will be here soon, and she will take me home.*

I could feel the breath of the orderly pushing my bed down the corridor. I could hear his soft footsteps. I listened as the electric door swung open and felt the gurney turn into the recovery room. The curtain hooks squealed as the curtain was pulled closed behind me. The monitor was rolled into position, and I relaxed, *it's over.*

The voice was soft, but still, I was startled. "Here we are again, Mister Smith. Sorry for the interruption. It happens."

My eyes opened wide. "Gabriel?"

Gabriel was standing beside the monitor. "Is the light better—the correct shade of gray? Do you prefer lighter or darker? I think a little darker this time. I remember the sun was hot on the back of your neck."

I stared at Gabriel in fear. "Am I dead?"

Gabriel smiled. "You still haven't learned. You

convinced yourself it was just a dream."

"I never—I mean, I did not know…"

Gabriel smiled. "The invitation has always been there for everyone to see. You are the one that claimed there is no God despite the revelation in creation. If creation's revelation was not enough, and truly it is, the Word has gone out—messengers, prophets, the Son of God Himself!. You could not miss it! His Spirit called to you in your heart. You chose not to hear."

I could feel my heart sink and my chest deflate. I whined, "The vision, the master was so angry. They say God is love. It isn't fair."

"The invitations were sent in love. It is His love that you reject. His love, far deeper than you understand—a costly love. He offers you love, yet you choose instead what he hates and cannot abide."

I sat up in the bed, looked down, and watched as sandals appeared on my feet. I heard Gabriel say, "Come with me,"

The curtain slipped open again. I found myself in the dark beneath a night filled with bright stars and a shining crescent moon. I was at the door of another Mideastern villa. I heard again the gentle splashing of a fountain somewhere in the shadows. A cool evening breeze carried the fragrance of rose of sharon mixed with the aroma of roasting lamb and the smell of sweet dates.

Gabriel spoke softly. "Master Luke has the warm and caring heart of a healer. But now you shall meet Master Matthew, once a tax collector; he comes from tougher stock."

Matthew appeared out of the shadows and greeted Gabriel. "Another dark one, Gabriel?"

Gabriel bowed before the white-robed, gold crowned Matthew, who turned to me and said, "Declare this in the house of Jacob; proclaim it in Judah: Hear this oh foolish and senseless people, who have eyes, but see not, who have ears but hear not. Do you not fear me? Declares the LORD. I placed the sand for the boundary of the sea. A perpetual boundary that it cannot pass; though the waves toss, they cannot prevail. Though they roar, they cannot pass over it. But this people has a stubborn and rebellious heart; they have turned aside and gone away."

Gabriel looked into my eyes and said, "It is darker, but still, you shall see, and you shall hear Matthew's lesson of chapter twenty-two.

I gazed into the open courtyard to the feast inside. I knew it was Jesus speaking his parable in the company of the wealthy. "The kingdom of heaven may be compared to a king, who gave a wedding feast for his son."

Matthew took my arm, and immediately we were in a palace so vast the ceiling was not visible, the walls beyond the horizon. Even in the darkness, my eyes struggled by the brightness of the king of majesty. I watched as he sent out his servants to those invited to the wedding feast.

As far as I could see, host upon host of servants bowed and flew off into the sky—countless servants all unquestioning in their obedience.

A single blink of my eye and they had all returned, each with the same report: "They are unwilling to come."

The king spoke, and every servant in the endless palace could hear his voice. "Tell those who have been invited, 'See, I have prepared my dinner, my oxen and my fat calves have been slaughtered, and everything is ready. Come to the wedding feast.'"

Matthew whispered in my ear, "Come, see what they say."

We appeared over the door of a house as the servant's knock was answered. The man shook his head no. "I'm off to the farm." The man glanced up into the sky. *Do I recognize that face?*

We were over a man walking down the street. He did not stop or turn to the servant. He said, "I have business" and kept walking. After the servant left, he turned for a glance. *He looks familiar.*

Next, we were above a vineyard. A group of men crushing grapes saw the servant approach. When the servant told them to come to the wedding feast, one called out, "It's the king's servant!" They surrounded him and came upon him. I could see one of them hold the servant's arms behind his back as others beat him. Again and again, they struck him and kicked him until he fell to the ground, unconscious. They threw him outside the wall of the vineyard.

The face of the one who shouted burned in my memory. "Please, let's go," I begged.

Matthew said, "Not yet, another servant has come."

I watched this servant beaten to death.

"Now, can we go?" I pleaded.

Matthew shook his head. "Wait. Here comes the son

of the king."

I looked and saw a fair and pleasant man walk into the vineyard. *Surely, they will respect the son of their king.*

The outspoken worker shouted, "This is the heir! Let us kill him and seize the inheritance!"

I could not speak. I was dumbfounded by the brutality of what I witnessed. Fists, clubs, and stones flew against the gentle young man until his broken and bloodied body was thrown on the garbage pile outside the vineyard wall.

Matthew asked, "How will the king respond to such brutality?"

I mumbled, "They should receive a severe judgment."

Matthew pointed, "You shall surely watch and see they receive what they deserve!"

As we watched, a vast army approached from every direction. With shields chest high and spears held out before them, they marched steadily towards the men in the vineyard. The soldiers said not a word as they maintained cadence marching in on the trapped men. I heard the screams as the vineyard workers fell in front of the army one by one, only to be trampled and cut again by the sword. Once they were all dead, the king's army marched off, burning the vineyard and burning the village. No one was left alive. I stared at the body in the center of the vineyard, the man who spoke out. His eyes staring up in death, looked back at me as if in a mirror.

Once again, we were in the endless palace of the king. The hall was filled as far as the eye could see with servants— too many to count. The king spoke, and every ear heard clearly, "The wedding is ready, but those who were invited were not worthy. Go, therefore, to the main roads and invite to the wedding feast as many as you find."

Matthew and I were gone with the servants. Immediately I found myself standing in the center square of the city. People all around me were being herded, directed through the city streets to the palace. *Where is Matthew? Why am I among the people? I am only an observer—I don't belong here!*

I stumbled along, and soon I was in the palace. I was no longer hovering above. I was walking on the beautiful white marble floor. I was pushed along, further and further inside. I passed table after table of wedding guests—each table decorated differently. I never imagined so many varieties of flowers and unique dishes existed. I could smell the food—my mouth watered in anticipation. The sights, the smells, and the sounds too! Glorious music—captivating melodies. My fears drained away. First, I felt peace, and with each step closer to the center of the hall, my spirit grew in joy.

I came to another aisle, no it was a river of water, gleaming and sparkling like crystal running to the center of the palace. I followed the river deeper into the palace.

At last, I arrived at a table with an open place. A servant pointed to a chair, and I sat down. I inhaled the enticing aroma. My eyes wandered over indescribable decorations. I lingered over the place setting—each piece encrusted with precious jewels. When my senses could accept no more, I smiled and looked at the others seated at the table. Each face shined with joy. Every wedding guest smiled, enraptured in the moment. Time did not exist—an eternal present, only the joy of the moment.

As I sat, I saw the king walking down the aisle, smiling as he looked over each guest. I smiled as he approached. He was magnificent!—handsome, gracious, resplendent in blinding white robes with jewels sending rainbows of colors around him. His crown was crowned with crowns. Words fail me. I cannot describe the glory of his presence.

The king came in front of my table. He stopped and looked at me. His eyes burned through me, and I felt ashamed. His eyes looking into mine, he said, "Friend, how did you come into here without wedding clothes?"

I looked at my clothes—the green hospital gown I was wearing. I looked at the other guests, each one in a white robe. My tongue stuck in my throat. I could not speak. I sat dumbfounded.

The king turned to the servant walking behind him and said, "Bind him hand and foot and cast him into the outer darkness. In that place, there will be weeping and gnashing of teeth. For many are called, but few are chosen."

I was shocked as Matthew took a rope and began to bind my arms behind me. I pleaded to Matthew, "No! Wait! I will put on the robe! Give me a robe! Please! Where can I get a wedding robe?"

Matthew kept wrapping the rope around me, pulling the cords tight as he knotted the ends together. He spoke as he bound me. "Did you not hear? The Son of Man will send his angels, and they will gather out of his kingdom, all causes of sin and all lawbreakers, and throw them into the fiery furnace. In that place there will be weeping and gnashing of teeth. He who has ears let him hear."

I heard Gabriel whisper in my ear, "Only those, who by faith have been washed in the blood of the Lamb, the redeemed, made righteous in the sight of God, are adorned in the white robe of a bride of Christ."

I began to weep, and soon I was wailing in despair and grief. I covered my eyes as they filled with tears. When I opened them again, I was instantly blinded by the bright light. I let the light engulf me. It penetrated my body and soul. My tears dried, and my crying stopped. The brightness dimmed, and the body in the operating room came into focus. The monitor was screaming its flat line alarm. The doctor held the paddles against my chest. I heard him shout, "Clear!" I felt the shock as I watched my body jump from the bed. I listened to the nurse cry out, "I have a pulse!"

I opened my eyes and watched the lights in the drop ceiling pass overhead. I saw the gap where yellow walls met the suspended ceiling. I heard the gurney push the doors of the recovery room open. I listened to the wheels and the breath of the orderly as he said, "Are you with us, Mister Smith? My name is Gabe, and I will sit with you through recovery.

I watched the blue curtains close behind the foot of my bed. I listened to the monitor beside me. I heard myself say, "I just want to rest awhile, Gabe, with my eyes closed."

Gabe replied, "You do just that, Mister Smith. Your wife has been waiting. If you don't mind, I will let her come and sit beside you."

My eyes closed; I smiled and said, "Yes, please."

A few moments later, I heard the curtain slide open as Hope came in. She came alongside me, leaned over, and kissed me. "You gave us quite a scare. The doctor said you had a cardiac event on the table. I prayed so hard! Thank God you're alright. I was so afraid I lost you."

She sat beside me and took my hand. I opened my eyes and smiled, "I remember seeing myself. I was above my body looking down. And there was this bright light. It was so bright."

"What else do you remember," she asked.

"Nothing. Just floating and watching them shock me—but mostly the light."

I closed my eyes again and squeezed her hand. "You prayed? I'm glad you did." Hope bent down and kissed me gently. I felt her tear against my cheek. My eyes opened to see her love.

I gave out one deep sigh, and I relaxed in her warmth. "Tell me—tell me again—how you love Jesus? When I get well, you must take me to church. I want the faith that you have found."

OCtObeR

The Art of Forgetting

Bree Indigo

There is something inside of me
inhuman and primordial
       a darkness coalescing
            sometimes hibernating
            always waiting
and it reaches with talons
       from the darkest depths
to claw its way up
           my
           throat.

I choke on it
       breathless
       suffocating
and I swallow the creature
            whole.

I am five years old
tugging at my turtleneck
under the polyester satin
        of the perfect Belle costume.
Still too young to blame myself
when Grama makes Mommy
return the store-bought costume
in favor of the one she found
        in the JCPenney's catalogue.
I throw a fit
        pretentious golden child
angry that Mommy wants to do my hair
        and not Grama.

Sometime after Halloween
(but before my birthday)
        I tell her.

                        I am still too young
                        to know better.

I am still wild and free
uncivilized and innocent.

                        I still shout in joy
                        and I scream
                        and I laugh
                        and I cry and
                                I tell her.

I tell Mommy about
that day in the blue house, upstairs
      in my white lace dress
      I am ready for Sunday school
         but my tights are pulled down
            and I was supposed to be safe
            and I was supposed to be protected
and Mommy looks me in the eyes
and tells me:
      "Go tell Grama what you told me."

I don't remember crossing the street but
I am standing in the kitchen
      not knowing it would be
      the last time for three years
         and I tell Grama.
In the fallout of my words
angry shouting and denials
I see something small and dark
      hidden in the shadows.
I am pulled away suddenly
and Mommy puts us into the car
      and we are driving away.
More confused and scared than before
I stare at the blue house
that would plague my nightmares
      the creature sitting
            quietly
            beside me.

I am eight years old
sitting on the couch
in our apartment across the water
        away from the blue house
        away from that room
playing with my cat
who, flighty on a full moon
left a scar on my arm
        I will carry all my life.
Mom looks at me
phone pressed to her ear
Grama on the line
and she asks:
        "So did it happen or not?"

The creature has been waiting
following me through
        hours
                and days
                        and years
of screaming and blame
        and accusations.
In those three years
I have learned
        the power of words.
I have been taught that
        I am why she and Daddy fight
        I am why her brother won't talk to her
                and my words are to blame.

And in that moment
that very *conscious* moment
    I blink
        I open my mouth, take a breath
            swallow the small creature
      and answer, feigning confusion:
        "I don't know what you're talking about."

We are back in the blue house, visiting
and the lie is clearly
enough for everyone to forget
    (or ignore)
enough for Mom to blame me
    (and for them to blame Mom)
because a five-year-old
wouldn't make that up on her own
and Mom has always been
    a little unstable.
I accept the lie
    accept the creature
    and make it part of me
so much so
that it isn't until
twenty-three years later
that I truly believe myself
    and my own memory
        because a five year old wouldn't make that up.
But an eight-year-old will lie
    to erase the past for everyone.

Everyone except her brother
     who won't forget
          what I accused their baby sister of
     who won't forgive
          Mom for choosing me over him
     who won't speak to her
          even though he is dying
     who won't see any of us
so when he shows up unannounced
               we hide.

Past the kitchen
     where I told
past the back door
     where the St. Bernard lived with his pet bee
past the door that led to the basement
     where I would first put a razor to my wrist
     at fourteen years old
we hide in the laundry room.

I can hear his voice
and I feel the creature stir
filling the room with
     an inky tension.
It grows, reaching
long sticky arms
filled with the truth
     and the lies
          and my silence.

I am eleven years old
        and my uncle has died
                a month before his thirty-third birthday.
He is a deep and dark sadness
        that holds my family
                still to this day.
Grief binds us together
        and strengthens the creature
                and erases what came before.

We stand outside the chapel
        next to the house
        where Great-Grama lived with her sister
                (after their husbands died)
        with the backyard full of dandelions
and I feel impossibly small
        holding Grama's hand.
She has summoned a strength
I still can't fathom
and she talks with the funeral attendees
        thanking them for coming
        remembering her son
but I am not sad because he is gone
        (a ghost who I don't remember)
                I am sad because
                        Mom
                        and Grama
                        and Daddy
                                keep crying.

And with his death
        the adults decide
                that we will move back.
There's no reason to hide
        no one to bring up dirty laundry
                nothing
                left
                but grief.

I am twelve years old
walking around the dark neighborhood
trick-or-treating, dressed as a vampire
when she tells me
how I ruined her life
        when I told.
Who decided that I would be
                        chaperoned by my abuser?
Why do I so desperately
                        crave her approval?
We don't talk about *before*
        and I don't know why
        she's talking about *before*
                        but I know enough
                        to keep my mouth shut.
She tells me
        how Grama beats her, black and blue
        covering bruises with makeup for Prom
                and how she couldn't volunteer with kids
                until her record was sealed two years ago.

The creature pulls my lips closed tight
        and I listen
        and I empathize
        and I break
                just a little.

I am fourteen years old
and my mother
        and my father
                and my brother
                        and I
move into the blue house.

By now I have mastered the art
        of forgetting.
If you tell yourself the same lie for long enough
        you start to believe.
It is only as an adult that I will wonder
        why anyone—*anyone!*— let me choose *that* room
                as my bedroom.

I start to have the same nightmare
and I wake
        (but don't wake)
frozen, unable to move
and an unseen force
        throws me across the room.
I panic and struggle and fight
        through quicksand to escape.

I wake out of the dream
open my eyes
          and try to scream
as a grotesque creature leers at me
its mangy fur matted with thick black oil
and it disappears as quick
          as it appeared.
I open my eyes
for what feels like
the thousandth time
and know that finally
          I am really awake.
When I drift off again
          the nightmare repeats.

          Seven years later
          I will discover that the nightmare
                  like so much I experienced
                  in that blue house
          is something many people
                  suffer from.
          The year I marry my wife
                  I never have sleep paralysis again.

I am fourteen when
I cut myself for the first time
in the basement in the blue house
but I am sixteen
          before it gets bad.

We live in an apartment again
and I slam my door behind me
emotions
        and words
                and so much I didn't understand
filling my chest
        and clawing
                to get out.
I sob but it isn't enough
and the creature fills my throat
stealing my voice
        and my words
                and my truth.
I pull the razor across my forearm
again and again
in the hope that
maybe
just *maybe*
        the creature will leak out.
If it can't come out
        through my mouth
maybe it could come out
        through my skin.
I cut deeper than I expect
        deeper than I wanted
        deep enough to scar
                opposite the arm
                my cat had attacked on a full moon
                        all those years ago.

I scare myself into caution
        though not enough caution
        to stop hurting myself.
It isn't until several months later
        my deepest cut healed
        (though still red and angry)
                that my mother learns my secret.

I stop cutting
        not because I feel any better
        not because I get help
        not because I care about my health or safety
but because of
        my parents' anger
                and disappointment
                        and disapproval
and an overwhelming sense
        that I was an annoyance
                and an inconvenience
                        at best.

It is this year that
my mother tells me
angry, in a manic episode
        that she wishes she hadn't
        had children.

                        The creature begins to fester.

I am eighteen years old
graduated from high school
        but still living at home.
I am reckless, alone
        my best friend abroad
        my father two years into a multiple sclerosis diagnosis
        my mother suicidal
the perfect storm coalescing
into very bad decisions.

When my ex-boyfriend
        just back from basic training
wants to hang out
in the middle of the night
        I don't hesitate.

I don't hesitate
until our clothes have started coming off
and I want to talk about
what this would mean
and he avoids my questions
and he says he doesn't have a condom
        and I change my mind.

I tell him no   *Are you sure you're a virgin?*
but he doesn't listen   He chuckles.
and the creature rises up   *Not anymore.*
telling me to keep my mouth shut
        and just let him finish.

The creature is strong
fed on years of my silence
and it fills my throat
        and my nose
                and my mouth
                        and my eyes
                                and my ears
and it lulls me to sleep
in the bed where I was just raped
with the boy who I thought
        would always listen.

The next day
I walk two miles
from his house
        to my part-time job.
I stop at a McDonald's bathroom
to change into my work uniform
and eat something
        before my shift.
In the stall I sit
my hand cautiously between my legs
and wince at the pain
and look at fingertips
        covered with bright blood.
I breathe
and stifle a sob
        and the creature grows.
                                I never tell.

I am thirty-one years old
and the creature still lies within me
    a darkness coalescing
        always waiting
to claw its way up my throat.

I have leaned into it
    smelled its musk
    nearly drowned in its depths
but in the drowning
I saw past the inky, oily façade
and finally understood.
The fibers of its fur
weren't fibers at all
    but words.
Every word I had omitted
    every word I hadn't said
        and every word I had said
            for someone else's comfort.

I have spent the last thirteen years
learning how to
    fight the creature.
I choke on it sometimes
    but then I pause, center myself
    and remember
        how to breathe.

The creature weakens
    with every word I write
    with every story I tell
pulled, strand by strand
    up my throat and
    out my mouth
I grasp the words
wrestling them to paper
    (or Word doc)
and bind them to the page
    with my truth
        and my voice
            and my words.

If I write for long enough
    if I tell all my secrets
        and share what I've lived
maybe
    just *maybe*
I will destroy the creature
        once and for all.

November

Veterans Day
Marshall Miller

he three college-aged students snuck into the Veterans Section of the Unity Memorial Cemetery and Park. During this November 11th, Veterans Day, the moon had almost disappeared as it entered the New Moon phase. Thus, the lack of moonlight and the overcast skies gave the three extra cover for their mischief.

James Dow led the trio through a hole in the back chain link fence, acres away from the caretaker's small house in the front of the memorial park. The cemetery had been in existence since the Civil War Days and contained buried dead from every conflict in which the United States participated. In recent years, First Responders and Police Officers who had also died in the Line of Duty became the newest internments if they or their relatives were Veterans. These actions had not been without controversy.

Thus, modern-day protests led the three local college students to sneak onto the grounds with spray paint and animal offal from the local butcher shop.

James had a near-permanent sneer on his face, put there (he claimed) by the hypocrisy of his well-heeled parents. James wanted for nothing, even fast cars and his choice of attractive members of the opposite sex. He believed he was intellectually superior and thus was the natural leader to Right The Wrongs, whatever that meant. Therefore, their mission in the Veteran's Cemetery.

His two 'playmates' for the evening were traditionally attractive young women, now dressed in tailored camouflaged fatigues he obtained. "See anybody?" asked blonde June Davis, she of the Large Rack and Bodacious Behind.

"No, June," James whispered back. "The only people out here is that crazy caretaker, Old Man Fogerty."

"Or the Cops," interjected the other female member of the trio, Susanne Chambers. She fit the sleek and sexy dark haired type of Femme Fatale. Susanne also had a mean streak a mile long that made James think she had a bit of Satan's Daughter in her.

"The only Cops are the ones dead and buried here. And I have their locations on my map."

James saw a flash of feral teeth as Susanne grinned.

"Best that we get along then, James. This foray is exciting."

"This will get the point across to all those assholes," James mumbled to himself as he led the tiny band to its appointed rounds.

James used his creativity to map out the chosen targets. For all his anti-social ideas, James was quite the artist.

His map of the targeted graves looked more like a painting than a plan. He quietly pointed out the graves to be 'visited' June stifled a giggle as she said, "This will shock old man Fogerty."

"That *old man*," hissed Susanne, "marching in that old uniform like some Civil War reenactor."

"The man is so ignorant he doesn't know the Buffalo Soldiers were racist oppressors to the Indigenous Tribes in the Southwest," added James. "Here, Susanne. You do the honors on this gravestone of this cop."

In a flash, a red graffiti adorned the gravestone of one Donald James, former State Policeman. And with that, the 'political act of resistance' picked up steam.

Some gravesites earned obscene insults, others 'fascist' or 'nazi scum.' The limited amount of butcher shop offal was reserved for pre-selected graves. One grave of a former police officer Zimmerman, adorned with a Jewish Star, received pigs' feet and blood.

"His asshole son is on the Force, busted me for underage drinking and driving," growled June. "Let's see who gets the last laugh now."

The last target was a combination statue of two figures commemorating the American Civil War. Depictions of a Union and a Confederate Soldier stood shaking hands. The plaque below reads, "Never again should Brother kill Brother over misguided loyalties. Soldiers of all colors and races must recognize the evils of slavery and prejudice. They must become a real Band of Brothers."

Despite the subject matter, the memorial was recent.

A biracial Gulf and Iraq War Veteran paid for its creation just before she died of cancer a decade prior. People still talked about why she did it.

"Fucking pro-slave idiot," said Susanne. "Let's see how sturdy this is."

The dark-haired woman pulled a small ball pean hammer from her bag and swung it at the Confederate Figure. There was a ringing sound as the three trespassers discovered the figures were of brass.

"Shit! Quiet," hissed James. "You trying to ring some chimes or something?"

"This is coming down, Jame, one way or another." Susanne tried to shove it over, only to find it deeply embedded in a stone pedestal. The woman began to curse, her voice rising.

"Hey, hold it down," interjected June. "Do you want someone—"

"To hear? Too late. Missy."

Three sets of shocked eyes fixed on the caretaker known as Old Man Fogerty.

The dark-skinned man held a massive horse pistol from the Civil War Era in his right hand, an old-style lantern in his left.

"Now, you three young assholes are going to come along friendly and easy like to my office up yonder. Then we wait for the police."

"I bet you that old piece of a crap pistol is just a non-firing replica, Uncle Tom," sneered James.

"Want to find out, Bucko?"

"Why do you talk like an old Western movie?" asked June.

"This is how I talked growing up, smartmouth."

"You're not that old," hissed Susanne.

"My age is not part of this palaver, Missy. Now, let's move along before you find out what Colt's Dragoon with fifty grains of black powder can still do."

"Now look, we are not going –"

The flash and the boom from the Dragoon pistol caused the three to jump and cry out. The lead ball projectile kicked turf up between James's feet.

"That may bring the police so they can see your handiwork. Now, *march*."

Susanne was on the Fast Pitch softball team in the previous quarter. Her aim with the hammer was exact. The ball pean head struck Richard Fogerty in his temple, and the older man collapsed.

"Run!" commanded James. "We are all wearing gloves, so it's his word against ours. Grab your stuff."

June walked up to the fallen caretaker and looked at him.

"Look at his head. I think you killed him.'"

James stepped over and cursed.

"That blood points to a cracked skull. Did you have to smack Fogerty so hard, Susanne?"

"Hell, he was the one with the gun. Come on, wimps. Let's move unless you want to answer an attempted murder charge."

James acquiesced to Susanne's demand, and the three

began to jog to the hole in the fence. They made the distance in record time, then stopped and stared.

"What happened to the hole?" Asked June.

"Come on. It's around here somewhere," said James. Five minutes later, and the eight-foot chainlink fence still had no hole.

"Alright. We'll climb over."

"There is barb wire at the top, James. They have had previous vandals, it seems."

"Susanne, we'll put our jackets over the barbed wire—"

"Hey, there is a second fence," said June. "Where did that come from? An that's concertina wire-"

There was an odd siren sound, then dogs barking. A voice called out, "HALTEN SIE JUDEN! HALTEN SIE!" A rifle bullet zipped by the three college students heads. They screamed and ran—

The fell into a muddy trench. Stunned, the three looked around. Rough hands grabbed James and yanked him to his feet. A grizzled face was inches from James.

"Where is your equipment, Soldier? And how'd you get these women here? This here ain't no Paris brothel. This unit is the All American Division."

A short whine, then a massive explosion threw the three college students into the mud. A stunned James tried to get to his feet and screamed when he noticed the remains of someone's intestines in his lap.

A flash and the two women and one man were in a helicopter. They looked around and noticed there were all

Vietnamese faces—men, women, and children. An American voice yelled in their ears.

"You all from the Embassy? You're lucky. This bird is the last 'copter from Saigon. Hope you three don't overload us."

Tracers zipped by the open side door, the helicopter violently twisted, and all three fell screaming towards the ground.

James, June, and Susanne thudded into the sand. As they laid stunned, Susanne looked to see an insect from hell coming right at her. She screamed just as a rifle butt smashed it.

"God damn camel spiders! Hey, what unit you from, or are you some jive-ass journalist visiting Iraq Land?" The Black female soldier glared her.

Another flash and the three vandals were stumbling into a rail fence.

"What the hell is happening?" said a panting James.

A man in a Confederate Uniform with a straightforward Officer demeanor walked towards the three people.

"Here, you local people must move. Meade's Union forces are just over there and—"

Cannonballs began to rain down, destroying the rail fence.

Another flash of light and three terrified college students laid on a rain-soaked street. Bullets ricocheted around them as a woman in a blue uniform rushed up, grabbing June.

"Get up! That crazy man is shooting at anyone and everyone. How did you three get through the perimeter?" The female police officer's head exploded into a red mist. June screamed.

A bright flash and the three protesting vandals lay next to the Civil War Memorial in the cemetery. They all screamed in unison.

"What the fuck just happened?" June yelled.

"Some bad drug trip," answered Susanne. James began to sob.

"Well, well, what do we have here?"

"You're dead!" James screamed at Fogerty.

"For over a hundred years, yes. I was a Civil War veteran next a Buffalo Soldier. Then I died."

"But, but—"

"You know those tales about All Hallows Eve, Halloween, the dead walking, spirits coming back because the veil between the living and the dead is lifted? The walls between now and the past disappear?" Old Man Fogerty laughed.

"You think it could not happen at other times? With other spirits?"

"That does not explain *you*, old man," hissed Susanne.

"Huh. Still with the attempted insults. You learned nothing from your recent travels."

A bright flash and Susanne was gone. James screamed again.

"The Veteran Dead, soldiers who died from violence in conflicts through history, have a bond. Even those who killed each other.”

"How can that be?” asked June. “You were enemies!”

"The bond, which also includes what you call First Responders, results from dying for 'something,' for a cause, a belief, while trying to help someone. Though there are those, like the Nazis, killing Jews, people torturing others for information which are profane and seem to affect those spirits' abilities to connect with others after they die and pass to what you would call The Other Side. There are tortured souls. Though, sometimes, they can heal.”

"How can you heal a Nazi, a racist, a fascist?” James spat out.

Fogerty laughed long and hard.

"Have you taken a look in the mirror lately? You just came here to cause the living some pain by defacing memorials to their family, their friends, their comrades only because you classified them as wrong and bad. But you hurting others is okay? Please tell this old soul why.”

"I'm fighting for social justice.”

"How is causing pain in a sadistic manner, social justice?”

James sputtered and seemed unable to answer.

"We just are trying to get people to change, to treat others better,” June replied.

"By treating others, complete strangers, badly.”

"You killed people in war,” James finally replied. “You helped oppress Apache and Comanche.”

Fogerty's eyes seemed to burn through James.

"You do not think I am paying penance for that? Tell

me, how would you deal with being kept alive as an older man, well after everyone you knew and loved, died?"

"So, you are a real Caretaker of Souls?" Asked June.

"Just the places which connect them as they work through their penance. And you have damaged those connections."

"Look, Sir, we did not know. We thought we were doing what was right."

"As most soldiers believe, or do what is necessary to stay alive."

There was silence as James and June tried to digest what this—spirit—told them.

The old Black man looked out into the dark for a few moments. Then he spoke. "You two have some penance to pay before Midnight. Every action has its results."

"What about Susanne?" asked James.

A feral grin formed on Fogerty's face.

"Watch," he said.

A bright flash and a naked, beaten, and cut body appeared. Susanne's once black hair was entirely gray. She saw the others, screamed, and ran into the night.

"What happened to her?" June sputtered out.

"You will have to ask her. Many people have their own private Hell."

James swallowed hard, then spoke.

"Look. We were wrong, okay? Can we make amends?"

"Don't ask me," Fogerty nodded towards the darkness. "Ask them."

A police patrol car eventually checked on the Unity Cemetery and Park at 11:30 PM. Officer Zimmerman told Old Man Forgerty there were reports of some screams and at least one gunshot.

"What happened, Mister Fogerty?"

"Some wild kids thought it would be funny to mess up the cemetery. Usually, they bother us at Halloween, or New Year's Eve. However, bothering us on Veterans Day? That's a weird one."

"Any serious damage?"

"Nothing I can't take care of. I caught the miscreants before they did anything more than yell, scream, and set off a firecracker. They did some spray painting, but nothing serious."

"You sure? I can call some people to help out-"

"Please, don't. That is why I get Caretaker pay."

Just then, Zimmerman's radio crackled.

"Excuse me," the officer said, and he stepped away. A minute later, he stepped back.

"We have a nude gray-haired female running around, screaming. I thought this was supposed to happen on the Full Moon."

"As they say, Officer, go figure."

Zimmerman laughed.

"Call me if you want anything."

"Will do."

After Officer Zimmerman drove away, a figure stepped in from the darkness.

"My son is doing well."

"Yes, he is. He may not have a lot of penance to do."

"That would be nice, Richard."

"How about the two remaining vandals?"

"They are beginning their penance and education. Come, have a look."

Old Man Fogerty walked back to the Civil War Memorial and saw two terrified college students sitting in the middle of a circle of shadowy figures. They had their eyes screwed shut as they sobbed.

"Ten more minutes, Richard Fogerty, Then Veterans Day ends."

The Caretaker fought back the desire to laugh. That would not be nice, could be said to deserve more penance. The two self-proclaimed justice warriors were experiencing the events which led the spirits to serve penance all these years.

Tomorrow, scrubbing off their spray paint would seem a piece of cake. Then, of course, there would be the next Veterans Day.

Old Man Fogerty grinned.

december

Test of the Tundra
Kristie Gronberg

Winter's long claws cut deep into Donna's lower back just below the hem of her cropped jacket, sending a shiver up her spine. She shrugged off the cold, undaunted, and climbed the concrete steps leading to the side entrance of her favorite bar. Her cherry red subcompact car chirped, headlights flashing in the night, as Donna locked it remotely with the press of a button. She paused to scrape the snow off her leather boots on the welcome mat laid out in front of the heavy side door.

It had been nearly a year since Donna had last set foot inside this building. The bar had been shuttered for months due to the pandemic that swept the globe early in the year. The initial closure came when the owner fell ill with the virus. Fortunately, she made a full recovery and none of her staff members had contracted the illness from her during the brief period when she had been both contagious and unaware. Still, the bar remained closed even after its owner's recovery. She had decided to invest her time and resources into renovating the place so that her business might come out of the hardest months of the pandemic in better shape than ever.

There was a part of Donna that ached to return to the bar as it had been before, with its familiar faux leather upholstered barstools and colorful posters, but that was impossible and so she clamped down on the feeling as if she could will it away. No one could go back to the way things had been the year before. Everything and everyone had changed. Perhaps that wasn't entirely a bad thing. Donna let out a long, frosty breath and allowed—or forced—herself to feel hopeful. Even a little excited.

After all, December had arrived to finish out the year and things were starting to look up. The bar was open for business again—had been for a little over a month—and there was no force in the world powerful enough to stop Donna from marching in there to claim a seat at the counter, order a stiff drink, and meet up with friends she hadn't seen in person since "pre-apocalypse times" as she liked to put it. For Donna, the madness hadn't ended when the gears of society started grinding forward again. She was a nurse.

And she was tired.

A bell jingled overhead as she pushed open the door and walked into the newly renovated bar. Donna sucked in a breath as she took in how the place had been gutted, rebuilt, and polished to a shine. Gone were the mismatched tables, chairs, and posters. A world of dark oak and laminate spread out neatly before Donna, bathed in warm light and swathed in holiday garland. On one wall was painted a realistic mural of a dark evergreen forest. Round and star-shaped sticky notes adorned the branches, each handwritten with a unique message. Donna's eyes lingered there and she paused mid-step to read a few.

I'm grateful for my friends and my fiancé.

I am grateful to still have a job and a home.

I'm grateful for my dachshund, Frank.

Donna smirked and chuckled softly, then turned her attention to the bar to look for her friends. Her dark brown eyes alighted on Scott, her friend from college, and his wife, Camille. Scott tapped Camille on the arm and nodded towards Donna. They smiled and raised their drinks in salute; Scott's, a bottle of hard cider, and Camille's, a short glass of amber liquid that Donna guessed—correctly—to be brandy. The couple's wedding rings, both simple silver bands, shimmered on their fingers in the soft light.

"There she is!" Scott called out to Donna. "Long time, no see. Let's get you a drink."

Camille set her glass down on the bar and stood up from her seat. Arms spread wide, she approached Donna and went in for a hug. Donna's breath hitched in her throat and she tensed for a moment before catching herself.

It's fine, she reminded herself. *You're safe.*

"It's so good to see you, Donna," Camille said. "We've missed you."

Donna relaxed and returned the hug with a tearful laugh. "I've missed you guys too. How have you been?"

Camille pulled back out of the hug and Donna caught a glimpse of sadness in her eyes, but the other woman shook it off with a bright smile. "Can't complain, really," she answered, vague and dismissive. She clearly intended to sound casual but the words didn't ring true. As Donna's lips parted to ask what was wrong, Camille barreled past the question before it could be asked with inquiries of her own. "How about you? How are things with Hope? Is she coming tonight?"

Donna's expression faltered. She shook her head, her dark brown hair washing over her shoulders in a gentle wave. "Ah, no, we broke up... A few months ago, actually," she admitted. "But it's fine. And, anyway, of course you can complain. It's been a hell of a year for everyone, right? So let's settle in, get a little drunk, and catch up."

Camille nodded and led the way back to the bar, where she passed a freshly opened bottle of cider from Scott to Donna. Camille hopped up on her barstool and patted the seat next to hers.

"Thanks for coming, you guys. I'm sorry we couldn't meet up sooner, but I just..." Donna struggled to find the right words. "I couldn't. Work's been crazy but, more than that, I've just felt worn out. But it's nice to be back here with you guys. It feels like coming home."

Scott raised his bottle. "To coming home," he said.

The trio clinked their drinks together, the gently colliding walls of glass singing a single silver note.

"To coming home."

In that same moment, a white-haired man with a well-kept beard raised his own drink from where he sat behind a game master's screen at a table in the corner of the room. On its outward-facing side, the screen depicted a panoramic view of a barren, icy tundra. The snow sparkled beneath the light of a waning crescent moon.

"Welcome home," the man said under his breath, and brought his glass to his lips.

No one noticed him.

A couple of hours later, Donna and her friends were shaking with laughter, tears rolling down their reddened faces. Despite Donna's earlier insistence that it was alright to vent, to complain, the group had quickly found themselves shying away from uncomfortable topics. It felt too good, being together again; too good to sully with the truth and the weight of it all. They laughed instead and, while they did so, it was easy to pretend all was well.

The white-haired man looked up from his gaming screen to check the nearby wall clock for the time. It was a quarter to ten. He sighed loudly and stood up to gather his things, neatly folding the screen before stacking a sheaf of papers and a large dice bag atop it.

The bartender, Tom, looked over at him. "Heading home there, bud?" he asked.

It was then that Donna, Scott, and Camille noticed the old man for the first time. He was short and stout with a round beer belly, dressed in a red plaid shirt and blue jeans with heavy black boots. There was something familiar about him, though they could swear they had never met him before. Maybe he was a local mall Santa, they guessed. He certainly looked the part.

"'Fraid so," he replied. "Looks like my group's not

coming tonight. Damned shame, too. I had quite the game planned for them. Real exciting stuff, ya know?"

Tom flashed the man a sympathetic smile. "I'm sure it would've been great, man. Sorry it fell through again. See you next week?"

The man shrugged. "I don't know," he confessed. "I'm getting too old for this. Our games are all I have to look forward to each week and I'm tired of folks just not showing up."

Donna, Scott, and Camille exchanged a look. An unspoken question hung in the air between them.

Scott was the first to speak up. "What kind of game is it?" he asked.

The stranger perked up at the question. "Oh, it's a tabletop roleplaying game," he explained. "The fantasy kind, with magic and monsters and dragons and such."

Scott nodded thoughtfully.

"It's one of the more obscure ones," the man added. "Test of the Tundra, it's called. You probably haven't heard of it. Why do you ask?"

Scott turned to Camille and Donna. "We've got time," he said softly.

"And it *is* the holidays," Camille added in agreement.

Donna hesitated, biting her lip, then nodded. "Yeah, it is. Okay. I'm in."

Scott turned to the game master with a mischievous smile. "If you need players and it's not too late, we're in," he said. "If you're willing to teach us, that is. I don't think any of us have ever played a game like that before, but we're quick learners."

"Actually, I have," Camille corrected him. "Granted, I was in middle school at the time."

"Who was your game master?" the man asked, curious.

"My older brother," Camille answered. "He was pretty good at it. We had a lot of fun. Playing your game might be a nice little walk down memory lane."

The game master's face brightened. "I'm sure it will be," he agreed. "And don't worry, this game has a very simple ruleset. Come sit down and I'll get you each set up with a character."

With that, the man turned and led the way to the table in the corner. He placed his belongings on its surface and began setting up once again as Donna, Camille, and Scott moved to join him. Each of them carried a drink in one hand.

"My name's Kris, by the way," the game master introduced himself.

"Nice to meet ya, Kris. I'm Scott and this is my wife, Camille, and our friend, Donna." Scott gestured to the two women in turn as they each took a seat at the table on either side of him.

"It's nice to meet you all," Kris said. "Thank you for volunteering to join me tonight. It's sweet of you to humor an old man like this. I do hope you get something out of this experience."

Camille allowed a goofy grin to overtake her face. "Well, I, for one, am excited," she said. It was rare for anyone to witness such childlike delight from her.

Donna couldn't help but smile, too, though a bit more shyly. She nodded. "Me too."

"Good. I'm glad to hear that."

Kris reached into his dice bag and passed out matching sets of polyhedral dice for each player to use. He then handed each of them a double-sided character sheet. "I think these characters will suit you well," he said.

Curious, Donna began to read hers over.

Race: Human

Class: Wizard

Level: 1

Name: Donna

Her stomach twisted as her gaze landed on it: her name, not written but *printed* on the page. She looked up sideways at Scott and Camille. Their faces had paled, expressions tense, eyes glued to their papers. Donna peered over at Scott's character sheet and saw his name printed there. She could only assume that, across the table from her, Camille's name was printed on her sheet as well.

But how was that possible? How could Kris have already known their names? Or that they would not only be here, at this exact time, but also agree to play his game?

Scott looked up from his character sheet to shoot an accusatory glare at Kris. The game master merely smiled, quite serenely, as mischief sparkled in his eyes. Scott opened his mouth to say something, but his words were stolen from him as a howling wind picked up outside. The doors and windows were thrown open, flurries of snow rushing into the bar and whipping violently through the air around its four patrons.

Their dice and character sheets were whisked off the table and into the air, yet Kris' gaming screen stood eerily still on the table amidst the chaos. It glowed bright white and blue.

Donna, Scott, and Camille shrieked in terror as the frigid air assailed them. The last thing Donna saw was Camille, desperately reaching out for Scott. More and more snow filled the room until all they could see was white. And then there was nothing as the flurries blinded them altogether, attacking their eyes, noses, mouths and ears with bitter, biting cold. Tears flowed from their stinging eyes and froze upon their cheeks. The howling of the wind grew to an earsplitting crescendo.

And then it stopped, just as suddenly as it had begun.

The trio blinked the powder from their eyes and looked around.

"What the actual fuck?" Scott asked breathlessly.

Sparkling plains of white spread out around them for miles in every direction. A waning crescent moon loomed overhead amidst a spectacle of stars in an unfamiliar night sky. The building they had just been inside was gone, along with all its furnishings, except for their table and four chairs. These and the gaming screen remained intact and untouched by the snow.

Donna shook her head. "This isn't real," she thought aloud. "It can't be."

Kris smirked at his players' bewildered expressions. Like the scenery around him, he had changed, too. He now wore a heavy fur coat and sealskin boots. Camille winced at the sight, only to realize that her own clothes had transformed as well, as had Scott's and Donna's. They were bundled up in warm furs from head to toe, but the icy air continued to bite at their faces.

"The game has begun, my friends," Kris announced. "This world of mine will test you. In order to survive, you'll need to work together. But if you wish to *live*, well, you'll need to open your hearts and minds. I wish you the best of luck. You'll need it."

Scott jumped up from his seat. "What's that supposed to mean? Where are we?" he demanded to know. His windswept hair stood on end as if alive with the force of his anger.

The game master shrugged. "Why don't you go find out?" he suggested, waving a hand towards the surrounding landscape. He then rose from his seat, folded up his gaming screen, and tucked it under one arm before calmly turning to walk away.

"Wait!" Scott shouted. "You can't just leave us here!"

Kris looked back at him with a cold, hard stare. "Of course I can," he replied.

A gust of icy wind sliced through the air between the two men, kicking up snow in its wake. Scott shut his eyes and threw his arms up to protect his face.

When it was over, Kris was gone. Though they could see for miles in any direction, there was no sign of him. Not even footprints.

Donna and Camille yelped in surprise as their seats began to give out beneath them. The furniture was losing its pigment and form, dissolving into snow. Scott looked back to find both women sitting on low snow mounds with a larger mound between them. He extended a hand to both of them in turn. Camille eagerly accepted the help and pulled herself to her feet with ease, but Donna merely stared at Scott's outstretched hand.

"This is a dream," she said. "It has to be."

Scott hesitated, then shook his head. "I don't think so," he said in a low voice. "You ever had a dream this vivid? And cold? Because I haven't. I don't know what's going on, but I think we need to find shelter, and soon. Let me help you up."

Numbly, Donna accepted his help and stood up. Scott was right, it didn't feel like a dream, but Donna still didn't know what to think. It couldn't be real, could it?

"Do you think that guy put something in our drinks?" Camille asked. "Maybe we're hallucinating."

This time, it was Donna who shook her head. "He never touched our drinks," she answered solemnly. Her heart sank as the words left her lips. There was no logical explanation for their bizarre circumstances. Except, perhaps, that Donna was having some kind of mental breakdown. Her stomach turned at the thought.

Camille cast furtive glances around them. "Okay, well, if this is real, then Scott's right. We can't stay here. So which way should we go?" she asked.

The trio peered out into the night. The pale moon- and starlight was reflected by the snow, a sea of glittering crystals which provided just enough light to see by. In the distance, a flickering amber flame was just visible.

Scott raised his arm to point out the pinprick of light. "There," he said.

Donna squinted. "It looks like a campfire," she observed.

"Where there's a campfire, there's people," Camille reasoned.

"Maybe they can help us," Scott suggested.

"Maybe." Camille bit her lip. "Or maybe they won't. They could be our enemies."

Scott raised an eyebrow at his wife. "'Our enemies'?" he repeated, skeptical. "What makes you think that?"

Donna nodded, suddenly understanding. "This was supposed to be a game," she said.

Camille frowned. "Exactly. And if that's what this is, then there will probably be enemies. They'll try to hurt us. Maybe even kill us."

Scott sucked in a sharp breath. "Okay, so, what do we do?" he asked. "We don't have weapons or anything. That guy left us here with nothing."

Camille was silent for a moment, contemplative. "What did your character sheets say?" she asked. An idea seemed to be forming in her mind.

Scott hesitated. "I think it said I'm supposed to be a fighter," he answered. "But, again, we don't have any weapons. And I haven't been in a fight in years. I'm an EMT, not some kind of gladiator."

Camille nodded thoughtfully, only half listening. She turned her attention to Donna. "What did your sheet say?" she asked.

"It said I'm a wizard," Donna answered. "But it's not like I have a wand or whatever."

Camille bit her lip. "You might not need one. Try to do something magical," she suggested.

Donna frowned. "Like what?" she asked.

Camille shrugged. "I don't know. Just like… take off your gloves, hold out your hands, and imagine conjuring a flame in your palms. Concentrate on the image and say any, you know, magic words that might come to mind."

"'Magic words'? Are you serious?"

"Yes! Just try it. Okay?"

Donna sighed. "Fine, I'll try."

She stripped off her gloves and held out her bare hands. Her breathing slowed as she envisioned bright, flickering flames nestled between her cupped fingers. She recalled the crackling, spitting sounds of a campfire and the feeling of heat on her skin, willing it to be real. Nothing happened, so she closed her eyes and tried again, using the darkness to focus on the image in her mind's eye. Still nothing. There was no hint of fire or 'magic words' which might conjure it.

Donna let her hands fall limp at her sides. "Sorry."

Camille bit her lip. "It's okay," she said after a moment. "We'll figure it out. In the meantime, we need to play to our strengths. My sheet said I'm supposed to be a rogue. Rogues are sneaky. So here's what I'm thinking. I'll scout ahead and find out what's going on where the fire is. Then I'll come back and we'll come up with a plan."

Scott looked at his wife with an expression of mild

horror. "You're not seriously suggesting you go alone?" It seemed like a question but sounded more like a statement of fact.

Camille shrugged. "If we all go, we're more likely to be seen," she explained. "We could be walking right into a trap or something. Let me check it out first, see if it's safe. Maybe I'll find something useful, too, like a weapon that I can steal without anyone noticing. If Donna can't use magic, then it's that much more important that we have another way to protect ourselves."

Scott shook his head. "Let's say you steal some kind of weapon without getting caught. What then?" he pressed. "Do you expect me to kill somebody with it?"

Camille's face fell. "No, of course not. But we'll be safer if at least one of us is armed."

"She's right," Donna agreed. "And, anyway, we don't have time to argue about this. We've gotta get moving or we'll freeze to death out here. Lead the way, Cam."

Camille nodded. "Try to stay a safe distance behind me. And stick together."

"Fine," Scott grumbled.

Tension hung thick in the air between Scott and Donna as Camille sprinted on ahead of them. As a dance instructor, Camille's footsteps were light and graceful, allowing her to move across the snow almost silently. She was little more than a willowy shadow in the night.

"What if they see her coming and we're not there to protect her?" Scott hissed at Donna.

The question landed heavily in Donna's stomach. She

didn't have a good answer for Scott, and that terrified her. If anything happened to Camille, they'd never forgive themselves. And Scott, well, he might never forgive Donna for supporting this plan.

Maybe this was a bad idea.

Camille, for her part, felt confident. This was exactly the sort of thing she had done in her brother's games. If she was careful, it would work. It had to.

A surge of excitement pulsed through her veins as she neared the campsite and its layout came into full view. She crouched down in the snow to study the scene before her. Camille counted two naked, humanoid figures huddling around the campfire amidst three deerskin tents. The tents were A-frame in shape and built low to the ground, presumably to survive strong winds. Each was just tall enough for someone inside to sit up but nowhere near tall enough for them to stand. Camille crept up behind one of the wide, squatting structures and peered around the side, careful to keep as much of her face and body out of the quivering firelight as possible.

The figures sitting by the campfire were eating and it was a garish sight to behold. Their faces were ghostly white with thin, alabaster lips pulled back to reveal teeth like bloodstained knives. They gorged themselves on dripping chunks of raw meat, blood trickling down their chins and onto the pure white snow. The nauseating, wet sounds of flesh being ripped from bone filled the air. Camille's stomach twisted in horror and disgust. A cursory glance around the rest of the campsite revealed signs of a struggle: disturbed snow, blood splatter, and a discarded sword. A pile of furs and dark hair laid off to the side of one of the tents, unmoving where it soaked in a dark crimson pool. It took Camille a moment to recognize it as a body; both legs had been torn off at the hip. Camille looked back at the ravenous duo and knew exactly what they were eating.

She had been right to expect enemies. Monsters.

The cautious part of Camille's brain told her it was time to report back to Scott and Donna. But what would they do then? They couldn't walk away from this camp. For all they knew, it was likely the only source of heat, shelter, and supplies for miles around. They had nothing and there was nowhere else for them to go. They needed this camp and they would need weapons to take it.

Camille's gaze strayed towards the sword resting on the snow, gleaming in the firelight.

Too risky. There was no way she could get to it without being seen.

Still, she had to do something.

Camille took a deep breath and quietly dipped into the tent she had been hiding behind through the back flap. Within, she found another body. The rumpled black hair was the same as the first, but this body was both intact and much smaller. It was a child, Camille realized with a shock. A boy, about eight years old. He laid on a bed of soft, brown fur. His head was turned to the side at an unnatural angle, face pale, blue-lipped mouth agape and glassy eyes wide with fear. A long knife laid on the ground beside him, just beyond his fingertips.

No! Camille's psyche screamed in horror. Though she did not know this boy, his death struck her like a blow to the chest, knocking the air from her lungs. She fought against the urge to cry out, to cradle the boy in her arms and mourn him as if he were her own.

There wasn't time. Scott and Donna needed her.

Camille kissed the boy's temple. A pair of hot teardrops fell from her eyes and into his hair. "I'm sorry," she whispered, her voice strained and thick with emotion.

She snatched up the knife and began to move backwards out of the tent. The deerskin flaps released her into the night with a soft sigh. Camille was not so quiet. Rattled and shaking from all that she had just witnessed, her usual grace eluded her. She stumbled backwards a few paces and then came to a sudden stop as she collided with something, or someone, large.

A pair of wiry, vise-like arms wrapped around her from behind and a screeching wail pierced the air, echoed by two others. Camille's own scream was lost in the cacophony.

"What the *fuck* was that?!" Scott shouted in alarm. His voice boomed through the night, dispelling any pretense of stealth. He took off running towards the campsite.

Donna followed close behind him. Her heart pounded in her chest.

"Let go of me!" Camille shrieked. She wriggled and fought to escape the creature's iron grasp, to no avail. It hissed and bore down on her neck with its wicked teeth. Camille was just able to twist sideways away from the bite and the creature's teeth plunged into her shoulder instead. She cried out in pain and lashed out with the knife, driving it up into the creature's right eye. A terrible howl tore itself from the creature's throat. Its grip loosened as it stumbled backwards, clumsily dragging Camille along with it. She recognized the opportunity to escape but was not eager to leave her only weapon behind. She yanked the knife free from the creature's eye socket, eliciting another blood-curdling shriek from it, and deftly slipped out beneath its arms.

Without a backwards glance, Camille ran. She prayed it was towards Scott and Donna. Fear and pain impaired her sense of direction as her eyes struggled to readjust to the night.

"Camille!" Scott shouted. Snow crunched under his feet as he raced towards his wife.

A wave of relief washed over Camille. She had never been so glad to hear Scott's voice. He came into view a moment later. The familiar sight of his silhouette propelled her across the snow, faster.

Meanwhile, two other silhouettes appeared behind Camille, lanky and awkward yet eerily silent as they loped after her.

"I'm here!" Camille called out, unaware of the danger closing in on her.

"Camille, look out!" Scott shouted in warning.

"Behind you!" Donna yelled. Fear thrummed beneath the surface of her skin.

Camille cast a furtive glance over her shoulder. The creatures were just a few yards behind her and gaining fast. She wouldn't be able to outrun them. And so she did the only thing she could think of, spinning around to face her pursuers and driving the knife into the nearest one's chest as it came close. It reared back, straightening to its full height of seven feet, and let out a deep, sickly coughing sound that seemed almost like laughter. The creature swung out at Camille with its long, thin arms. She sidestepped the first swing, but the second caught her squarely in the chest, knocking her to the ground.

"Camille, *no!*" Scott screamed.

The creature was on her in an instant, shrieking and spewing blood in her face as it attempted to pin her down. Meanwhile, the creature's companion lumbered past the two of them. It turned its attention to Scott, head cocked to one side, total darkness pooled in its sunken eye sockets.

"Oh, fuck!" Scott swore as he recognized the creature's intent. It was going to kill him.

But it didn't matter.

He had to save Camille.

"Scott!" Donna screamed his name as he ran headlong into the path of the creature which held him in its sights.

Scott feinted right, spun on his heels, and punched the creature in the ribs as hard as he could. He heard the ribs snap under his knuckles, felt the ribcage cave in from the blow, yet the creature continued, unconcerned. It laughed its sickly, wheezing laugh and turned to swing at Scott, batting him aside as if he were nothing. He fell to the ground and began backpedaling on his hands and feet, desperate to put space between himself and the terrible monster that would be his death. Yet, even then, he spared a sideways glance at Camille.

She thrashed and screamed beneath her attacker. Her shoes churned the snow as she kicked out wildly. The creature grabbed her face with its long, bony fingers and leaned in close. It breathed death into her face, rancid and suffocating, as it appeared to study her. Tears streamed from her eyes and the creature's face split open in a wide grin. It relished in her fear.

Donna felt helpless as she watched the scene unfolding before her. Her friends were going to die and she would die with them. Fear flooded her stomach, her mind, her heart. It filled her body with a sickening, burning energy—both hot and cold at the same time—that threatened to devour her. The surrounding air crackled as blue sparks danced over the skin of her hands. Without thinking, she extended her arms and screamed in a language she did not even understand. Pale blue light shot out from her fingertips and arced towards the creatures. Their bodies went rigid, mouths twisting in agony as the light struck them. If they screamed, no one heard it. The only sound for miles was roaring, rumbling thunder.

And then, there was silence, terrible and absolute.

The creatures laid lifeless on the ground. Tendrils of black smoke rose from their smoldering bodies, carrying the acrid smell of burning flesh.

Donna had done it. She didn't know how, but she was relieved. The monsters were dead and her friends were safe. She was safe. It was over.

Except it wasn't.

"What did you do?!" Scott screamed. He scrambled to

his feet and rushed towards Camille. She laid on the ground beside the fallen creature. Neither moved.

Donna's heart sank and the blue sparks returned to the surface of her skin, skimming her arms and hands with a featherlight touch. What *had* she done?

Scott shoved the monster's corpse away from Camille and gently shook her shoulders. "Camille? Cam, wake up!" he shouted. When she didn't respond, he moved to check her pulse.

Nothing. She wasn't breathing, either.

"Fuck!" Scott swore.

Donna watched in pained silence as Scott began performing CPR on Camille. He delivered thirty chest compressions and two rescue breaths, then another thirty compressions and two breaths. Still, Camille did not move.

"Dammit! Come on, Cam! Come back to me!" Scott yelled.

Even in the dim light, Donna could see the strain on his face.

"Get over here, Donna!" he called for her.

She hesitated, weighed down by the guilt and fear in her stomach, but only for a moment. A few seconds later, she stood at Scott's side, looking down on Camille as he continued to pump her chest. Her face was splattered with blood.

"I need you to be our AED," Scott explained gruffly. "You did this. You can fix it."

Donna's eyes went wide. "I... What? How?"

Scott leaned down to breathe for Camille. When he came back up, he began working to remove her coat and shirt.

"You're going to shock her again," he instructed, miming the motion over Camille's exposed chest. "Right there. Now!"

"But… I don't know how to control this! What if I hurt her?"

"She's dying, Donna! Do it *now!*"

Donna did as she was told, bending down to place her hands upon Camille's chest. She felt an instant change in the direction of the electrical energy in her body. The blue sparks no longer danced erratically across her skin but instead pulsed down her arms from her elbows to her fingertips. At first, nothing else happened. The power Donna had wielded before seemed to have lost its intensity. Her breathing hitched and a jolt of fear passed through her.

Camille is dying because of me.

The terror of that thought overtook Donna, seeming to ignite something inside of her. Her eyes rolled back, her hands glowed blue, and foreign words poured from her mouth of their own volition. She had no control over the power as it slammed into Camille's chest in one massive surge. Camille's body spasmed, Donna gasped and pulled away, and Scott moved in to resume administering chest compressions.

As he leaned down to breath for Camille, she squirmed and moaned.

Relief washed over Scott, rounding out the sharper edges of his face. "Camille!" he cried out. "Are you okay?!"

A low whine escaped her lips, but that was all.

Scott bit his lip. "I think she's still unconscious," he announced in a low voice, "but she's alive."

Donna hugged her arms to her chest, fighting back

tears. "Thank God," she said. "Scott, I'm—"

"Save it," Scott snapped. His tone brooked no argument.

Donna flinched. She bit her lip and her throat seemed to swell.

"I'll carry her into the camp," Scott muttered. "You keep an eye out for any more of those... things."

As Scott fixed Camille's clothes and scooped her up into his arms, nestling her head against his shoulder, Donna looked out into the sea of snow around them. If there were more creatures out there, they were lurking out of sight. Not a comforting thought, Donna admitted to herself. Her fingers tingled.

She looked down at the corpse by her feet. Its face was turned to the night sky, unseeing eyes fixed on the stars above. Donna felt a strange sense of sadness looking at it. She comforted herself with the fact that it wasn't Camille. The knife the rogue had found was still buried in the monster's chest. Its smooth bone hilt glowed faintly in the moonlight. Donna wrapped her fingers around it and yanked the knife free.

The creature shrieked, seemingly returned to life. Donna's own scream was cut off as the creature's arm shot out at her, hand wrapping around her throat. Sparks jumped from her fingers to the blade of the knife and, instinctively, she thrust it down into the creature's head. The monster gasped, whimpered, and then stilled. Its arm fell limp at its side, fingers curled in death.

Donna waited for a long moment before pulling the

knife out again. This time, there was no reaction. The corpse was really a corpse this time, it seemed.

Donna shuddered.

Her gaze fell on the other monster's prone body. It looked dead, but she decided to make sure. She bent down and plunged the knife into the void of its left eye socket. The blade pierced the creature's brain with a soft squishing noise. Gagging, Donna yanked the knife out and stood. She watched the corpse for a second, still disbelieving her eyes.

Everything was so surreal. A part of Donna still believed she was dreaming, but that did little to ease her fears. She wouldn't let either of her friends die, even in a nightmare, if there was anything she could do to stop it. But what if there wasn't?

What if Camille never woke up?

Donna shook her head to dispel the thought. She looked up from the corpse, scanned the horizon one last time, and then took off at a jog after Scott and Camille. When she caught up to them, she took the lead, keeping a wary eye out for danger.

"What happened back there?" Scott asked.

Donna wasn't sure which 'what' he was referring to. She decided to assume he meant when she'd hung back to retrieve the knife, and not when she'd nearly killed Camille.

"At least one of those things wasn't totally dead," Donna explained. "But they are now. I made sure of that. And I grabbed this." She held out the knife. The blade was coated in a thin film of gore. Scott glanced at it and grimaced. Even so, he seemed to take comfort in the sight.

"Good," he said. "Keep it handy. We might need it."

Donna nodded wordlessly.

Apart from the apparent lack of living occupants, the campsite was much the same as Camille had left it. Half-eaten chunks of raw meat littered the ground, hastily dropped by the creatures when Camille had been discovered. Scott and Donna were more accustomed to blood and gore than Camille, but even they found it difficult to keep their stomachs when they discovered the mutilated corpse that Camille had initially mistaken for a bloodied pile of furs. They realized, as she had, where the meat on the ground had come from.

Donna used the blade of the knife to lift the flaps of each tent. She peered inside, checking for any creatures that might be lying in wait for them. There were none.

But there *were* more bodies.

Three in all, one for each tent in the campsite. Two adults and a child. It was difficult to tell the gender of the mutilated one, but Donna guessed it to be a man, presumably the father of the dark-haired boy.

The third was a red-haired woman. A look of panic was frozen on her face. She appeared afraid but not for herself, despite the large chunk missing from her neck. The woman had lost a significant amount of blood. It soaked her clothing, bedding, and hair. Upon closer inspection, Donna confirmed that the injury was a bite wound, and a gnarly one, at that. The creature's razor teeth had torn through one of her carotid arteries. She likely would have lost consciousness within seconds of it being severed and died within minutes. Whether it was blood loss or lack of oxygen to her brain that had done her in, Donna wasn't sure. It might've simply been shock.

After she had finished checking the tents, Donna cleared a spot on the ground for Camille next to the campfire. Scott gingerly laid her down on a bed of bearskin taken from one of the tents. A peaceful expression came over her as the firelight flickered across her face. Donna noticed then that the fire was beginning to die down, casting a tighter and fainter circle of light against the darkness. She glanced around the camp and found a sealskin bundle nearby. It contained thin, dry pieces of wood. She added a few pieces to the fire and stoked it while Scott stroked Camille's hair.

"We shouldn't have let her go alone," he said suddenly. "We should've been there."

Donna took a deep breath and let it out, slowly. "Maybe," she said. "We don't know what would've happened, Scott. It might've been worse."

Scott tensed. His fingers froze in a tangle of Camille's hair. "Worse than you almost killing her?" he demanded, his voice dangerously low. He kept his eyes on Camille's face, but Donna could feel the heat of the glare he was suppressing.

"Those things were going to kill you both!"

"So, what, you thought you'd beat them to the punch?" Scott sneered. His face twisted in anger and his free hand balled into a fist.

Donna shook her head in dismay. "Of course not! But I had to do *something*, Scott. So I did. I don't know how. I told you, I can't control it. It just happened. I didn't mean to hurt her. I was trying to save her."

Scott sighed. "Let's just hope that's what you did."

Donna decided to give Scott some space and time alone with his wife. She used snow to clean the filth from her knife, then set out to gather what supplies could be salvaged from the camp. There wasn't much, but she found the essentials: jerky, a partially frozen waterskin, two small blankets, an iron cooking pot, a tinderbox, and a small jar containing some sort of healing salve. She also found two more knives, one on each of the adult bodies, and a sword.

Donna carried her findings in her arms and placed them in a pile near the campfire. Scott looked up but said nothing. That was fine with Donna. She unfurled one of the blankets and laid it gently over Camille.

"Here," Donna said, holding out the second blanket to Scott.

He stared at it warily, almost as if he didn't trust it. "What about you?" he asked.

Donna shrugged. "I'm fine."

Scott shook his head. "No, you're not." He sighed. "I shouldn't have said what I did. I'm sorry. You were just trying to help. I know that." His voice was soft, tone sincere. There was something like defeat in the slump of his shoulders.

"It's okay," Donna said. "I'm sorry, too."

Scott hesitated, not knowing what to say. He wasn't ready to forgive Donna, not while Camille's life still hung in the balance. Eventually, the words "I know" fell awkwardly from his lips. As they hung in the air with his frosty breath, a look of regret came over his face.

Donna found herself slipping into her nurse mode.

"We'll do everything we can for her," she promised Scott with a soft, sympathetic smile. On anyone else, the expression might've appeared artificial, but Scott saw a measure of his own heartache mirrored in her eyes.

He fixed her with a knowing look. "That's what we always tell them."

Donna nodded, swallowing hard. "I know," she admitted, "but we will."

"Yeah. We will."

"Take the blanket. I'm gonna get us some water."

Donna found a patch of clean snow on the edge of the campsite and filled the iron pot. She placed it near the campfire and sat down to wait for the snow to melt.

Scott and Donna were quiet for several minutes. The silence was neither comfortable nor uncomfortable. It just was. Donna was afraid to break it, but she didn't have to.

"My mom died," Scott announced suddenly. He seemed as startled by the words as Donna was. She'd had no idea.

Scott grimaced. "It was a few months ago," he muttered. "She got sick."

"Scott..." Donna struggled to find the right words. "I'm so sorry."

"I tried to tell you," he continued. "I called a bunch of times, but you didn't answer. And it's not... it's not something I knew how to say in a voicemail or a text. After the fourth time you sent me to voicemail, I got a text from you saying you'd call me back later. But you never did."

It was true. Other than her girlfriend, Hope, Donna

hadn't spoken to anyone outside of work during the peak months of the pandemic. Whenever her phone rang, her stomach twisted and she felt sick. She never answered unless it was work or Hope calling. She ignored all other calls or sent them to voicemail. It didn't matter whose name came up on her caller ID. For reasons she had trouble putting into words, she simply couldn't find it within herself to talk to them, even though it might've been nice to hear their voices. She had told herself that work was just too stressful, too draining.

After the pandemic was over, things would be better. She would be better.

But, now, she was finding out months late that Scott's mom was dead, while Camille laid unconscious on the ground.

Donna's head spun on its axis as she tried to process all of it. Tears stung her eyes.

When she didn't respond, Scott continued. "I needed you and you weren't there. And do you know what the worst part of it all is?"

Donna shook her head, too choked up to speak.

Scott swallowed hard before answering. "I was working when my Mom called 911," he recounted. "She was having trouble breathing. She had to be taken to the hospital, but I didn't get to be the one to transport her. And once she was there, she wasn't allowed any visitors. Not even family. No exceptions, not even for EMTs. Pandemic rules, you know. They suspected she had the virus and then it turned out that she did. She died in that hospital, alone. I just... I should've been there. I mean, I know why I wasn't allowed to be. But it feels like I should've been there."

Tears streamed down Scott's face. He looked down at Camille, seeming to sleep peacefully. Her breathing was even, her cheeks rosy from the warmth of the fire.

"And now, I just look at Camille and..." The words trailed away as Scott's Adam's apple bobbed up and down. A couple of minutes passed before he spoke again.

"We should've been there," he said finally.

Once the snow had melted somewhat, Donna boiled it and allowed the water to cool to a safe temperature. She poured half of it into the recently-thawed waterskin. Scott then took the cooking pot from her and began tending to Camille. He wet a small rag he had found and carefully cleaned her bite wound. Donna stoppered the waterskin and passed him the healing salve. He grimaced, but accepted it nonetheless.

"I hate not knowing exactly what this is," he muttered.

Donna sighed. "Me too, but it's all we have."

"I know. Hopefully it helps, whatever it is."

Camille whimpered as Scott applied the salve. Her eyes fluttered open.

Both Donna and Scott felt their hearts leap at the sight. "Camille?" Scott said her name gently.

"Oh, ow," Camille groaned. "Oh, God, why does everything hurt?"

The truth sounded so bizarre that Scott wasn't sure how to put it. "We were attacked by those monsters," he began. "Do you remember? One bit you."

Camille blinked several times to clear the fog from her

mind. "Shit, yeah," she said. Her eyes went wide. "I remember. There was a bright flash and then I... blacked out, I think. What the hell happened? Are we safe?"

"We're safe for now," Scott said. He planted a kiss on her forehead. "I'm just glad you're okay. We weren't sure you were going to wake up."

"What happened?" Camille repeated. "What was that light?"

Scott's gaze flicked up at Donna and Camille's followed. "You tell her," he said.

Donna hesitated. Her heart jumped up into her throat. "I, uh, guess you could say I did the wizard thing," she explained, poorly. "I don't know how, but... I shot lightning out of my hands. I didn't mean to hurt you, I swear. I was trying to save you from those things."

Camille's gaze slid away from her and across the campsite to where the mutilated corpse still laid in a pool of blood. Her eyes went wide and she gagged, then sat bolt upright. Vomit poured from her mouth, soiling her clothes and the bearskin rug beneath her.

"Fuck," she coughed. "Ugh. This place is awful. It's sick. We can't stay here."

Scott shook his head. "We'll leave as soon as we can," he assured her, "but you have to get some rest first."

Camille's eyes filled with tears. "You don't understand. I can't be here, Scott. How am I supposed to sleep surrounded by bodies? If we're going to stay, you have to bury them."

Again, Scott shook his head. "We can't bury them. We don't have anything to dig with and, anyway, the ground is frozen," he explained patiently.

"We can't just leave him like that!" Camille shouted.

Scott's brows furrowed in confusion. "Who? That guy over there?" He gestured to the legless corpse.

"The boy," Camille sobbed. "You have to bury him, Scott. You have to."

Scott's eyes flashed as a horrible realization struck him. He looked down at Camille with eyes that were sad and soft. "You're right," he agreed. "We do. We will."

Donna stared at them, perplexed. She'd just admitted to magically electrocuting her friend and now that same friend was crying over the death of a boy she'd never known. Why?

The grave look on Scott's face told her all that she needed to know.

A *miscarriage*, she realized numbly. Donna hadn't even known Camille had been pregnant. Maybe no one knew. More likely, though, this was just another tragedy she had missed.

"I'll help you bury them," she found herself saying. "I have an idea."

Donna's idea was simple. She and Scott worked together to dismantle one of the tents. They then carefully wrapped the bodies in deerskin and buried them in snow on the edge of the campsite, marking the small family's grave with a cross fashioned from the tent poles. Donna hoped that the deceased would approve of their burial, that it would bring them peace, but she had no way of knowing what this world's customs were. Still, this was the best they could offer.

Once it was done, Camille slept, exhausted from all that she had been through.

"I missed a lot, didn't I?" Donna asked when she was sure Camille was asleep.

Scott huffed. "Yeah. You did."

"I'm sorry."

"I know."

Donna and Scott took turns watching over the campsite. Hours passed and then, finally, the sky began to fill with light. The sun shone on the backs of mountains, throwing their shadows across the landscape. As the sun emerged from behind them and into the sky above, the world came to life in a splendorous display of color and light. Donna squinted at the base of the mountain range. A large city was nestled at its feet, constructed of stone and cleverly designed so that its high walls and towers were nearly indistinguishable from the mountains behind it. Nearly.

"A city," she pointed out to Scott and Camille. "Maybe we can find help there."

Within an hour, they had packed up and were ready to go. Scott and Donna wore the disassembled tents in bundles across their backs. Camille, still weak from the previous day's events, carried only a knife for self-defense. Scott and Donna each carried one as well, and Scott wore the sword in its sheath on his hip. As they made their way towards the distant city, a white dragon soared across the sky and disappeared over the mountain peaks.

It took most of the day for the trio to reach the city. When they finally arrived, they were met by armed guards. Black masks concealed the lower halves of their faces. They regarded the group with narrowed, suspicious eyes. Camille's face shone with sweat and she panted heavily as she approached, arms linked with Scott. She leaned on him for support.

"Halt!" the leader of the guards commanded them. "Come no closer. What is your purpose in coming here?"

Scott cleared his throat nervously. "We're looking for shelter, and my wife needs to see a doctor," he explained. "We were attacked last night by... some kind of monsters. One of them bit her."

The guard made a disapproving noise. "I see. Unfortunately, we cannot allow you inside. The creatures you encountered are known as the Pale. They carry a deadly sickness in their bodies and their bite is fatal. Your wife won't survive more than a few days, I'm afraid, and then she will become one of them."

A chill passed through the group, and it had nothing to do with the biting cold.

"I'm going to die?" Camille asked in a small voice.

The guard nodded. "Yes, ma'am. I'm sorry."

"How can you possibly know that?" Scott snapped.

The guard sighed. "Because she's been bitten and she clearly has a fever. I'm sorry, but her days are numbered. There's no way around it."

"What about magic?" Scott asked, desperate. He looked sidelong at Donna, remembering her wild displays of power.

"There is no cure, magical or otherwise," the guard insisted calmly. "Now, please, you must go. Anyone who is confirmed or suspected to have been infected by the Pale is prohibited from entering the City of Stone. If you refuse to leave, we will have no choice but to remove you by force."

"Where are we supposed to go?" Donna asked. "We don't even know where we are."

"There is a cave south of here where you might find shelter." The guard pointed in the direction. "Now, go!"

Donna, Scott, and Camille traveled in silence, their hearts heavy. They found the cave within a couple of hours. It was small, dark, and dank. Animal bones littered the dirt floor.

Camille leaned against the stone of the cave mouth and sank to the ground. Her face was pale, her breathing uneven. "This was supposed to be a game," she laughed without humor as tears rolled down her face. "And now I'm gonna die here. Aren't I?"

Scott shook his head resolutely. "No," he disagreed. "Absolutely not. If this is a game, we can win, right? How do we win?"

Camille turned her eyes to the heavens and sniffled. She swallowed hard before answering. "You don't win a game like this," she told him. "You play until you die."

And that's exactly what they did.

When Camille began to change, neither Scott nor Donna had the heart to kill her. Scott plunged his sword into his own gut instead. He refused to live in this strange, foreign world without her. The last thing Donna saw before the world went black was Camille, or what had once been Camille, screaming as the cave erupted in a crackling burst of blue lightning.

"Not the ending I expected, I must admit," Kris said as his three players came back to their senses. "Truly tragic, but sweet in its own way. And you did so well, developing your characters! You faced your fears together and unburdened yourselves of some of your pain. That's exactly what I was hoping to see from you. I daresay you'll have grown closer as a result of this experience. Wonderful job, everyone."

Donna, Scott, and Camille blinked in confusion. They looked around and saw that they were, once again, in the bar. The furniture was free of snow, as was the floor of scattered dice and papers. Their character sheets rested neatly on the table in front of them, each covered in handwritten notes, including health trackers which put their health at zero. Tom the bartender seemed unperturbed as he cleaned a pair of empty glasses.

"What happened?" Camille asked. "Did we die?"

Kris smiled sympathetically. "Oh, yes," he confirmed. "That's the risk you take with this sort of game. But you know what? Every ending really is a new beginning. And, anyway, what matters is that you had fun. You did, didn't you?" The game master's face brightened.

The trio stared at him in stunned silence.

Kris looked up at the wall clock and gasped. "Oh my,

look at the time!" he exclaimed. "It's officially Christmas Eve. I really should be going. The missus will worry if I'm not home soon. I have some things to wrap up before my big work trip. It was wonderful meeting you all. Thank you so much for your time. Merry Christmas!"

And with that, Kris whisked his belongings off the table and disappeared through the side door which Donna had used to enter the bar. The attached bell jingled merrily in his wake.

Donna, Scott, and Camille exchanged startled looks.

"What the actual *fuck?!*" Scott half-shrieked, half-whispered.

"That was real, right?" Camille asked, struggling and failing to keep the panic out of her voice. "We can all agree that was real?"

Donna took a deep breath and let it out, slowly. "I think so. It felt real. All I know for sure is I'm glad you're both okay... I'm so sorry, for everything. Can we talk?"

thirteen

A Permanent Solution
David Mecklenburg

he alpine scenery moved by Ms. Fentahn in all of its vast contrast: rocky outcroppings, splayed meadows of a pure, unfouled green, and the towering fractured peaks of white snow thrusting up against a blue sky. But she did not look at the scenery moving by with any sort of contemplation of its sublimity, or even novelty. Yes, the view was very different from the drab grey buildings of her former home in the Flatlands; she would not have found a single point of common reference, but she had other things on her mind. And really, wasn't the "moving scenery" merely an illusion of the train's motion and one's own changing perspective? Ms. Fentahn's world was changing and the train ride was literally a vehicle of change. Rather than study the view, Ms. Fentahn—Lusan was her first name— simply did what many people do when they are facing new and entirely uncertain fortunes—she perseverated on the past.

She thought of her former home and the empty cradle sold off to help finance her new professional wardrobe. She remembered the face of her husband, blissfully lying upon the hard cedar board. He had never looked as peaceful as that in real life for he was a fitful sleeper prone to mouth-breathing and bad dreams. To save money, the kindly mortician slid the body of her husband, gently and with reverence, into the crematorium without a coffin. Lusan remembered the soles of his feet for that was the last she saw of him, as she remembered him.

"Mr. Yamatang does a good job. I don't think your husband looked better." A large and heavy hand, fleshy beneath a black glove, rested on her shoulder. Perhaps for too long. It was the hand, the glove and the voice of her husband's former employer, Mr. Phutee. "It's important because your last glimpse of him is how you will remember him."

And then there was the metal clink of the latch on the oven door and that was the end of it, for while she thoughtfully dispersed his ashes in the river that ran through their city, that act of closure did not feel quite right, for Mr. Phutee was there as well and was fond of touching her.

Mr. Phutee's touching then violated her memories. It was friendly at first, but his attentions regressed. He touched her hair, complimented her on her scent which was nothing more than simple vanilla. He bade her to sit on his lap finally one day and began to fondle her breasts.

"You don't have to worry, Lusie," it was his pet name for her. "I will take care of you." There was to be an apartment he leased that was to be her home and it was obvious the rôle of mistress was to be hers. She felt his manhood stiffen below her and felt sick.

"Do not cry, Lusie, I will take care of you."

The train reached a long straight grade. She had looked at a map earlier, for Lusan Fentahn liked to know where she was going, but the only thing that could pass through her mind was the memory of Mr. Phutee and his mahogany desk. The desk was a show of power, not only for its intricate inlay work, nor astronomical cost, but the fact he had so many subordinates that the ordinary detritus of business letters, ledgers, files and other flotsam remained entirely absent. She was the only adornment on the desk that day.

Her stomach turned on this memory. At the apothecary's shop, she bought a camphor douche and an employment periodical. That night she found the solicitation for an accounting clerk, a woman, (it was very specific) of a certain age to assist in the administration of a tuberculosis sanitorium at a distance and altitude she hoped would separate her from her former life forever.

The dark, half-timbered houses of Zahlindroma surrounded the train station where she waited for her ride. The employee of the Sanitorium who fetched her was unremarkable, efficient, and quiet and they quickly arrived at the funicular railway that ascended up to the Zahlindroma Sanitorium.

Now that she was in the close proximity of her new situation, she remembered the curiously queer nature of her interview. The woman who performed this function was less interested in her accomplishments and abilities, although they were politely acknowledged with requisite professionalism, but rather her age and the circumstance. Through shrewd questioning the interlocutor laid bare Lusan's place in the world.

"My brother takes care of my father and mother at the family farm in Castorp."

"No, my husband and I did not have any children."

"His mother disapproved of the marriage."

"My former situation is quite untenable now."

"I have no other income."

These answers flowed out from Lusan with such insistence and force that she trembled inside at what the world would do to her if she did not sign the employment contract straightaway.

After she had climbed the Sanitorium's steps with her baggage, she expected to see many wan and beautiful, yet moribund souls wandering through the dark hallways with the glowing large eyes she had read about, but most were frail people. Many of them were losing hair or had violent tremens as they attempted to walk to dinner.

The Director of the Sanitorium, Dr. Kofnen and his assistant, Ms. Kinrote greeted her and whisked her off to the offices where she would be working. Dr. Kofnen was a stout, hearty man with a shock of iron grey hair, square-framed glasses, and a habit of waving his right hand in the air. Lusan would eventually be able to interpret the contextual signals of his hand's positions quite well such as pointing heavenward in joviality, or horizontally rigid in times of consternation. Assistant Director Kinrote was the opposite. She was tall, thin and had terrible posture, perhaps from a lifetime of stooping over to chastise and correct. Her skin was quite unlike Lusan and Dr. Kofnen's rich brown, for it was pale and made all the more unreal by a cloth face mask. She coughed and abruptly excused herself for a spot of blood had begun to bloom where her lips should be on the mask. Dr. Kofnen leaned toward Lusan and whispered:

"An employee as well as a patient, I'm afraid. Incurable."

Lusan spent her first days in the usual adjustments of settling into an entirely new place, a new bed, new routines, new food, but she met these with welcome, even if they took place in a rather institutional space. The Sanitorium was clean and mostly white. The walls were painted white. The dining hall where many of the patients ate was white, painted in enamels, with porcelain tiling.

Lusan's duties at the Sanatorium were straightforward and she was grateful to her new employers for the fresh piles of work allowed her to forget her past. The books had been in disarray for a while, since Ms. Kinrote's time had been continually pulled in different directions and occasional flareups of her condition rendered her bedridden at times. Lusan possessed an excellent mind for figures and accounting and the ability to hold certain sums in her head, along with the alignment of such sums both in terms of the nature of the expenditure or receivable and its placement within the chronological framework of the fiscal year.

Her quarters were in a small apartment building built away from the main hospital and joined to it by both a tunnel and a covered walkway. The tunnel was straight, well-lit and not terribly romantic or terrifying for it was there because the snow would overwhelm the walkway during the deep winter. She had two small and comfortable rooms: a bedroom with wardrobe (she did not need many different kinds of clothes) and a washstand and mirror, and a sitting room where she could read or conduct hobbies. Director Kofnen was quick to suggest she take up something. "Botany may be a good one, were it not for our short season here, but there are many others. Philately is one which allows the indulgent to travel the world from an armchair."

The Director was a jovial albeit somewhat nervous man. Aside from the linguistic supplement of his frequent gesticulations, he frequently toe-tapped as well. And although he often seemed nervous around her, he seemed to genuinely care about her situation—were the quarters sufficient? Was the work manageable? Was her temperature and other health in good condition?

"You must forgive me asking that. Something of a professional habit, Ms. Fentahn. But you seem to have a strong healthy constitution. Has Dr. Moh said anything of your physical?"

"My physique?"

"No, your physical. You've had one, haven't you? We

want to make sure you're healthy Ms. Fentahn. We did not bring you all the way up here to waste away as a patient after all. You're particularly important for the future of the Sanitorium."

"Oh, no I have not even really met Dr. Moh."

Dr. Moh prowled the halls in a black smock with a stethoscope around her neck like a rosary. She had a head of long black hair, rather lustrous and beautiful that was always bound up in a thick braid that hung to her waist. A serious woman of little humor, she tended to the female patients and would gaze at you through her thick, smoked-lens glasses with curious eyes whether you were a human being, a geode or a translucent fish brought from the deepest trench in the ocean. But she was polite and obliging although she did not warm to Ms. Fentahn. This troubled Lusan at first, until she realized Dr. Moh treated everyone this way.

"Your vital statistics are all normal and your lungs sound fine. You have very healthy skin. Your red eyes are a mild form of conjunctivitis, do you sleep well?"

"I have never been a good sleeper."

"Most likely you will sleep better here. The air here tends to do that once you acclimatize although some never do. Your pelvic exam is good. You haven't had children and it doesn't look like you contracted any venereal diseases."

"I should hope not."

"Indeed, you don't want to end up like the patients here."

"But I thought…"

At that moment there was a shouting and screaming from Dr. Moh's waiting room.

"Oh gods, it's Saterp again," Dr. Moh said. "Nothing to worry about. Hallucinates frequently, almost like delirium tremens at times. He thinks there are frogs and centipedes trying to rape him. If you will excuse me a moment."

Lusan saw through a sliver of the open door a man, or it had been a man, spinning around and around, like a cat chasing a tail that had long ago been cut off. She blinked and could not tell where his forehead was because it seemed to bulge out in all four corners of his head, like round protuberances covered with thin strands of corn silk.

She heard the voice of two orderlies as they bound him down. He screamed some more and then was quiet.

When Dr. Moh returned, she found Lusan sitting upright, her hands crisply folded like napkins.

"Far far gone. We have to give him morphine to shut him up now. What is the matter?" Dr. Moh asked.

"I have never heard of anyone suffering from tuberculosis like that."

"Tuberculosis? Miss Fentahn, Mr. Saterp is in the deep and final throes of tertiary syphilis. Surely they spoke to you about that."

"Who?"

"I see. They didn't. That fat ponce left it to me. Let me explain this briefly, for your own health. While there are some patients here who do indeed suffer from various infections of *Mycobacterium tuberculosis,* most of them suffer from *Treponema pallidum.* That is why they are here. Their families are ashamed of them and cannot cope with the sort of displays like Mr. Saterp performed out there."

"That is why we so seldom see them."

"Precisely, although some are perfectly functional people. Sad really and quite intriguing that the disease can manifest itself in so many ways. Not everyone is a mass of gummas and insanity like Mr. Saterp."

Lusan spent the next month diligently working and avoiding contact with the patients, whom she was now afraid of, not as much as vectors of infection but overwhelming figures who had lost much of their humanity and their families. Lusan could not be sure if the kindly old lady in the white dress who painfully walked by her would fly into a storm of rage and terror.

"Someone needs to take care of them, Lusan and your candor in this matter is of utmost importance," Dr. Kofnen finally admitted. "But I think we can trust you to be one of us. For many, their beloved uncles, aunts, fathers, mothers, or children are at a respectable Sanitorium such as International Berghof. It is what they tell their friends and other relatives."

Well, I am under no obligation to injure the patients or their families' reputations. I am doing a service by saying nothing. She thought on her walks. When she had finished her work, Lusan would walk some of the pathways around the Sanitorium, up the steep hills, going a little further with each voyage until one night the cold came up and brought with it prodigious amounts of snow.

"She's won against the summer, again. I wonder if

some day She will never relent and the world will remain as you see it now," Ms. Kintrope said this one day as the two women were looking out the window.

"Who?" Lusan asked.

"Her, Lady Winter. I am being metaphorical Ms. Fentahn. Do not take me for one of our patients. My only malady is the traditional kind that sends people to the mountains, but I will never be able to return down there. The air would kill me in a week, so the secret of this place is safe with me. And what about you?"

"Ma'am. I don't have anywhere else to go whether it is the flatlands or here."

"Yes, another orphan of the world." Ms. Kintrope said somewhat melancholically. "Such a pretty young widow. And all alone." Ms. Kintrope looked at Lusan briefly in the threat of unmistakable grief.

And Ms. Kintrope was right. The snow did not relent. It came and piled up high and made even passage down to the village somewhat difficult. Avalanches would stop the trains, and everyone felt the isolation. The management kept the place warm, for Lusan herself knew how vast the supply of coal was in the lower basements and boiler-rooms; she had calculated it based on its transmutation into the figures of money.

Soon, Lusan found herself making use of the tunnel between the staff quarters and the main building complex. The halls felt more deserted as the patients remained in their rooms. There was no proscription against her wandering through the hallways, and so Lusan began to take this as a form of exercise.

"Well and enough," Dr. Moh said to her one morning during Staff Coffee. "But you may see some things you'd rather not. Then again, how long are you planning on staying here? You are young and attractive, why have you not found another spouse?"

Lusan had, against all her anticipation, felt a growing friendship with the very direct Dr. Moh. At times, Dr. Moh appeared to have come from some other world, a parallel one to ours, or so Lusan often thought, rather happily after a while because it was now Lusan's role to explain the life of humans.

"I loved my husband dearly. I do not wish to be with another man."

"What about a woman then?" Dr. Moh asked. "Sapphic love can be more lasting, and it doesn't result in children."

"I'm afraid I don't know where I would begin," Lusan said laughing. The thought of bonding her life to another woman had never really crossed her mind, although she had felt strong affection for other women throughout her life and, truth be told, felt strongly enough to have this affection people her fantasies and desires at times in dark night and other forms of solitude.

"Be careful, or you will live up here forever" Dr. Moh said with something that almost appeared to be a grin.

Had Lusan been a bit more worldly and experienced, she may have taken Dr. Moh's remarks about "living here forever" and "Sapphic love" as a kind of overture, but Lusan was not all that worldly or given to second-third-or-fourth guessing the emotional stratagems of others. However, Dr. Moh's braid seemed to shine with a greater gloss after that day, and her conversation did not seem to reside solely within the cold clinical descriptive realm of her profession.

Yet Dr. Moh's *other* comment about "living here forever" catalyzed a great deal of Lusan's thoughts in those first weeks of winter. *What am I going to do? I hadn't thought that far ahead. How could I, I was in such a state, what with Mr. Phutee and my poor husband's ashes barely cold...* Up and down the halls she thought of these matters.

One night, long after supper she wandered alone into the upper reaches of the Sanitorium. "Do I really want to live here forever?" She asked the cold wind which seemed very loud and Lusan saw that a door stood open onto a small balcony caked in snow. With effort against the stubborn drift of snow, she closed the door. Lusan looked down and saw the snow trailing toward a wide-open interior door of Room #505. Inside the room it was quiet. She stood long there, shivering and trying to make out the sound of a breath, or a whisper, or anything. There was only the wind, now reduced to its usual, insistent, but muted volume. She looked into the room.

The snow draped over everything like the sheets one sees put over old furniture in closed up houses. It was on the washstand, the bureau, and the bed frame. And there, lying on his back, was some remnant of a man. The gummas had swollen so on the right side of his face so that he could not have opened that eye, but the other side still had traces of humanity, of a handsome cast at one time. The left eye was open in an expression that seemed one of alarm and wonder.

His crooked mouth opened wide and his tongue lolled out. The cavern where his nose had been was already filling up with snow, so that he looked almost as if he were powdered by the confectioner's caster than by death. He did not move and Lusan knew he was profoundly, solidly dead.

"You are sure you did not see anyone?" Dr. Kofnen asked.

How it could have happened was still a mystery to Lusan as she sat there, wrapped in a blanket before the office fireplace with a mug of grog. Dr. Kofnen, Dr. Moh and Ms. Kintrope were all there.

"No, no one."

"There were only Ms. Fentahn's footprints in the room. The snow could have been as virgin as that outside your office, Dr. Kofnen," Dr. Moh said.

Of the three, only Ms. Kintrope said nothing. She looked at Lusan, or rather through her, as though there was a far country or memory a thousand years away.

Lusan was allowed a few days of freedom from work, which she spent in her bed, propped up with pillows under the eiderdown drinking some decoction of Alpine herbs. On the second day of her convalescence, Dr. Kofnen came for an hour of questions, most of which Lusan answered with "I do not know."

"Well, it certainly is a strange case. A man frozen dead, although that particular patient did not have much time left. It was probably a blessing. What made you go up to that floor in the first place? Do not worry, I am not about to punish you, there is no rule against it. Did you hear anything?"

"No, Dr. Kofnen. I had gotten used to walking here, the paths and trails around us are thick with snow, so I was just wandering the halls instead."

"Doing the rounds? Ha, well, there's no harm done to you."

"It will not happen again." Lusan said.

"I certainly hope not. We can't have all of our patients freeze to death. Think of the lawsuits."

"No, I meant my wandering."

"You are not in trouble, Ms. Fentahn. But tell me, you are quite alright? You aren't going to leave us? You were settling in so well."

"No, you have all been most welcoming."

"Yes, even Evelyn has warmed to you."

"Evelyn?"

"Dr. Moh, I apologize."

The next day Dr. Moh herself attended to Lusan.

"I feel fine."

"As well you should." Dr. Moh was looking at the thermometer she had plucked from Lusan's mouth. "I don't detect any real shock to the system: strange considering what you have seen."

"It was…"

"Yes? Tell me. I am interested, professionally you might say, as to what you felt like, Lusan. It's not every day one sees that, although it's not uncommon here."

"Uncommon?"

"Oh, nothing. The mountains. A man freezing to death. If that is what actually happened."

"What else could it have been?"

"I am not talking about some hunter getting lost in the snow. While there is no doubt the extreme cold killed that man, the way it did it was most interesting. There was no sign of struggle. In fact, the patient looked almost…"

"…grateful. No. Enchanted."

"Yes, something like that. You may call me Evelyn if you wish."

"I would like that, but that sounds impertinent."

"No, Lusan, it is not. Tell me. There is something you want to say."

"Dr. Evelyn, it was—I feel awful saying this, a man died."

"Yes, but nothing you can say will hurt him nor offend me."

"It was beautiful."

"Beautiful?"

"Yes, you know how beautiful the world outside can be when the fresh snow has draped over everything, when all the sharp edges are gone and there is nothing but the snow rolling like waves that do not move?"

"You are not as prosaic as you would first seem." Evelyn Moh looked at Lusan for a while, as searchingly as though she were examining her for an illness. Finally, she said. "Is the beauty why you do not wish to resume your walks? Dr. Kofnen mentioned it."

"Yes. I'm afraid I will find it again."

"Perhaps you were meant to."

Far more than any room, resplendent in an unnatural

furnishing of snow, these words chilled Lusan as she thought about them over the next week. She did not yet go wandering through the halls at night but decided that the daytime was sufficiently safe.

Occasionally she ran into patients, but none were out of control, even if many were obviously in some sort of orthopedic pain or off in a distant world. Room 505 had been cleaned out and now contained a woman far gone in the disease. She cried out at times about the bats, none of which Lusan could see and Lusan had learned that the terrible old "cures" of Mercury treatments had prematurely brought on senility and dementia.

In time, Lusan felt as though she knew everyone on sight as the days grew darker, and so in the evening, when the lights were still on in the corridors she would also walk. The artificial lights were comforting—they cast no queer shadows nor concealed mysteries. They revealed people as they simply were. Some were wasted, twisted things, while others, owing to the strange quixotic nature of the disease maintained a convincing facsimile of their former selves. And perhaps this is why, with her knowledge of the staff and patients she was struck by the novelty of the beautiful woman she came across one evening on the third floor.

She was unlike anyone Lusan had seen. She passed some ways in front of Lusan at a "T" in the halls, yet even at that distance Lusan could see the woman's full, beautiful lips, her delicate nose, and her black eyelashes that were so long they swept over the top of her high, full cheekbones, for the woman looked down. She moved gracefully, as though she were not actually walking but gliding. Lusan hurried to the intersection of the halls to see her better. The woman was not entirely thin, but nor was she fat. Lusan noticed her slender waist and curving hips, for she wore a long white silk dress that shone like thousands of small stars or jewels and it hugged her body tightly. She had flowing black hair, so long and thick that it swished down to the floor. She stopped and turned. Effortlessly, she held out her hand and someone inside the doorway she had stopped before opened it and the woman glided in.

"Good Gods another one!" Dr. Kofnen burst into the administrative offices and Ms. Kintrope looked up with a start.

"Ms. Kintrope, please!" Dr. Kofnen said militarily. "We need to speak."

Lusan could not catch all of the conversation in the Director's office, although some of it was shouted. "Was anyone on the third floor last night?!" There were muffled answers and Lusan felt her throat grow thick.

Another patient had frozen to death in Room 345.

No one had seen anything save for poor Lusan. She thought and fretted for several days and one night stood at her window watching the snow fall and brushing her hair. She was trying to screw up enough courage to approach Dr. Moh, whom she trusted the most, when she saw the woman. It could be no other.

She was gliding, the same as before over the courtyard. And even though the lights on the exterior were dimmed in the thick snow, and even though the wind was blowing hard enough to send the woman's hair out like an opulent sable banner, and even though it must have been terribly cold, the woman wore only her beautiful dress. But it was a robe of sorts, Lusan realized, because it was open and fluttering around her naked body for Lusan also clearly saw a piercing light, cradled between the woman's breasts. Was it a necklace? How did it shine so in the dimness, like some icicle that burned with an inverse heat of profoundly cold light? These thoughts, like the woman's swift course over the snow, came to an abrupt halt as the woman stopped and gazed up at Lusan.

There were more bodies. More shouting in the Director's office.

"When will she make an end of it?!"

"When she comes…" and Lusan could not make out the rest of it. It was only Ms. Kintrope in with Dr. Kofnen now, for Eveyln Moh was conducting physicals.

"Ms. Lusan!" the Director said loudly. Lusan jumped in her chair but realized it was his normal, boisterous volume but the door to his office was now open.

"Yes, sir?"

"Have you seen anyone strange in the building on your walks?"

Lusan's stomach turned beneath her ribs like a convulsive puppy. She had to think quickly and had been dreading this question for she was an honest woman. But what could she say? That she had seen a half-naked woman, the most beautiful woman she had ever seen, walking through the snow as though it were Midsummer's eve? Or that she had seen the same woman glide into Room 345? Or the singular fact that, knowing the condition of its prior inhabitant, the visitor had opened the door without even touching it?

"Um, no. Sir. It's terrible" she added hastily. Dr. Kofnen looked at her and walked over.

"I know you get out and around. I had hoped you had perhaps seen something."

"No, I'm afraid not."

"Well, be on the lookout. If you see anyone strange, try to figure out who it is, but be safe. Don't do anything foolish, you understand. If you can somehow follow her, then do so, but be discreet." Dr. Kofnen blinked, as if he were thinking of something else to say and then said: "the Beelbatt Family is threatening a lawsuit. Any help you can give the Sanitorium would be most welcome."

Lusan did not see the strange woman again that night, but she sat up for a long while looking out over the courtyard. Perhaps she could make up for her previous silence by finally seeing the woman and reporting it the next day. But her vigil proved fruitless and she fell asleep on the window seat.

The next few nights were the same and her work began to slip a bit in the daytime. The office was suitably distracted itself with the general dismay over the uncanny freezing deaths, save for Eveyln Moh who noticed Lusan's bloodshot eyes.

"Not sleeping well again?"

"No. I'm... having trouble falling asleep."

"I see. It's usually easier to fall asleep in your bed, than the window seat."

That night, Dr. Moh's words endlessly rang like out-of-tune bells. *How did she know that?* Could she have been the woman? Her hair was long and black, bound up in the braid, perhaps it could have reached the floor if let down? The shapeless physician's smock she wore could easily conceal a goddess-like figure. No, Dr. Moh was short and the woman she saw was tall. Lusan decided that she would find out once and for all.

And that is why she wandered the hallways. Even after lights out, the white walls and porcelain tiles made it easy to find her way. But there were shadows, certain pillars, or arches cast them, and Lusan studied the shadows for the flutter of a white dress or long black hair. She did not peer into any private rooms, for most of them were locked now, although that had not stopped the deaths. She went further and looked in the great kitchen, the boiler room, the examination rooms, the office, but there was nothing. In the empty dining hall she sat down and put her arms upon the table and bowed her head in thought, searching over the image of Dr. Moh. Perhaps even Kintrope? No. That was certainly not her. She wondered what would happen if financial ruin cast her back in the world. Feeling entirely alone, Lusan began to weep, trying to remember what the pot of irises looked like on the wall behind her old house.

That is why Lusan did not hear the gliding approach. Her solitude broke only when the long thin hand, without blemish or disproportion, touched her hair lightly, so lightly that it felt more of a draught in that place.

"Lusan, do not weep for the life you have left behind."

How utterly gentle was that first touch. Surprise and shock melted in Lusan's bones and disappeared like souls when the body finally releases them. Lusan turned to look into a misty cloud, in the center of which the woman stood, gazing at Lusan with her eyes more terrible, more beautiful than Lusan could have imagined for they were as deep and black as lustrous ink. A cold light, a livid resonance of frozen fire burned between the woman's breasts and Lusan saw that it was not a necklace, but rather a delicate chain made of crystals that gracefully swept down from platinum clips on each of the woman's nipples and wavered in Lusan's earthly breath upon them, as though she were blowing gently upon a morning spider's web first kissed with dew.

The woman took Lusan's hands in hers and gently lifted her to her feet. The woman tilted her ethereal face to the side and Lusan mirrored her movements for they were to kiss and nothing in the world would come between them and that kiss.

They glided through the dining hall and down the main corridor. In the blue darkness of the night, they continued their journey toward the grand front entry doors that stood open. Outside, the woman gently lifted Lusan's hand and they moved over the snow as silently as an owl flies above it. They followed the pathways beneath the fir trees and Lusan understood their creaking language beneath the Atlas-burden of the snow. They moved beneath the stars brightly shining in a sky that was far clearer than any Lusan had seen. Up the mountain they went, past impossible crags and over crevasses that would have swallowed armies of men, until at the highest glacier they reached an ice cathedral far taller than the labored piles of stones that men call churches.

The woman removed her own and Lusan's clothes gently and lovingly, not quickly or languidly for those are the adjectives of time, and Lusan had abandoned her acquaintance with that human framework of experience. Time moved in the inscrutable slowness of glaciers or the quickness of a sudden blizzard as Lusan stepped into the beautiful woman's arms.

Could we really understand how their corporeality unfolded into ecstasies of exploration? Could we understand the progress of water as it became a tongue of ice, pushing against the fragile, labial beauty of a frozen peony? Would the broad caress of snow across the aching stone give us some glimpse of love made upon implacable mountain peaks? These are but a few of the stumbling phrases that attempt to traverse the slopes between metaphor and the transubstantiation of Lusan Fentahn.

She did not die, unless one expands the description of death as a transition into a mutability that is paradoxically beyond the horizon of being we call time. For a brief moment, we could not understand in terms of duration, Lusan and her lover lay together in elemental conjugation.

"I don't ever want to leave."

"You do not have to, Lusan. Thank you." And the woman gently removed the platinum clips of her chain and placed them on Lusan's nipples—the first and last sharp pain she felt.

"I don't?"

"No, you are my replacement. Why did you think I had them bring you here?"

The bright light of the ice around them, an albedo that was almost blinding in the first kisses and tumults began to dim from white to the blue of snow within hollows of footsteps, to the darker blue of the ocean, to the sapphire of the sky at late dusk until the blue became no more and Lusan slept.

Although her slumber should have continued until the first flakes of autumn snow called her, she awakens. She had never been a very good sleeper after all. She leaves the high glaciers, and, for what we would call a moment, goes down amidst the last patches of her element that remain beneath the deep shadows of the firs. She watches the train move down the valley.

A woman named Yuki, for that name was as good as any, sits on that train, with her black hair now cut above her shoulders. The wool jacket and simple dress fit her well. She relishes the feeling of real clothes and smells the air. While it is clear, and piercing, she can still detect the waking smell of rot that has begun to work upon the dead leaves, animals, even the tiniest flakes of decomposing pollen now that spring has arrived.

There is a bouquet of columbine in her hands and Yuki finally understands what the faint, first brown creases upon the flowers mean. She smiles at this symphony of life consuming itself, to reproduce and begin the process again. Yuki stretches her hands to the ceiling of the train and smiles because she understands that she is finally dying, even if it will take many turns of the sun to finally do so.

author biographies

JANUARY

A *PNWC* and *Bumbershoot* award-winning poet and *Seattle Times* bestselling novelist, Jennifer DiMarco first toured nationally as an author when she was nineteen years old. Her resume of publications includes contemporary drama, science fiction, high fantasy, and mystery novels as well as poetry collections and stage plays. For the last ten years, DiMarco has worked as a filmmaker, writing and directing more than a dozen feature films, half a dozen mini-series, and more than a hundred short films. She lives in the Pacific Northwest with her wife, author and composer Brianne, and their children, author and illustrator Maxwell, and producer and actor Faith.

FEBRUARY

A writer since childhood, Maxwell DiMarco still holds onto his creative spirit at twenty years old, creating stories in both prose and visual form. A dedicated editor for Blue Forge Group, Maxwell gets his inspiration from a wide variety of sources and his favorite stories are those that straddle the line between serious and humorous. When not browsing the Internet for factoids and unique series to enjoy, Maxwell enjoys drawing on his tablet, gaming, and listening to his favorite soundtracks. He's a huge believer in community, acceptance, and seeing the world from all perspectives.

MARCH

A mom first in all things she does, Amber Rainey just happens to also be an author, actor, and award-winning filmmaker. She lives in Texas with her engineer husband, precocious son, and two cats, who vie for her lap while she writes. Amber has yet to find a medium she doesn't enjoy so she writes novels, short stories, and screenplays. Her first novel, *Eternal Willow*, can be found online at Amazon. You can visit www.amberrainey.com and www.tiny.cc/amberrainey for more about Amber and her work.

APRIL

J.W. Capek has always appreciated the art of storytelling from grandmothers, radio programs, community theatre, and books. After teaching high school and developing the Senior to Senior Intergenerational Telecommunications project, J.W. began writing her own epics. Her debut novel, *The Deerwhere Awakening*, creates a science fiction world with quantum computers, epigenetics, and three unique sexes: Female, Male, and Uniale. Continuing *The Deerwhere Codex* series of the twenty-fourth century is a Northwest story of survival in *Adrion's Passage*. The anthology of the Uniale experience was released this year as *Ever Aequum*.

MAY

Mark Robijn is an author, screenwriter, filmmaker, and short story writer. His love of writing began in junior high when you wrote his first science fiction story and has continued to grow ever since. One of his screenplays was a recent quarter-finalist in the Page Screenwriting Awards, and he won the Scriptoid TV Writing Challenge in 2015 for Best Pilot for an Original TV Series.

JUNE

Michelle Lee is a novelist and short story writer. The first five books in her series *The Raven's Journey* have been published this year through Blue Forge Press and can be found online at Amazon. She writes faster than her publisher can keep up, so look for more urban fantasy and contemporary novels from Michelle Lee coming soon!

JULY

Angela Faro is an artisan of many skills who resides in Washington State. She is an author, an award-winning filmmaker and actress, a musician, singer, and journalist. Her previous writing includes a novelization of the *Ghost Sniffers, Inc.* episode *Wild Things Waking*, various short stories, poetry, and articles for *Arts Ex Machina Magazine* and a reoccurring column in the *Northwest Karaoke & Entertainment Guide* called *The NW Film Focus*.

AUGUST

Hailing from Tacoma, Washington, Lauren Patzer has been an information technology guru, actor, writer and film producer among other pursuits. His love of horror began with an overnight, could not put it down, reading of *The Amityville Horror*. First happy memory with horror was nearly scaring the life out of his sister while she was watching *The Exorcist*; high school was truly the happiest of times. When he's not spending time with his wife, three daughters and grandson, Lauren reads the works of Joe McKinney and Joe Lansdale.

SEPTEMBER

David Martyn lives in Gig Harbor, Washington with his wife, Karen. Retired from a career in the Maritime Industry, he can keep watch over the ships passing to and from Tacoma and the Vashon Island Ferry. David believes God reveals Himself and sets us on a journey of discovery that brings us to the revelation of God's Word, to the very heart of God. His love of Scripture, which burns in our hearts, has been strengthened by years of home Bible Study groups which brought him insight on Bible passages and confirmation of God working in the lives of His people. It is David's hope that his stories awaken the seed of revelation God planted in the reader's heart.

OCTOBER

Bree Indigo is a poet and songwriter. She enjoys astrology, exploring Washington State's Olympic Peninsula, and local mushroom foraging. Her favorite authors include Madeleine L'Engle, Ellen Hopkins, and Laurie Halse Anderson. Indigo lives with her wife and their children in the Pacific Northwest. Her first memoir, *Unreliable Narrator*, is forthcoming by Blue Forge Press.

NOVEMBER

Marshall Miller retired from Homeland Security and police enforcement to more deeply explore the human condition and what drives us a species. Framed with the arrival of alien Apex predators who see us as little more than a food source, Miller is best known for crafting his series, *The Tschaaa Infestation* that dares to ask: Are we truly superior and do we deserve to survive? Find out more about his work at www.tiny.cc/marshallmiller

DECEMBER

Kristie Gronberg was born and raised in Western Washington. Kristie graduated from Olympic College with an Associate of the Arts degree in 2019. As a child, Kristie always aspired to be a writer. She used an educational computer program for children to write a collection of short stories at the age of 7, dedicating it to her elementary school. *A Story of Stories* was later "published" when it was added to the school's miniature library. The joy and sense of accomplishment Kristie felt drove her to continue writing.

THIRTEEN

David Mecklenburg was born in Sacramento, CA. but at the age of 22 he moved home to the Pacific Northwest, where he received his MFA in Creative Writing from the University of Washington. In short fiction, novellas, poetic essays and novels, he unveils worlds upon worlds in the fabulist tradition that reveal the multivalent condition we call being human. His short fiction has appeared in Silver Blade Magazine, Adelaide Literary Review, The Dark Fiction Spotlight among anthologies, such as Blue Forge Press's Unnerving series. His longer work includes The Nightingale's Stone, a fictional memoir, along with Graphic Illustrated Essay collections such as Hyperborea, and Deukollectrum, available from Blue Forge Press. For more information, please visit:

www.davidmecklenburg.com

www.ingramcontent.com/pod-product-compliance
Lightning Source LLC
Chambersburg PA
CBHW060236100726
47907CB00003B/651